PRAISE FOR
MY FAVORITE TERRIBLE THING

"*My Favorite Terrible Thing* is one of my favorite books of the year! Insightful, emotional, and utterly surprising. I devoured this deeply psychological novel in one sitting and immediately wanted to read it again. Madeleine Henry is brilliant!"

—Wendy Walker, bestselling author of *What Remains*

"A twisty, evocative novel from a gifted writer with a smart, fresh voice. I loved it!"

—Sarah Pekkanen, #1 *New York Times* bestselling author

"A gripping novel that explores the tenuous line between fiction and reality. Lyrical prose, compelling characters, and pacing that keeps the pages flying by make *My Favorite Terrible Thing* a not-to-be-missed triumph."

—Liv Constantine, internationally bestselling author of *The Last Mrs. Parrish*

T0108124

MY
FAVORITE
TERRIBLE
THING

OTHER TITLES BY MADELEINE HENRY

The Love Proof
Breathe In, Cash Out

MY FAVORITE TERRIBLE THING

A NOVEL

MADELEINE HENRY

This is a work of fiction. Names, characters, organizations, institutions, places, events, and incidents are either products of the author's imagination or are used fictitiously. Any resemblance to actual persons, living or dead, or actual events is purely coincidental.

Text copyright © 2024 by Madeleine Henry
All rights reserved.

No part of this book may be reproduced, or stored in a retrieval system, or transmitted in any form or by any means, electronic, mechanical, photocopying, recording, or otherwise, without express written permission of the publisher.

Published by Little A, New York

www.apub.com

Amazon, the Amazon logo, and Little A are trademarks of Amazon.com, Inc., or its affiliates.

ISBN-13: 9781662517440 (hardcover)
ISBN-13: 9781662517433 (paperback)
ISBN-13: 9781662517457 (digital)

Cover design by Laywan Kwan

Cover image: © lindamka / Shutterstock; © Ljupco Smokovski / Shutterstock; © Ricardo Reitmeyer / Shutterstock; © studiocasper / Getty Images

Printed in the United States of America

First edition

*for everyone
who's a prisoner
to great stories*

ONE

"I have one hundred shadows."
—*Claire Ross,* The Starlit Ballet

A loner is consistent. The ruts are deep.

I've been staring at the same broken mirror for nine years. There's one crack across the middle, like an axe gash. Or a flat mouth with glass teeth. When I face my medicine cabinet, the crack scratches out my eyes. I can't see their shape—close set, almond. Can't see their color—deep brown that looks black in the shadows.

I'm getting dressed for work, facing the shattered line. My eyes, missing as usual. Both sockets, carved out of my reflection. It's hard to tell who I am from the remaining scraps of flesh. My neat hairline, crooked nose, and thin lips are all crystal clear. But on their own, they could belong to anyone. I smooth my crimson sweater and take one last look. It's almost as if the mirror is taunting me. Turning me into a blind investigator. An eyeless private eye. It would be easy enough to replace the glass. There are a couple of hardware stores here in Riverhead, Long Island. But by now, I'm used to the break.

The only person who sees it is me.

~

Southampton still doesn't feel real, even after working in the area for a decade. Driving through it now, the houses look like shingle-style castles. Each is a sprawling blend of weathered wood and glass under an asymmetric roof. The homes are so immaculate—with so many pillars, second-floor balconies, and guest cottages—it's as if they were written into existence by F. Scott Fitzgerald. Not built by people with permits, budgets, and other constraints.

I'm getting close to Cooper's Beach.

No one else is on the road this morning.

House after house appears to be vacant. It takes a truly grand estate to look gorgeous when it's dead empty, as these do. Most houses need to be lit up and filled with people first. But these are so well kept and geometrically satisfying, they look aspirational even while they're closed up for the colder months. I anticipate every one before I pass it in my Honda Accord, each property as familiar as if I grew up on this block. I've come to know this town as well as anyone who belongs here, a list that includes some of the world's most darling celebrities: Jerry Seinfeld, Steven Spielberg, and, at one time, Claire Ross.

I park at the beach and step outside.

I'm still the only one here, half a mile from my next job at Jill and Wyatt Campbell's waterfront address. Jill hired me a few weeks ago, suspecting that Wyatt might be sleeping with his yoga instructor, Millie. He is. Millie visits their house twice a week and spends up to three hours there every time. I set up cameras to catch them in the act, but the place is twenty-one thousand square feet, and they only have sex in the least predictable spots. They're staircase people. Hallway people.

Now I have to film them by hand.

I walk through sand clumpy with old rain. A gray wave slides up and down the beach, skirting my faded sneakers. Winters in the Hamptons aren't as snowy as they are wet and empty—and while it's not quite "winter" yet, the word is my personal shorthand for the off-season. For the long, desolate stretch after everyone disappears. After the lifeguard stands have been packed up and stowed away, leaving the oceans unsupervised.

I reach the dunes outside the Campbells'.

A boardwalk cuts through the green, leading to their porch. Jill bought this shingle-style the year her app, DateBooth, went public. She remains its popular CEO, working around the clock to bolster its 90 percent success rate, responsible for over one hundred thousand relationships last year. Meanwhile, Wyatt quit his job the week of their wedding. He's now little more than the life of every party, amused by destroying relationships, one tryst at a time.

I walk past their boardwalk, all the way to the far corner of their lawn. From there, I spot Wyatt and Millie inside. They're laughing and holding hands on their way up to the second floor. Wyatt's body is classically athletic, from his broad shoulders down to his thick calves. He's balding prematurely, leaving him with a U-shaped hairline. It gives his handsome face a misleading air of wisdom, as if he's done his time and learned from his mistakes. Millie, on the other hand, has lush, dark hair with a streak of pink. She has a natural look, just bare skin and Lycra.

I walk around to the front door.

Find Jill's key under the mat.

At least Wyatt hasn't taken Millie into the primary bedroom, where he and Jill sleep between her business trips. If I had to guess, though, I'd bet that's an accident. Wyatt doesn't seem like the premeditative type. He's spontaneous, risk prone, and, unfortunately, very funny. I find myself laughing at his jokes when I play back his and Millie's exchanges. Unlike Millie, however, I've learned by now that bright charisma is usually a warning sign. The most mesmerizing people tend to be the most deceptive.

I step inside.

On the second floor, Millie moans.

I drift toward the sound, through the open kitchen. Copper pots gleam overhead, dangling from the high ceiling. It's unsettling how much heartache can fit into homes this enormous. I start the video on my phone and creep upstairs, testing out each step before trusting it with my weight. Millie's moaning is too loud, performative. Still, I inch closer. I follow their noises all the way to a guest room, where they've left the door wide open.

On the threshold, I get them both in the frame.

"You're so fucking hot," he says.

She squeals.

"So *fucking* hot."

It does wear on the soul to live inside this many shallow affairs.

I can't help but imagine how Jill will react when she sees her husband screwing Millie in high definition—especially when Jill paid for this bed, for these sheets.

A floorboard winces under me. Wyatt stops moving. For one frozen second, no one makes a sound. I hotfoot off the threshold, down the hall. When someone creaks out of bed, I bolt downstairs and race out the front door. It's only when I'm sprinting into the parking lot that I dare to look over my shoulder. The only person here is me.

~

The weather is never quite the same, going from the Hamptons to Riverhead. It's just as crisp here, half an hour inland, but we get different storms than they do. I feel some freezing rain on its way, the air dense and damp. I'm a few steps from home when I see my neighbor Lauretta smoking on her second-floor porch. The age spots on her face look like bran flakes swimming in milk. She leans forward in a faded blue hoodie and sweats. Now in her mideighties, she's as strong willed as ever.

"Hey, you!" she calls.

She blows a long puff through yellow teeth.

Lauretta's never actually said my name. I'm not sure she knows it. Meanwhile, I know more than hers. I know that Lauretta Decker Jones dropped out of Queensborough Community College in 1965, even though she tells everyone that she graduated from Cornell. Of course, I never bought that story. Lauretta was no Ivy Leaguer, no more born to privilege than I was. It took only a background check to prove it to myself.

I wave from the parking lot.

With my free hand, I rearrange books in my purse, feeling for my keys. I always keep two or three novels with me. Having plenty of literature in mind, ready to elevate any moment, gives me dignity no matter what—even when I'm taping other people's *fuck-me-harder*s. Even when I'm steeped in their secondhand air, when every breath I take is one they've already licked. I find my keys under an old, soft spine.

"Again with the costume."

Lauretta points at my outfit with her cigarette, holding it like a dart between two fingers. Today, I'm in a V-neck sweater over a white oxford. A braided leather belt secures my khakis. I look elegant, as usual, apart from the sneakers.

"You know I work in the Hamptons, right?"

"Yeah, playing dress-up." She takes a drag. "Hate to break it to you, kiddo, but the only person you're fooling is yourself. I've done a couple more spins around the sun, so trust me when I say: you should just get on with your own damn life." Lauretta's always doling out advice, weaponizing the intel that she gleans from her porch. The indomitable Cornell grad, opining from on high. *Just be yourself.* The irony isn't lost on me.

I head into our building.

The hallway ahead of me is so poorly maintained, I wonder if it matters to anyone. Frizzy maroon carpet, clinging to dust balls and long stray hairs. Nicks in the walls that look like tiny gray headstones. I do want to move out of here, move up in the world. The hardest part about being a great detective, though, is the lack of recognition for a job well done. Most of my work is domestic surveillance—one spouse hiring me to watch the other—so no matter the lengths I go to, my clients won't admit what I've done.

My dream is to solve a great case, one so well known and deeply layered that everyone will finally see what I can do. There must be a good chance of finding one like that out here, working with high-profile clientele in the Hamptons. I have what it takes. "Doubt" isn't the right word. Because the key to this job isn't doubting—it's *expecting* the worst. It's looking for rot, skeletons. It's knowing that everyone is easily wounded and vengeful. That when it gets dark, everyone likes to watch fire burn. My cynicism has been shaped by a lifetime of being overlooked, starting with parents who drank until it killed them when I was a teen. I've never been wealthy, well connected, or pretty enough for anyone to curry favor with me. Every day, I see how people act when they want nothing from you.

Every day, I sink deeper into my ruts.

I step into my modest one-bedroom, right under Lauretta's. The best part of this apartment is the packed bookshelves. I have every genre except nonfiction, which feels too preachy. I get enough of that in real life—people who think they're better than me, telling me what's true. My favorite novels are *The Starlit Ballet*, by Claire Ross, and *The Goldfinch*, by Donna Tartt. I have multiple copies of each and quote them like prayers.

Lauretta yells to another neighbor.

The Cornellian knows everyone.

Technically, I never went to college. It didn't make financial sense, taking on that much debt for a degree that might never pay off. Besides, my bills wouldn't wait for me to write term papers on Shakespeare's political plays. The closest I got to higher education was cleaning college kitchens around Boston. Between shifts, I'd slink into classes, blank faced in the crowd of students, my backpack hanging off one shoulder. I'd sit in the back of lectures, just for the Melville, Emerson, and Woolf. Just to listen. I like to think I have an unofficial bachelor's degree from multiple universities. Even though I have nothing to show for it—yet.

~

That night, I send Jill the video and lean back on my sofa.

Jack Kerouac captured this feeling in *On the Road* when he described people shrinking in his rearview mirror. He understood the silent goodbye. I probably won't hear from Jill again, except to get paid. I charge $3,000 for most jobs: the first half when I start, the rest when I finish. It's enough to cover rent, groceries, and books but not enough that I can get sick without anxiety. Usually, I do my best to swallow coughs, drown sore throats. Ignore any pain.

Window bars stripe the parking lot.

Fitful headlights tear up the dark.

I liked Jill. She was punctual and considerate. She didn't talk over me, didn't ask me to do anything that's not technically my job. Sometimes, the line between private investigator and personal assistant blurs when the client isn't used to hearing no, when they're not used to remembering what everyone around them actually does.

A former client, Katie-Rose Landry, once asked me to take care of the "bug problem" in her basement. At that moment, we were in her kitchen, where everything was sparkling, even the water. She looked immaculate in champagne-colored lipstick. I had a hard time believing there was anything crawling downstairs. I could've said no, but Katie-Rose was nice to me. She remembered my name. In a world where no client's ever acknowledged me in public—not even with a polite nod—I'm good to the few who are good to me.

So I visited her basement. I didn't expect to find anything more than a centipede curled into a hard, doomed swirl. As it turned out, her basement was blooming with bugs. Most of them were dead and scattered like chia seeds, tinting the floor dark brown. Some thrived in open boxes of her cable-knit sweaters. The rest were airborne. One landed in my hair. Naturally, I found the right aerosol among Katie-Rose's endless supplies and sprayed the life out of that place. It wasn't until I got home that I realized: fighting something small is more unsettling than fighting anything my own size. For weeks, every tingle made me strip down and wash my clothes, unsure if there were eggs in the wool, larvae sliding through the stitches.

"Can you shut the fuck up for like one time?" a neighbor shouts.

"Can *you*? I'm not even talking!"

"I'm done! I'm done!"

"I don't want to go through this again!"

The walls in this building are so thin, I hear every fight between the couple next door. Sometimes they spit such venom at each other, I feel poisoned myself, stunned and weak with spreading numbness.

My phone starts to ring, almost drowning them out. It's bright on the sofa, branded with an unknown number.

I answer with my name.

"Hi, Nina," the caller says. "It's Miranda Ross."

My world stops. Miranda Ross. That's the name of Claire Ross's mother—as in, *the* Claire Ross, the author of *The Starlit Ballet*.

"Hello?" she asks.

"Hi, how can I help you?" I manage.

"I assume you've heard about Claire."

I tell her that I have.

Over two months ago, thirty-year-old Claire was reported missing on the day of her wedding in East Hampton. The world might not have noticed, except that Claire wrote one of its most popular love stories. The tabloids couldn't have asked for a more heart-wrenching setup: a symbol of love to millions, vanishing on her wedding day.

That morning, Claire's bedroom was found empty, with the door locked from the inside. One of her windows was open, letting in a chill. The police worked on her case for over a month before ruling that there was no evidence of foul play. The Ross family maintains that Claire was kidnapped, but they don't have a shred of proof.

"I'm a friend of Abigail Waters," Miranda says.

Abigail also lives in East Hampton. She hired me this year to find the Picasso stolen from her living room. The painting showed a woman's face split into a dozen pieces, rearranged in a grotesque but fascinating jumble. For a moment, I thought it might've been my great case—except that Abigail didn't want anyone to know it was stolen. If she had to replace it with a fake, she didn't want anyone to be the wiser. Once again, my work went unnoticed.

"She's in the Maldives with her husband, but we've been playing phone tag about you. She hired you to find the Picasso?" I tell her that's correct. "We've just been on completely different sides of the clock. Today, she finally sent her gardener over with your card and a message. As I understand it, Abigail said your methods were unusual, but you'd lead us to Claire. She said you were our best chance, actually. As I'm sure you know, the police got nowhere with Claire's case. We're losing our minds." She exhales sharply through her teeth, a short whistle. "Are you based out here?"

I tell her that I am.

"Do you think you could swing by the house, and we could talk face-to-face? If we can come to an agreement—I don't know what your usual rate is, but I'd be happy to start at fifty, if that sounds fair. That would be for finding Claire, of course, but I'd still pay half for a thorough investigation." It takes me a moment to realize that she means fifty *thousand* dollars. In the brief pause, she appears to panic: "Honestly, I'd go higher."

"Your rate sounds fair," I manage.

"Are you free tomorrow?"

TWO

"The windows frame Yosemite Valley, a green version of
infinity. Maybe it's not a stretch to have fifteen thousand
years inside my head, after growing up with views this
deep."
—*Claire Ross,* The Starlit Ballet

The next morning, I'm up an hour before my alarm. I shower and make
Starbucks instant coffee, one packet of french roast stirred into warm
water. I fry two eggs and slide them onto a plate, but I'm too energized
to eat anything but the whites. When I'm done, the yolks are ragged.
They look like the remains of butchered daisies.

I scrape them into the trash.

Claire's case feels made for me, perfect for me. I don't just know
books. I know hers. I spent the night rereading parts of her debut, *The
Starlit Ballet*. It follows two soulmates who reincarnate and find each
other in every life across historical eras. They find each other in ancient
Rome, then off the coast of Madagascar in the Golden Age of Piracy,
and then in Philadelphia during the yellow fever epidemic in 1793.
They continue to find each other and fall in love as different people, in
different places, through to the year 2903 in Yosemite National Park.
The Starlit Ballet was translated into forty languages and optioned by
Netflix. It's in development with an A-list cast, including Zendaya.

I read her book when it came out last year, then watched Claire
sweep late-night and morning shows as a guest. She had a pink pixie

cut, elfin face, and big clear glasses. She was beautiful, but when she opened her mouth, you forgot what she looked like—which I guess was the point of her book: what matters transcends skin and bones. Her greatest asset was her mind. On every show, she taught the audience something—about the Colosseum, about how pirates tortured people at sea—and she did it all gently. She acted exactly like the kind of person you'd expect to be behind her novel. It made her the fixation of a fanatical fan base.

Then, she disappeared.

I get dressed with fast hands.

I haven't felt this good since I was on college campuses. Steeped in *The Portrait of Dorian Gray*, mahogany banisters, and geometric quads. With bright kids who carried as many books as I did. Back then, I had no idea that I was preparing for my future clientele. I still take style cues from that time, over ten years ago. I'm still the truly harmless version of Tom Ripley, slipping into a well-bred character. Tweed, houndstooth, and blazers in the fall, paired with suede boots. Pastels and linen in the spring, with woven handbags. All year long, raincoats with tartan linings. I still can't afford the brands they chose, but I copy them enough to get by. Now, I work closely for Hamptonites without ever making them uncomfortable, without ever drawing attention to the wide gap of lifestyles between us.

Today, I'm in a long-sleeve polo tucked into high-waisted khakis. It's a classic look with equestrian undertones. My hair fills a clean low braid, which lets me sidestep the challenge of taming it. Abigail had a hairdresser blow hers out at home every week, and another woman would paint Abigail's nails at the same time. I don't wear any polish, because it chips too easily, and I've noticed that chipped nail polish is a bigger faux pas than none at all.

I look in the mirror under the gash.

And it's Nina, the elegant detective.

The one they assume went to college, even without realizing that's what they assume. The one they trust because she seems a little bit like them. The one who slips in and out of their lives, because that's what she's always done. Because she's learned how to make a living out of being forgettable. Out of being white space.

Out of being everyone and no one.

~

I drive faster the closer I get to Miranda's house. It's all I can do to keep from speeding down Further Lane, the luxuriously wide road through central East Hampton. I pass earth-toned estates with covered pools, an empty golf course with its flagsticks removed for winter. It's almost nine in the morning now, the earliest I could suggest. Gray clouds drift through a silver sky, shining like the inside of a seashell.

Abigail's house appears on my left. Wide and white with closed black shutters. Potted plants by the front door wrapped in burlap, expertly mummified. Her Picasso should be back in its place on the other side of the entrance, among the world's greatest paintings and effectively in storage. I picture Abigail in the living room again, wearing a floor-length Missoni kaftan, sipping lemonade with mint frozen into the ice cubes. She used to model, back when models had to be stick thin. She still has the small bones, the whittled look.

Eventually, I turn right.

According to my GPS, Miranda's place is at the end of this road, right on the ocean. I drive between dense hedges. It's a long, bumpy ride all the way to her square wooden gates. They part slowly. Miranda's home is even more striking in person: a mammoth, chocolate-brown shingle-style on a wide lawn. I roll into the pebble driveway. In the distance, her grassy yard becomes a belt of sand dunes, which becomes the wild ocean.

The front door opens to reveal Miranda Ross. She's tall and slender but soft around the arms, as if her body isn't an obsession. Her hair is gray at the roots and combed into a champagne-colored ponytail that runs down her back. Her oxford shirt, creamy sweater vest, and long pearl necklace are elegant over khakis. It's a chic take on beachwear, but the look appears to require minimal effort: no makeup on her face, no color on her nails, and an outfit that's loose enough to slip on. In the photos of Miranda that I found online—from before Claire disappeared—it's clear that this is generally how she used to present herself too. The only difference is that now, I can feel her aching from here.

I park, careful not to drive on a single blade in her perfectly trimmed lawn. As I step outside, wind captures a strand of my hair and whips it around. We're so close to the ocean, I hear waves breaking. I smell tiny crabs burrowing in sand, seaweed on the shore. I mute my own awe that I'm here, that I'm shaking Miranda's hand. Up close, she has a heart-shaped face with prominent cheekbones. They cast their own tiny shadows.

I introduce myself as Nina.

"Nina Travers?" she asks skeptically.

"That's me."

"You're so young."

Her disappointment is as subtle as her outfit. I'm tempted to defend myself and say that I'm almost thirty, that I've been doing this job for nearly a decade. My first clients trusted me because they assumed I was born with a cell phone in one hand, a laptop in the other, and could use my innate tech wizardry to meet their surveillance needs. Since then, I've been referred often enough that I get almost all my jobs these days based on merit. I've had enough experience that I can do this work as well as the seasoned pros.

"Welcome," she says sadly.

She leads me inside.

The foyer is flooded with natural light, even today. I follow Miranda past a seashell-framed Hermès beach towel, into a living room with lofty ceilings. The glass wall in front of us gives a panoramic view of the ocean. White birds hover in place over gray waves. It's beyond immersive. This room has such a wide lens, so rich with the landscape, it feels Thoreauvian. Or it would, if Thoreau had ever lived in the Hamptons.

The decor here is mostly white and its sibling shades. On either side, full bookshelves are accented with conch shells, hydra-like pieces of coral, and small but glittering crystal sculptures.

Miranda continues with measured steps, a combination of grace and heavy emotion slowing her down. She sits on an ivory armchair and offers me the sofa. As soon as I take it, she starts to cry. I lower my gaze to the glass-top coffee table between us. It supports a pyramid stack of books, *The Starlit Ballet* on top.

She follows my stare.

"Did you read it?" she asks.

"Who didn't?"

She nods with understanding, then wipes her eyes. Drops trickle down her palms like beads of melting wax. Normally, my client leads our first session together. They are, after all, commissioning my services. But Miranda's too deep in her grief. She keeps dabbing her eyes. Her hands keep getting wetter, as if she's drowning.

"Maybe we could start with, in your own words, what happened that day?" I ask.

"Right."

Miranda hasn't had any plastic surgery, so sadness deepens every line in her face. Her pursed lips crack at the corners. I read that she graduated from Yale with an art history major in the eighties, then had a career at Sotheby's before quitting when Claire was born. Now, she serves on the board of half a dozen charities. She's involved in causes that range from ALS to conservation in the Serengeti. Despite her plush home, I'm tempted to believe that she's unsuperficial at the core. That could explain some of Claire's depth.

"September eighteenth," I prompt quietly.

"It was just Claire, her sister Kira, and me in this house." Claire's Wikipedia page notes that her dad, Andrew Ross, died fifteen years ago of a stroke. He was the third-generation heir to a manufacturing fortune. "That morning, I was upstairs, and the girls were—" She points at the left wall. Her expression is so severe, it's as if she found them right there, body parts shelved among the books. Spines with spines. It takes me a second to grasp that she's gesturing behind it. "They slept across the hall from each other whenever they were here."

"Can I see?"

She nods heavily.

I follow her out of the living room and down a wide hallway, in the direction she was pointing. She stops between two doors.

"This is Kira's room."

She turns one handle to reveal a queen-size bed under a princess canopy. There isn't much space left around the bed, just enough for a slim bench and bookcase. The bottom row is filled with copies of *The Starlit Ballet*—crisp, unread hardcovers.

"Claire's a year older than Kira," Miranda says, "but growing up, people thought they were twins. They had the same pixie cut. They were almost the same height. I put them in matching outfits for every holiday: velvet dresses at Christmas, pink overalls for Easter . . ." It's common for families here to color-match their kids. It can make them look like armies, impenetrable, uniformed. I understand this world too well to be an outsider, but I'll never be a true insider either. I guess that puts me on the fence, somewhere with a good view. Miranda's still talking about her girls as children, as if they froze at six years old. She must be avoiding what's next. "Sorry," she says, interrupting herself. "It's hard to be back. I've been living in a friend's cottage out here. Last night was my first one in this house since . . ."

"You slept here?"

"I did my best."

I don't ask how that felt. I imagine the only sound was the rolling ocean at the edge of her lawn. It churns in the silence between us now, deep and indifferent. Eventually, Miranda shuts the door and turns to face its mirror image. She grips the handle.

"And this . . ."

She trails off.

Steps back.

"I'm sorry," she says.

"May I?" I reach for the door.

Miranda tells me to wait.

I pause with my fingers on the knob, every muscle still.

"Would you mind signing an NDA?" she asks. "I don't think it's right to go any further without one, given who Claire is."

I manage to smile politely and give an agreeable "Of course," even as my chest sags. Miranda looks relieved. She holds up a "one second" finger and takes off down the hallway. I've signed nondisclosure agreements before. They prevent me from sharing anything that I learn over the course of an investigation. Here I am, on the edge of my great case—and soon, I'll be legally bound from mentioning any of it. That reality is deeply sensory. It feels like a gnat in my hair. It sounds like my warring neighbors.

Above me, Miranda's sandals clop across the hardwood floor. Every step echoes as she descends the long staircase and returns. She brandishes a piece of paper overhead before extending it to me. I pull a pen out of my back pocket and glance through the document. The language here is standard. It makes sense that Miranda would want one, given Claire's global fame—but one line at the end is different: "In the event that your work leads to Claire's whereabouts, all provisions of this Agreement will survive, except that Miranda Ross will publicly honor your contributions."

"Is there a problem?" Miranda asks.

I tell her no, but my voice shakes. There's a ripple through the syllable, breaking it in two. I sign my name with more care than usual, sculpting every letter through to the final *s* in Travers. She tucks the final document into her pocket.

"May I?" I ask, reaching for the handle.

She nods yes.

I open the door to a room that's twice the size of Kira's—with a better view. Kira faced the family pool, but here, two windows frame a dark ocean that seems to run to the end of the earth. It's such a stunning but haunting visual that I remember Edgar Allan Poe's poem "Annabel Lee." The words are just as beautiful, just as cold.

A wind blew out of a cloud, chilling

My beautiful Annabel Lee . . .

To shut her up in a sepulchre

In this kingdom by the sea.

"The left window was open." Miranda points at it. Her pale finger is perfectly straight, knuckle flat. "Otherwise, nothing in this room's been moved. No one's been in here since September except for the crime scene 'investigators.'" She scoffs. "The only thing they did right was they didn't turn this place upside down. When they were gone, it was as if they'd never stepped foot in this house. In more ways than one. So everything's . . ."

"The way she left it."

I take slow steps forward, my awareness heightened not just because I'm working, but because I'm in Claire Ross's room. Her bed's a queen, with a wooden headboard. The grain like brown waves stunned in place. Her comforter forms a scrunched C shape at the end of the mattress, as if she just kicked it off, lifted the window, and ran away from everything— with nothing. The decor is as elegantly beachy as the rest of the house, including a starfish-patterned rug, a powder-blue chaise longue, and a bookcase with jars of seashells for bookends. I can almost see her on the chaise, reading a book with her emerald stare.

"Kira woke up at eight that day and walked across the hall." Miranda is well behind me now. "She knocked. No answer. That was strange because Claire's always been an early riser. She gets up with the birds, before seven on the weekends. Kira tried the handle, but it was locked. Then, she went and made coffee in the kitchen. She said it felt weird for Claire not to be up yet, on her *wedding*, of all days. So she left the kitchen, walked around to the window"—she points again at the left one—"and climbed inside."

"Kira found the window open?" I confirm.

"Yes, but Claire was nowhere." Her pitch rises. "Kira ran out through this door and shouted for me upstairs. She was hysterical. We yelled everywhere for Claire. Searched the whole house. Ran down to the beach and shouted her name. I called the police at 8:17." She crosses her arms, as if she's holding herself together. "And she's still missing. Every morning, I wake up and remember all over again that she's gone."

"Do you mind if I take photos?"

She motions to go ahead.

I photograph the window, asking if the police found any blood or body fluids. Miranda shakes her head no. I photograph the bed next, asking if they found any finger- or palm prints. Another sad shake. I pull a flashlight out of my pocket and shine it on the carpet under the windows. The blue-and-white fibers are tight, clean.

"What about footprints?" I ask.

"No, nothing. The police said that they didn't see 'any sign of a struggle' either." Her contempt is clear even though it's understated. "There were no signs of anyone but Claire. So they decided she ran away. That certainly made their lives easier. It isn't against the law for an adult to do that. They could pack up and go home."

"But you don't think she ran away."

"Why would she?" Miranda demands. "Leave all of us—and Roger, on their wedding day? Leave her whole career? Why would she do that?"

I walk to Claire's bedside table and survey the lamp, notepad monogrammed with an *R* over an anchor, and mug full of pens. Writers tend to care about their pens. These are sleek black Jetstreams, probably a few dollars each—nice, but not top of the line. I imagine that Claire might've written some of *The Starlit Ballet* right here, crumpled unsatisfactory pages, and thrown them away. I peek inside the wastebasket—empty.

"Speaking of Roger," Miranda continues, "I should mention that I invited him and Kira over too. They both happened to be in town this weekend for a charity event, and I figured you'd want to meet them. They should be here soon."

She glances at her silver Tank watch.

I transition to the topic of her wedding planner. I read that she'd worked with someone named Eliza Briggs. Keeping my tone deferential and a touch graceful, I ask if I could speak with Eliza too. "Wedding planners know more than you think."

Miranda pulls an iPhone out of her back pocket.

"Eliza lives not too far, in Sag," she says, texting. "We had dinner together last night. Roger could pick her up on his way over." I gather that she's used to having people bend to her will, that her polite suggestions are as powerful as other people's ultimatums. She pockets her phone. I shine my flashlight across the floor, looking for signs of dragging.

"How did you tell your guests about Claire?" I ask.

"I sent an email to everyone, including the vendors, around noon. I told the truth: Claire is missing and there won't be a wedding. I asked people with any information to please come forward and help us find her." She clasps her hands.

"Did anyone respond?"

"People sent their condolences."

I imagine how Miranda's heart must've leaped with every new email, only to find that it was just another line of regrets.

"Did anyone show up to the house that day?" I ask.

She thinks about it.

"It was just us here. Why?"

"Sometimes, people return to the scene of their own crime."

Her eyes widen.

"Strange but true," I say.

"Like I said, just family."

I turn my attention to Claire's bookcase. It's filled with versions of *The Starlit Ballet* in different languages. There must be one copy here in every translation. In the top-left-hand corner, the spine of the American edition is black with a yellow, serifed font. Most of the foreign spines are dark, too, but the fonts vary.

I wonder if Claire arranged these or if this is Miranda's handiwork. Domain is a gray area, staying in someone else's home. Especially when they're family. I read in a magazine feature about the case that Claire spent most summers here with her mom. Multigenerational living is normal in this part of the Hamptons, where homes start at $10 million. Besides, parents always have the space, in the form of guest cottages or extra rooms so superfluous, they don't even have names. They're just *rooms*. When you're an adult spending months at your parents', though, who's really in charge of your bedroom?

I walk over to Claire's closet and open the double doors to find a bureau and U-shaped rack full of hanging clothes. In her TV interviews, Claire always wore a black turtleneck and slacks, which she called her "creative person's business formal." The clothes here don't look like anything I've ever seen her wear: pastel polo shirts, linen bermuda shorts, and golf skorts. Hamptons camouflage? It's hard to imagine her gabbing with other women in these outfits on the beach. She had an intensity that didn't turn off—but "intensity" isn't quite the right word. It was an unrelenting earnestness. She was too sincere. Her gaze practically vaporized all bullshit on contact. It made you say what you really believe.

I walk into Claire's bathroom, asking if the police took anything from the scene. Miranda tells me just a hairbrush, for DNA. Eventually, she leads me back to the living room, where she sits in the same chair as before. Our tour appears to have drained what little color there was out of her skin. Behind her, whitecaps and gulls are the brightest things on the horizon.

"So the police didn't take anything else?" I confirm.

"Just the hairbrush."

"Not her journals?"

Miranda pauses.

"Journals?" she asks.

"Claire said in a couple interviews that she journaled every day."

"No. They never mentioned those."

I pull a notepad and pen out of my pocket, flip to the first blank page.

"How were Claire and Roger leading up to the wedding?" I ask, clicking the pen.

"Made for each other."

I wait for more, pen tip on paper.

She tells me that they'd been together for five years. "He was like a son to me, spent almost every holiday with us. He joked that he was going to take *our* name, be a Ross." She smiles for a moment. "I'd never seen Claire so happy. When they started dating, she came out here more often, instead of holing up in Manhattan and writing that book day and night. She still cared about her writing, of course, but she relaxed her grip on it."

"Was she on bad terms with anyone?"

She bites her lip.

"Nothing out of the ordinary."

"What was ordinary?"

She pulls up one sleeve and scratches her forearm.

"A little tension in the family before a wedding is normal."

"I never said it wasn't."

"Are you married?" She glances at my left hand.

"Not yet."

I smile hopefully, doing my best to signal that we all have traditional family values here. As if my parents are still alive and eager to throw me a wedding. As if my kids will end up matching too. Dressed in ruby red on holiday cards and wearing black patent shoes. I usually don't have to lie to my clients. They just fill in the gaps on their own. On the rare occasion that they do probe into my personal life, I'll sometimes invent a boyfriend. *Charles. We met at school.* I've gotten so good at it, it's not even acting. It's gliding.

"Then you'll have to take my word for it," Miranda says. "Weddings are hard—not because it's hard to choose a dress or choose a cake. They're hard because you have to reconcile different cultures across families and with*in* a family." She interlaces her fingers. "It was just over little things. They seem so petty now." She starts to cry, and it's so heartfelt, I'm tempted to reach for her hand. "Things like . . ." She shakes her head, apparently in disbelief. "Roger's mom was indecisive. And—I can't even talk about it. It was all so trivial."

"I'm afraid I need to hear you talk about it."

She fidgets.

"The tension was mostly between Claire and her sister," she admits slowly. "But I don't want you to get the wrong idea. It was run-of-the-mill sibling rivalry, with some wedding stress. Do you have siblings?" She seems to hope that I do.

I nod yes.

"Two brothers."

"It might be different with sisters." She sighs. "Claire is very particular, and Kira . . . isn't. She would do things that upset Claire, but it wasn't malicious. They just have different personalities. Claire kept saying Kira didn't care about the wedding, that she was trying to sabotage it, but that's not true. It's just that *no one* cares as much as Claire does. She wrote a book about soulmates who love each other across thousands of years."

"What do you think happened to your daughter?"

"I think someone has her."

Knock. Knock.

There's someone at the front door.

Miranda excuses herself on her way out of the living room. Once I'm alone, I stand and peer down the hallway after her. A tall woman steps into the foyer. I can only see an inch of her around Miranda's silhouette—the yellow crown of her head, one arm of her black fur bomber jacket. It's an enormous coat, broad and boxy. As if it's meant for the cold blooded, the ones unable to keep themselves warm. I step back as they hug.

Footsteps approach.

Before I know it, Kira strolls into the living room. I recognize her from some of the features that came out after Claire went missing: spray-tanned and heavily made up. Her straight nose looks contoured. Its edges are darkened, effectively shaving off bone. She has a wider jaw than Claire, almost square shaped, both ends pointed. Kira moves quickly, long legged in brown leather pants. Her high-heeled boots announce every step. Her whole look comes off as pretty in a firm, aggressive way that values sex appeal over natural beauty.

In one of Claire's interviews, she mentioned that before she sold her book—while she was still scraping by, with the dream of being an author—her sister tried to convince her to write for TV. Kira works in marketing for HBO, and she kept saying *that's* where the money is; nobody reads anymore, and when people get home from work, all they want to do is eat dinner and watch shows. But Claire explained that she was always more interested in the life of an author, because they work alone. TV writers collaborate.

"I'm Kira." She extends a hand.

I share my name.

"Abigail said we should bring you in," she says skeptically, sitting a cushion away from me on the sofa. Her blonde waves smell a little like burned hair, curls left in the iron a beat too long. She takes off her jacket and stores it in a heap beside her, watching me closely the whole time. "Do you mind me asking what you do exactly?"

"Kira," Miranda chides.

"It's hard to learn much about someone whose work is private," she defends.

"Does Abigail have her painting back or not?" Miranda asks.

"I work mostly on domestic surveillance investigations." I frame them the best I can. "Less frequently on missing persons cases and theft."

Kira eyes her mom.

"For *me*," Miranda pleads.

"All right," Kira says, surrendering. "Let's get this over with."

Her edge is surprising.

In Claire's interviews, she was always so compassionate. You'd think that succeeding as a fiction writer would require some narcissism—that anyone who believes *their* imagined story to be worth twelve hours of *your* time must have an inflated ego—but Claire didn't project any self-importance. She was soft in a way that melted even the most sarcastic late-night hosts. Meanwhile, Kira's crossed arms and sharp chin dare me to prove that I deserve her attention. I ask for her version of September 18, which matches Miranda's. She must have it down cold, with the number of times she's had to tell it.

"Do you mind if Kira and I talk alone for a minute?" I ask Miranda.

"Yes, I do."

"Okay, then," I say smoothly. Plenty of clients overrule me, and I don't have an ego about it. I prefer to be mild, even when contradicted. Especially when insulted. As far as Miranda's concerned, I want to have a light touch. I'll be nothing more than a wave on her beach. "So, Kira, why'd you go in through the window?"

"What do you mean?" she asks.

"What was going through your mind?"

She avoids my gaze.

"I thought something bad had happened."

"What?"

The ocean rolls.

"What did you think happened?" I probe.

"The worst."

Her chin drops until she's looking at her black silk shirt. Sharp collar. Top two buttons undone. Sleek enough to appear soaking wet. *The worst.* She looks glamorous even with a terrible idea in mind, leaking slowly out of her mouth.

"Which was?"

"I thought she might've killed herself."

It's hard to read Kira as she says this. She's clearly had some Botox, which keeps her forehead firm, unreactive. Her eyebrows are straight brown stripes. There might be some fillers around her mouth, too, plumping up faint lines that could've whispered something.

"Why would she do that?" I ask.

"I don't know."

Miranda starts to cry.

"Can I please speak with Kira alone?" I repeat to Miranda, more softly.

This time, she nods yes.

"I'll put something together in the kitchen," Miranda announces. "For when Roger and Eliza get here." She leaves the room.

It's just Kira and me now.

She turns a pavé diamond ring around her middle finger, while a tennis bracelet sways under her wrist. The only jewelry that Claire ever wore was her engagement ring, one pearl on a silver band. In an episode of *The Tonight Show*, Jimmy Fallon asked Claire all about the proposal. Plenty of interviewers did. Everyone had high expectations for her real-life romance, since she wrote about permanent connection, about a love stronger than death. As the camera zoomed in on her ring, Claire admitted that she'd had a say in the design. She'd told Roger that she didn't want anything flashy, that she didn't even want a diamond.

Kira's glittering joints suggest she thinks differently.

"Abigail said that your methods were 'unusual,'" she says eventually.

"Makes sense."

"What does that mean, exactly?"

"I solve difficult cases by really getting to know the people I'm working with," I explain. "So I ask a lot of questions that might seem off topic. I spend a lot of time with my clients. It helps me get a full picture of their lives."

She rolls her eyes.

"Why do you think you're so resistant to working with me?" I ask.

"Excuse me?"

I wait.

"Because my mom is a wreck about this, and I don't want anyone fucking with her."

"Why are you less of a wreck about this?" I ask.

She checks her nails.

"Your mom hired me to find Claire," I say, feeling like a school-teacher. Like the nature of my job has changed again in order to satisfy client need. Kira continues to stare at her hand. Her gaze falls below her nails, toward the creased belly of her palm. "Your mom asked me to come here, sign an NDA, and start working today. I would imagine that if you really want to please her, then she's made it pretty clear how she wants us to interact." Her icy front doesn't crack. "I'm just asking for an honest conversation, that's all."

No response.

"I imagine that it wasn't always easy to be Claire's sister," I go on more gently. "As I said, I'd like to get a full picture of your lives. Not every detective does that, goes as deep into the past, into things that don't seem to matter. I'm not just interested in September eighteenth. I'm interested in your side of the story, starting long before that day." Kira relaxes a barely perceptible degree. The mass of fur peeking around her arm still looks like a sleeping bear. "So, you and Claire grew up going to the same schools?"

Very slowly, she nods.

"Until college," she says.

Both girls went to Phillips Exeter Academy, the prep school in New Hampshire, before Claire went to Harvard and Kira to Tulane.

"How was that for you?" I ask.

"It had its ups and downs."

I wait for more.

"My whole life, I've been following in Claire's footsteps," she says quietly, pinching a tiny wrinkle in her leather pants. "I've spent the past twenty-eight years trying to do things as well as Claire." She laughs sadly. "Trying and failing."

"That must've been hard for you."

She shrugs and drops her hands.

"Were you close as kids?" I ask.

"Yes, but . . ."

"But?"

"Claire was always different," she admits.

"How so?"

"She was an adult as a child, and a child as an adult." It's articulated with more indifference than I would've expected from Claire's sister, especially at a time like this. I write the words down exactly. "So, even as a kid, she was *sensible*. Too *sensible* for everyone else's bad decisions. That meant she wasn't eating the sandbox with the rest of us idiots. Then, she wasn't skipping class to smoke under the bleachers. Then, she wasn't trying to get drunk on Listerine. She was rule abiding, and not begrudgingly. *Gladly.* As if she was thirty years older and had already made all our dumb mistakes. Didn't need to learn from them twice.

"*I*, on the other hand, was always giving Mom another reason to worry: talking back to teachers, running off in the dead of night . . ." I hear other transgressions left unnamed. "When we got out of school, though, things changed. Claire wasn't the more responsible one anymore. She was intent on writing this book. This dreamlike, fantastical book. When she told people the premise, it sounded like she was radioing in from another planet. It obviously worked out for her. But for a long time, I was worried. When everyone else was building a career in the real world, Claire didn't. She stayed in the world she imagined." It's interesting that Kira claims they were close, because all I hear is tension.

"I asked you about the eighteenth already," I say, "but I'm curious: When you went into Claire's room that morning, did you move anything?"

"No." She recoils.

"Right, I didn't think so."

"Then why'd you ask?"

I ignore the jab and plow ahead.

"Because I'm looking for her journals."

"Claire didn't keep journals."

"She did," I say confidently. "In interviews, she mentioned that she journaled every day. So, I'm just wondering, what makes you so sure she didn't?"

"I—I never saw her."

Kira crosses her legs. The leather squeaks, as if it isn't quite real.

"Few people ever *see* someone write in their diary, right?" I ask.

As an answer, she stares me down.

"What do you think happened to your sister?"

"I think that she's missing. And it's not a crime to be missing."

"Your mom thinks someone took her."

Miranda appears as if on cue at the threshold. She holds her own hands nervously. There's a thought rippling through her lips, slowly taking shape. Kira and I watch her until she reveals, "Eliza and Roger are almost here."

THREE

"For someone with my condition, it's a gamble to fly down this road. Then again, I know what the crash would feel like. I've felt my ribs pierce my lungs, my aorta tear on my spine. I've had my heart displaced on impact, and I'm still here."
—*Claire Ross,* The Starlit Ballet

Before anyone else arrives, I want more time in Claire's room.

Miranda guides me back there but stops short in the hallway. I glance sideways to find her frozen in place. A Slim Aarons–type photograph hangs on the wall beside her. It's a bird's-eye view that captures sunbathers around a pool and a diver poised to jump. I'm sure that it's supposed to be a glamorous scene, but without lights on, and without windows in this hallway, the black water looks ominous.

"I'll leave you to it," she says.

She waves goodbye.

I take the last few steps alone.

Claire's silver doorknob is loose. It's surreal to think that she must've had her own hand right here, felt exactly this. I wonder how she would've described it. In *The Starlit Ballet*, her style is radically simple. She writes as if she's deeply aware of the constraints on your time and has something specific to say. Her sentences are carved down to the bone. Still, they're gorgeous and fascinating because of *what* she's communicating, not *how*. She proves that great writing isn't about words, but ideas.

In almost every interview, Claire was asked to give advice to aspiring writers. It looked like everyone wanted her roadmap to artistic success—if not to realize their own dreams, then to demystify her. To understand the mechanics of her wild ride, the factual nuts and bolts of it. Claire had a few different answers, but one was, "You need to rip your story out of real life." She said that all tensions in a novel, all emotions, have to come from somewhere real in order to resonate with people. "Careful," she warned, "because if you do it right, you might rip your*self* out of the real world too." Almost too prescient.

I'm drawn back to her bookcase, where I study the titles: *Il Balletto Stellato*, звездный балет, 星光芭蕾. I pull the last one off the shelf, wondering if Claire scribbled any secret in the margins, if she circled any meaningful words. The spine crackles as if it's never been opened.

I slide the book back in its place, then face the windows. They're double hung and gridless, giving nearly unbroken views of the water. I approach the one that Kira found lifted. There are no dents in the sill, no chips in the white paint. I unlock the bottom panel and push it up, letting in a breeze that cools the blood in my cheeks.

I thought she might've killed herself. A few high-profile author suicides come to mind. Virginia Woolf filled her own pockets with stones, walked deep into a river, and never came back. Ernest Hemingway shot himself in the head at home in Ketchum, Idaho. Sylvia Plath left milk and cookies out for her children, then put her head in the oven.

What did Claire Ross do?

I leave the window open and return to the bookshelf, where I peek between titles for anything she might've left behind. Eventually, my fingers find *The Goldfinch*, *The Little Friend*, and *The Secret History*—Donna Tartt's entire oeuvre. Claire raved about Donna in multiple interviews. In her Q and A with *Vanity Fair*, Claire said she admired Donna's grit, persevering on each book for a decade. That's almost how long it took Claire to write *The Starlit Ballet*. Claire must've felt a kinship with Donna. Marathoners.

I step away from the shelves.

Back in Claire's closet, I unzip one of the garment bags and find her wedding dress. It's a strapless cut by Monique Lhuillier with an elaborate lace pattern and leafy off-the-shoulder sleeves. I touch one of them, surprised. I would've expected Claire to choose something simpler—a plain white slip, for example—but dresses like this don't happen by accident. This would've required multiple fittings and thousands of dollars. This is a dress that Claire chose well in advance and spent time on away from her work.

"She was supposed to wear my earrings too."

I jump, dropping my hands.

Miranda steps into the closet.

Usually, I do a better job of blending into a tasteful home, as smoothly as a cashmere throw—even when I'm alone. That means not leaving a trace. Not a coffee cup on the counter. Not a fingerprint on the bathroom door handle. As if I don't have a body at all, and I'm just a hired mind. I almost *never* touch anything fragile or emotionally important to a client without their permission. But if Miranda saw me holding Claire's dress, she doesn't seem bothered by it. She opens the top drawer of the bureau and removes a velvet satchel. She unties the strings and tips it over to release two pearl studs in her palm.

"I wore these when I married her father," she says. "'Something old, new, borrowed, and blue,' right? These were going to be her something borrowed." Her eyebrows stitch together, mourning the idea. The pearls have a ghostly tint in her hand. "Her something blue is still upstairs in my jewelry box. A sapphire tennis bracelet. We'd talked about other options, but none of them ever really set her on fire. She thought she was just going to tuck a blue ribbon into her shoe. A one-inch scrap, like debris from a first-grade project. She deserved something more exciting, didn't she? The bracelet was going to be a surprise."

"That's very thoughtful."

She nods, putting the pearls back.

"Sounds like you put a lot of work into planning this," I say.

"These things only happen once."

She holds my gaze.

"Roger and Eliza are here."

~

After shutting the window, I find everyone in the foyer.

Eliza must be the thirtysomething with fiery red hair. Her royal-purple maxi dress swishes around her ankles. She greets me with an energetic handshake and perky smile.

Behind her, Claire's fiancé, Roger Galvin, is more muted in a faded green polo and khakis. The short-sleeve verges on white, as if he's worn it out here for weeks and it's encrusted in salt. I've seen photos of him, but none captured how downbeat he is, how he seems to sink in on himself. If he stood up straight, he'd be over six feet tall, but there's a slight hunch in his shoulders. He has a short haircut and ears that stick out on either side. Brown bangs cover his forehead, gathered in loose curls. In photos, those were always gelled to the side. Roger's large nose is just imperfect enough that he comes off approachable, maybe even kind.

He shakes my hand without much pressure.

We trade first names.

I watch him as Miranda ferries us into the living room.

After someone writes an epic love story, it's tempting to think that her own relationship must be supercharged. After all, Claire convincingly described a connection that transcended different eras, different identities. That must have shown up in her personal life. Did she and Roger have a love as powerful as the one in her book?

Miranda offers everyone something to drink. Only Kira speaks up, asking for orange juice. As Roger, Kira, and I take seats in the living room around a generous spread on the coffee table—wheels of cheese, seedy crackers, little pickles in a white ramekin, and thin slices of salami—Eliza follows Miranda into the kitchen. Roger leans back in his chair, ignoring the food. I remember reading that he's an accountant in New York City. He's worked at the same firm since he graduated from Davidson College ten years ago.

"So, you found the Picasso?" Roger asks.

"I'm sorry, but I can't talk about past clients."

He nods sympathetically.

Kira lathers jam on a cracker.

"Abigail said her methods are 'unusual.'" Kira doesn't look at me as she cuts a thick slice of brie and layers it on top. "She's here to ask us questions about ourselves. She says the better she knows us, the better chance she has of finding Claire."

"Whatever it takes," he says soberly.

I study him. His soft cheeks—rounded as if his mouth is full—are the one exception to his wiry build. Everywhere else, he's lean. Roger ran cross-country in college, and it appears he's hung on to the figure. He's unusually pale, especially next to Kira, but I'm trying to see him the way Claire did. What about him got to her? Gently, I ask how he and Claire met—Hinge, he tells me—and for his first impression of her.

"I thought she was too pretty for me." His brown eyes well, making his irises look syrupy. "Sorry, it's still hard to talk about her. Ever since . . ."

I read the weather was beautiful on September 18.

Clear blue sky. The clouds had vanished too.

"What do you think happened to her?" I ask.

"I think what Miranda thinks," he says, shooting a cautious glance at Kira. "That's why we're still looking. It doesn't make sense. What I believe"—he taps his knee for emphasis—"is that if she'd agreed to a bodyguard, she would be here right now. I asked her, 'Please, Claire, get some security for the weekend,' but . . . she refused."

"Simple as that?"

He nods yes.

"I usually deferred to her. She was—Claire Ross." His shoulders shrink up to his ears. "I knew she needed a professional with her, maybe even a team. I mean, 302 guests, plus vendors? Someone was going to let it slip. The wrong person was going to find out." His eyebrows pinch together. Their thick inner corners taper fast, the ends like dark stitches. "But Claire killed the idea. She was adamant there's no such thing as a famous author. She had a line, 'Books are famous—authors aren't.' She said she'd only been stopped on the street *twice* for a photo. I told her that was because she barely went outside. She didn't understand she was at risk." He holds both his kneecaps. "I just *know* someone took her."

"Who?" I ask.

"One of the Starlites," he says, referring to Claire's superfans. They coined the term as soon as her book came out, uniting behind it on Reddit, fan sites, and social media. "It felt like millions of them were in love with her. You don't understand—or maybe you do. When people read a book, they want the author to be the essence of it. So, Claire was the essence of true love for these people. She got hundreds of love letters, love poems, even tortured written proposals from people she'd never met."

Starlites are known for their strange addiction to her. Plenty of books get fanfare. But in Claire's case, the fixation is on *her*. For Halloween, book events, and conventions, Potterheads dress up as Harry Potter and Hermione Granger. Twihards dress up as Bella Swan and Edward Cullen. But Starlites dress up as Claire Ross. It makes her line "Books are famous—authors aren't" feel recklessly unaware. I've heard of authors tuning out the world in order to hear their own ideas. Did Claire tune out the Starlites? How many dangerous fans did she meet while her mind was somewhere else?

"Did she complain about any stalkers?" I ask.

"No. But like I said, she didn't get out much. She was always writing. For all she knew, there could've been a hundred thousand Starlites standing on our block, just looking up and watching her breathe." I picture yellow streetlamps, a dark mob of bodies, and two hundred thousand eyes gleaming at night.

"Did you see any of the love letters?" I ask.

He nods yes.

"Anything that worried you?" I ask.

"The number of them."

"Did you ever see her write back?"

He repeats the last two words to himself, then tells me no.

I transition to the subject of Claire's journals and ask if he ever saw her write in any. Again, he repeats the last two words. He takes long enough with the question that I can tell he's never had to answer it before. All his time with the police, the press, and no one asked him this. He glances up at the ceiling, eyelids clipping the tops of his irises. It's refreshing to see him respect me, after my face-off with Kira. Eventually, he shakes his head.

"No, why?"

"She said in a couple interviews that she kept journals." I glance at Kira. She pops two pepperoni coins into her mouth. "Claire said that she wrote in them every day." Roger looks surprised. "She went on about it, said it was a great place to mine for material. A lot of her journaling found its way into *The Starlit Ballet*."

Eliza emerges with two crystal tumblers of orange juice. The citrus is aggressively bright. Tropical splashes in a neutral room. She gives Kira one with a pleasant smile, then pats her on the shoulder. Eliza sits next to Roger, close enough that she could touch him too. She seems at ease here. Technically, we're both hired help. But she seems woven into the fabric of the family. *We had dinner together last night.* Maybe that's because as a wedding planner, she's called in for the best moments in people's lives. Meanwhile, I'm part of the worst. She's a midwife to celebration. I'm a midwife to tragedy.

"Please excuse me," Kira says.

She leaves without her juice.

Eliza and Roger face me expectantly.

In my prior cases, I always interviewed people alone. It's not just the group setting that feels new; it's the cheese plate, the crystal glasses, and the fact that an event planner is sitting right here. What's usually a solemn meeting is now strangely festive. Lavish, even for the Hamptons. I wonder how Claire felt in this environment. She was always so heads down and hardworking, uninterested in a life of leisure. She seemed more likely to respond to the legendary Ernest Shackleton ad, "Men wanted for hazardous journey. Low wages, bitter cold, long hours of complete darkness. Safe return doubtful."

I ask Eliza how long she's been a wedding planner.

"I'm more of a 'luxury event' planner."

"'Luxury'?" I probe.

"We work with budgets of at least $300,000. We just booked our first million-dollar wedding next year." I hide my surprise like a well-guarded therapist. Someone who keeps their judgments to themselves, so the person in the armchair will say more. I've heard of million-dollar weddings, of course, but they're still a mystifying species. I can't even visualize one. "'Luxury' also refers to our level of service. We hold our clients' hands through everything. *We* track RSVPs, et cetera." She takes a tangy sip. "It's usually a fun job. I work with my two best friends. Frankly, I have to because I can be disorganized. Forgetful, believe it or not. Everything an event planner shouldn't be. But we help each other, filling in all the unforgivable gaps. We each lead only four events a year, which means we have to be choosy. So, before agreeing to a wedding, we interview the bride to screen for red flags."

I ask for some examples.

"When people care too much about the wedding, and not enough about the marriage, for one thing," Eliza says. "Or when the bride doesn't mention the groom at all. That happens more than you'd think." A jaded look. "But Claire barely said 'I.' Even with her vocabulary, that word just wasn't in it. Roger was such a presence on our call, I felt like I knew him. Roger, from Chattanooga, Tennessee. Roger, who wanted a white cake with vanilla frosting. Who wanted traditional vows. Whose ten fraternity brothers would be his groomsmen. Some brides are all about themselves, but Claire was all about Roger."

"How was Claire throughout the planning?" I ask.

Eliza reflects.

"Relatively hands off," she admits. "But at this level, to be perfectly honest, my clients are the moms. It's their money, and they know it." Her smile softens the blunt remark. "And this was Miranda's first wedding, so she was extra involved. First-wedding moms always are. By the time we get to their second or third, they say, 'I trust you, Eliza—'"

A cabinet slams shut in the kitchen.

Kira emerges in a huff. She strides toward the sofa and plops down next to Eliza—so close that Eliza scoots over. Kira flashes us a smile that does not lift up at the ends. It's just one hard line. Seconds later, Miranda enters the room with red eyes.

She fixates on Kira.

"We are going to find your sister," she says with authority, apparently picking up on a conversation they were just having in the kitchen. "I don't know why you're making this even harder than it needs to be. We're not going to tell Nina to go home."

Kira makes a fist.

Only I notice it.

"I'm just saying that if Claire ran away, she doesn't want to be found," Kira says.

"Why would she do that?" Miranda shouts. "Why?"

Kira stares at the rug.

Miranda looks at me.

"I will do my best to find your daughter," I say cautiously.

Kira crosses her legs into a tight spiral.

If I didn't know they were sisters, I never would've imagined it. It's not just that Kira's nails are bright red with a gel manicure, while Claire never got hers painted, or that Kira's wearing layers of makeup for a meeting about her missing sister, while Claire went on TV without a touch-up. It's deeper than that. Kira's cynical. Meanwhile, Claire worked alone for years on the most idealistic book I've ever read.

"She didn't *run away*," Miranda says.

She plucks an empty sleeve of crackers like a weed and leaves with it. I'm tempted to tell Miranda that although the prospect might feel personal, it isn't. If Claire ran away, that decision would say more about her than anyone else. Authors are known for their love of solitude. Maybe Claire got scared on the morning of her legal union to someone else. J. D. Salinger ran from the limelight after *The Catcher in the Rye*'s wild success. He requested that all future editions of the book be canceled and his author photo removed from the jackets. Marcel Proust spent seventeen years of his life alone, the final three in a soundproofed room.

It's counterintuitive, though, that someone who wrote about *love*—about the power of a deep connection to transcend space and time—would abandon her fiancé, her family, and all her wedding guests. It would be heartbreaking for the world to learn that the woman who gave them a glimpse of true love put those closest to her through hell.

"You ever worked on something like this before?" Roger asks.

"I unfortunately can't discuss that."

He and Eliza nod.

"You know, if you're really trying to know Claire—what she felt, believed, thought about . . ." Roger pulls *The Starlit Ballet* out from under the pickles and holds it up. "She spent more time with this than with any one of us." He puts the book back down. "It's a download of her consciousness for the past decade. Have you read it?"

http://www.reddit.com/r/ClaireRoss

r/ClaireRoss posted by u/B3LI3V3M3 2 mos ago

FINDING CLAIRE: MEGATHREAD

`MEGATHREAD`

☆☆✳ PLEASE SHARE INFORMATION RELEVANT TO HER CASE. ☆☆✳
We know her better than anyone.
We should be able to find her. ☆☆✳

Current Megathreads:

ENCOUNTERS
PHOTOS

Sort By: Old

speakVOLUMES · 2 mos ago

I HAVE MEMORIES THAT DON'T BELONG TO ME.

CLAIRE'S LIFE LEADING UP TO SEPTEMBER 18:
We all know that Claire barely left her apt on East
68th St. (She worked all day from home, including
weekends. Had her groceries delivered. Had her
toiletries/kitchen/cleaning supplies delivered. Ate
virtually all her meals there. Didn't paint her nails.
Didn't get her hair done. Didn't go to a gym outside
her building.) Modern Day Salinger.

We know from ENCOUNTERS that she really only
left to go on walks with Roger, a few times every
week. I can personally confirm this. My parents live

in their neighborhood (East 61st), so whenever I was on break from school, I'd follow them.

Most of the time, Claire and Roger walked to Central Park and back. During the week, they'd set out in the 6:30-7:30 p.m. range. On weekends, they'd leave between 1 and 3 p.m. Each walk took them 30-40 minutes. Claire wore the same outfit almost every time: charcoal sweatpants (no brand, the material looked synthetic), Adidas slip-on sneakers, baseball cap. The only stops they ever made were for coffee on the weekends.

They were honestly very affectionate. Not super *in love* or *obsessed* with each other—I never saw them make out. Or kiss, actually. But they seemed comfortable. They were always holding hands or linking arms. Never argued. The only thing that was a little weird was they never looked at each other full-on. They stared straight ahead the whole time. (For context: they're the only people I've ever *watched* walk. So maybe this is normal?)

PageByPaige91 · 2 mos ago

If she only saw Roger, does that make him our top suspect?

DES10NYY · 2 mos ago

For people saying the walks sound too boring to be true: NYC is always changing. You can never go on the same walk twice

paper-s0ul · 2 mos ago

The same clothes?
Why the same clothes

speakV0LUMES · 2 mos ago

I HAVE MEMORIES THAT DON'T BELONG TO ME.

I don't think she was wearing the exact same *pair* of
sweatpants over and over again. She must've had
more in her closet than that

Then again, I don't really know

PageByPaige91 · 2 mos ago

Maybe she was saving up for something.

secret7admirer · 2 mos ago

I have phantom Claire

CLOSER3ADER · 2 mos ago

Leave her alone.

readMeRoss · 2 mos ago

☆☆✳ **WE ARE HER BEST CHANCE
DON'T YOU WANT TO FIND HER** ☆

one-more-sin · 2 mos ago

Exactly ☆ She saved us all ☆
Now, it's our turn to save her ☆

xxjjkk66 · 2 mos ago

CCCcccccccccclaireeeeeeeeeeeeeeeeeeeeeeeeeeee
eeeeeeeeeeeeeeeeeeeeeee ☆☆✶☆☆✶☆☆✶☆☆✶☆☆
✶☆☆✶☆☆✶☆☆✶☆☆✶☆☆✶☆☆✶☆☆✶☆☆✶☆☆✶☆☆✶☆☆
✶☆☆✶☆☆✶☆☆✶☆☆✶☆☆✶

ClaireBearXX · 2 mos ago

Me too. I feel her with me

rabidhole · 2 mos ago

YOU KNOW WHAT IT'S LIKE TO DIE?

We can't just look at Claire's lifestyle generally speaking. We need to look at her specifically in the *weeks/days leading up to her wedding*. Did anyone else here live on her block? Did you notice anything right before Sept 18?

paperbackribs · 2 mos ago

I manage a restaurant in Amagansett (5 minute drive from East Hampton). The Rosses ordered takeout from us on Monday Sept 13th. They used a fake name but I knew the address. (Doesn't everyone?) I was in front-of-the-house clothes, but I had someone cover me so I could deliver the food myself.

Drove my own car.
Don't know what I was expecting.

When I showed up, their gates were shut. On the other side, their house was all lit up. Not a dark room in the place. It looked like a small group was in the dining room on the first floor. Six or seven people standing around a table.

I had instructions to leave their food on the gate's call box. So that was (unfortunately for us) the closest I could get. Of course, I took my time about it. Kept staring at the dining room. They were in the middle of a discussion. It didn't seem angry or heated, but everyone there was *invested*. Everyone except Claire, actually. She was off to one side, leaning against the wall. I'm sure it was her. Can't miss the hair. Like blood on snow. Looking back, it's strange that she wasn't in the huddle? She was three or four steps away, staring at the floor.

COSM1CALLY · 2 mos ago

What did they order? ☆☆✳

paperbackribs · 2 mos ago

1 chicken parmigiana 1 caesar salad, dressing on the side 1 cheesy garlic bread 1 chicken paillard 1

vegetarian lasagna 1 greek salad, dressing on the side 1 salmon special

mixChief_ · 2 mos ago

Hard to know what to make of it.
That could've been her family around a seating chart, debating where to put the weird uncle. Or it could've been the florists. Photographers. Lighting crew. Anyone in the wedding, planning the weekend . . .
Still. Off to the side?

scar-tissue6 · 2 mos ago

A true fan would've given her the food by hand using a l l t e n f i n g e r s

PageByPaige91 · 2 mos ago

What was the fake name?

paperbackribs · 2 mos ago

Atticus

solmated · 2 mos ago

SINCE WE WERE VIKINGS

Claire and Kira were in East Hampton that Friday Sep 17. They worked out at Barre3, at the 8 a.m. class. It was clearly Kira's idea. Both slots were in her name.

Claire had to sign a general liability waiver before we started.

☆I was
the teacher.☆

During class, though, Claire wasn't . . . there. Not mentally, I mean. She was late on almost everything. At first, I thought it was my fault. I assumed I was messing up cues. Because, you know, *Claire Ross*. She taught me 12 colors I'd never seen before. She taught me how much I can feel, pulled me out of the shallows and *held me underwater until I could breathe*. But everyone else was roughly on time and in sync with each other. I started to get worried. It almost looked like she was having a stroke. She was *that* distractible, wrapped up in something. Part of me wanted to single her out and ask if she was okay . . . Maybe I should have.

mixChief_ · 2 mos ago

You really should have.

FOUR

"Now, I'm remembering too many organs: a whole kidney in the palm of my hand. A fatty heart rippling in an opened rib cage. A stomach on a steel surgical tray, both ends leaking."

—*Claire Ross,* The Starlit Ballet

"Yes, I've read it," I admit to Roger, Kira, and Eliza. All three of them face me on the sofa, and suddenly, *I* feel like the one who's being interviewed. The mirror on the wall above them reflects tiered, frothy waves sliding across the beach. Green dunes slice up the wind. When Miranda returns, she sits on the chair beside me, evening the balance a little.

I turn to Kira.

"Did you read it?" I ask.

"No." She reaches for a pickle and crunches through it.

"Why not?" I ask.

"I don't read fiction."

Miranda is stony. As if this horse has already been beaten.

"Did you?" I ask Roger.

"Claire asked me to read it the week it came out. That's what she asked all of us." He has a habit of shrugging when he talks. It comes off modest, as if he's quietly undermining his own contributions. "To be honest, I don't think she cared *when* we picked it up, so long as we waited for the official release. She kept the manuscript . . . private."

"Private?" I ask.

"She wouldn't let anyone read her drafts. Not Miranda, not me. She'd write on her laptop, edit printouts. And when she was done, she'd shred them. We must've gone through six or seven shredders. She kept grinding too many pages at once, clogging the teeth. I think she was being a perfectionist. Every word needed to be in place before we saw it." He keeps his chin angled humbly toward his chest. "Sometimes, it felt like she wasn't even writing. She was *building*. It wasn't creative. It was architectural. And if she didn't put those 120,000 words in order, the structure would collapse. Kill everyone inside." He covers his lips with three fingers, as if he's preventing himself from saying more.

"What did you think of it, Nina?" Miranda asks.

I can feel her ache for praise.

"It was the most brilliant, most deeply felt book I've ever read."

Miranda half smiles.

"What was your favorite part?" Kira asks skeptically.

"Long answer or short one?" I ask.

"Long."

I nod, accepting her test.

"The opening chapter takes place in Yosemite in 2903," I say, shifting into my newest role: literary critic. "There, Logan struggles with seeing too much at once. He's overwhelmed with flashbacks to hundreds of moments throughout history. Then, the book cuts to a series of stories. They take place in ancient Rome, seventeenth-century Madagascar, and then eighteenth-century Philadelphia. Each is told by a man and ends in the middle of the narrative. Sometimes, right in the middle of an action. The middle of a sentence.

"In part two, a woman tells the second half of each story. When those are complete, an angel visits the last woman with a question: 'Are you ready to go?' The angel explains that she and her soulmate have been reincarnating for thousands of years, and the goal of their time on this planet has been to evolve into old souls. They're supposed to grow spiritually—meaning, to lose interest in this world and become unreasonably kind. The angel asks if she'd like to leave Earth now that she's matured, while her soulmate continues to evolve. But Chloe won't leave her partner. She chooses to stay and reincarnate with him until he's ready.

"The book continues from her perspective. Her soulmate makes *some* progress going beyond himself. But he doesn't fully mature until his life as a professional cyclist. Then, he survives a crash so dramatic, his outlook turns on its head. Now, after thousands of years, he can finally put himself second. He can find causes and ideas more important than his one microscopic life. When the angel returns to take them away, they ask for one more life together. And this time, they'd like to keep their memories.

"Cut to Yosemite again, where you realize that Logan, the boy from the beginning, is one of the two soulmates we've been watching. He's kept his memory, but he can't handle it. There are too many memories, from too many past lives." Roger's mouth parts at the scope of my recollection. "Eventually, he and Cady—that's her name in this life—meet. She helps him make sense of his memories, and they live out their final life side by side."

A brief silence.

"I asked for your *favorite* part," Kira says, unimpressed.

"All of it. It's the most complex, most soulful book I've ever read."

"Thank you," Miranda says earnestly.

"I know the book was successful before," I say. "Not to be crass"— people who grew up with money hate to talk about it; maybe deep down they're uncomfortable with their privileges—"but I have to imagine it's only selling better in her absence?"

Small nods.

"Did she have a will?" I ask.

"No." Miranda shows disdain for the idea. "Enough about wills. That only matters if—but we're going to find her." Without a will, if Claire was declared legally dead, the state would hand her assets over to Miranda, her closest living family member. "But I would make sure it all went to Roger," she adds, as if she can read my mind. "It's what

Claire would've wanted." I look at the man who might receive royalties into perpetuity for the most successful book of our time. He avoids everyone's gaze, his shoulders slumped, staring at the floor.

~

On the drive home that afternoon, I pick up a McDonald's Quarter Pounder with Cheese. It warms my thigh as I merge onto the highway. I've been eating these burgers for so long, the salt in my blood might've come from the beef.

I take slow bites.

As a kid, I appreciated the consistency of McDonald's. There was one across the street from our apartment in Boston, where I'd go after school and stay for as long as I could. That place was reliable. Every burger came out exactly the same, down to the number of sesame seeds on top. The people who took my order were sober. No one there ever slept all afternoon, drenched in light, wearing tight-laced sneakers on a daybed. No one there ever needed a drink so bad, they sipped blue dish soap in front of me.

My dad was in the marines until his discharge before I was born. He had a lean face, long chin. Wore green military jackets at home. When he wasn't drinking, he had incessant physical energy. Part of him was always moving—a bouncing knee, jittery thumb. He could be paranoid, prone to conspiracy theories. He insisted that we had to be *prepared*—not for anything realistic, like rent. But for a nuclear apocalypse. World War III. He kept canned soup under his bed and tended to the supply like a lifeless garden.

My mom drank just as much but managed to work. She usually had a job—hostessing at a Hilton, selling perfume—but none lasted for more than a year or two. Then, her temper would intervene. Her manager would rebuke her—tell her she couldn't smoke inside, for example—and she'd turn in vicious self-defense. Then she'd come home and crash on the living room daybed. She'd watch daytime movies and the evening news for weeks, bottles around her mushrooming. When she felt up to it, she'd eat cloying foods, especially sugar and red jam on white bread. She'd repeat *Fuck you, Jenelle*, or whoever her last boss had been, while pushing the TV back with one foot. It would teeter at a perilous slant.

My parents divorced when I was eight.

Mom and I stayed in our place. She was the one already on the lease. She was the one who paid rent. I remember that apartment with its cracking ivory paint. It looked like we were in the belly of a brown spiderweb. Nothing was clean, not even on her good days. Every surface was littered with cookie wrappers, open magazines, clear bottles, and strangled beer cans. Our building was full of cabdrivers. I could hear their conversations in the hallway about hours, neighborhoods, and noteworthy passengers.

For the next ten years, I only saw my dad when he needed another loan. Every time, he'd take me out to a Mister Softee truck, then drop me off in person so he could ask Mom for a couple hundred dollars. That's how I lost my taste for ice cream. To this day, I can't even have a milkshake, because the sweet cream reminds me of those slimy afternoons, when his hair was slicked back and his mind was somewhere else. He'd be rapping his knuckles, his brown eyes hyperactive. It wasn't until I was a teenager that Mom cut him off, and then he resorted to stealing. On three separate occasions, he broke into our apartment through the fire escape and took the cash under Mom's mattress.

When I was eighteen, I woke up to the sound of my mom shrieking in her room. Everything was black. I couldn't see to the end of my bed. As soon as she stopped, I heard a man fighting to breathe—doomed gurgling. Short groans. He was in Mom's room too. Something heavy hit her floor and cracked. I jumped out of bed and ran to her, straight through the dark. I try not to think about it. But I remember calling 911, crying for my parents, crying for myself, and then trying to understand. My dad must have come back to steal. In her drunken confusion, my mom must have tried to kill him. He must have fought back.

At the time, I was too consumed with the imperative to survive to be able to mourn them deeply. Mom didn't leave enough money to fulfill the rest of her twelve-month lease. So I couldn't sit with my own emotions for long. I couldn't grapple with what it meant to lose my entire family, flawed as they were. Instead, I had to decide whether or not to sell her old wedding band. Whether or not to wear her clothes. Even when I was alone in that apartment, eating the last of the red jam in the fridge with a spoon, flashbacks to them were scarce. Dad listening to a stolen police scanner in the corner. Mom's strange bruising—her shoulder would turn purple whenever she slept on one side for too long.

For the next four years, I worked as many jobs as I could, including two washing dishes in college kitchens. Those were nonstop shifts. I had more pleasant options, but not on college campuses. Not where I could sneak into lectures on Elizabeth Bishop and Virginia Woolf. It took me a while to work up the courage, but eventually, I was sitting in on three to four English classes a week. It helped that everyone else there was my age. And I took care to sit in the back, with up to fifty rows between the professor and me.

Those classes were worth—everything.

They gave me a community, even if I wasn't really a part of it. Every time I left "Romanticism" or "Moby Dick," I found myself in a crowd of undergrads, our backpacks knocking, and no one ever tapped me on the shoulder to ask if I was lost. I enjoyed being an ungraded A student. And the *books*. They gave me something that lasted through two eight-hour shifts in a row, cleaning liquid at the bottom of trash cans. Picking up 176-degree forks. Reaching for knives in gray water. I kept up with the syllabi for all my stolen courses. I read everything that I could, especially stories like mine. When an author described something well, they understood it. And that was something. To this day, I love books like people and believe that great novels have souls—including *The Starlit Ballet*.

I'm not the only one.

Popular reviews for the novel are superlative. The first on Amazon proceeds under the headline, "I would die for Claire Ross ☆☆✳." The first on Goodreads begins, "*The Starlit Ballet* isn't a book, it's a ☆ transformation. Once it gets inside you, you'll never be the same again. ☆" The top opinions are all overrun with star symbols, badges of Starlite loyalty. The jumbled ☆'s make their wild claims look even stranger, like snippets of font in their own language. Or words they invented to describe how Claire makes them feel. Because the Starlites are more than fans; they're evangelists. They swear her book isn't just good; it's biblical.

I take the Riverhead exit, drive through town.

My mind keeps drifting back to Roger. His gentle respect. Clumsy appendages—big ears, long hands. Before Claire went missing, he kept his distance from her public life. He never graced any of her TV appearances. He was never quoted in any feature about her—not even the ones that interviewed her at home, when he might've been in the next room. People always assumed that he and Claire had something special because of the depth in her book. But really, no one had a grounded sense of what they were like as a couple.

I try to picture them together. What did they talk about over dinner? I try to imagine it down to the words they might've used, how they might've sounded. Claire's voice was deep, confident. She never said anything that her whole body didn't believe. Her chest was involved, giving every sentence a husky backbone. Her hands were emotionally invested. Her thighs and knees were active listeners. Meanwhile, Roger's energy didn't animate much below his neck. I liked him, but watching him didn't make me feel more alive.

I try to picture them having sex. Claire was sensual. Not for any physical reason. Her sensuality came from how deeply she probed her own mind, how far down she reached into her own viscera. Her life story touched everyone's latent desire for more. It was elevating to know she'd fought so long for her dream. It got the blood going and heart pumping in a way that was more than sexy. It was passionate, gritty, and real. Meanwhile, Roger was shy and humble. Even at his most decisive, there was doubt on the edges of his words.

I can't picture the sex.

Or romance.

Did Claire Ross, with *her* standard for love, really lose her heart to timid Roger? Did he balance her—was that it? Did he make her feel normal?

I need to talk to him alone. After we chatted as a group for an hour this morning, and then toured the house, he and Kira left to get ready for a charity dinner that Miranda will host tonight at the Parrish Art Museum. I got their cell phone numbers. We all planned to meet again tomorrow morning for a tour of the property. Roger and Kira can work remotely, so they're happy to stay in town while I get the investigation underway.

I should reach out to him separately—or find those journals. They won't just shed light on Claire's relationship. They could explain how she managed to thrive in a mansion with fragile oyster plates on the walls. White sofas that looked like they'd never been wrinkled. Books that had never been read. A few times, I got the sense that I was on a film set. Chairs rented, props hollow. Ready for the cast.

I pull into the parking lot for my building to find Lauretta near the front door in a limp green parka, struggling with two bags of groceries. Outside, it's chilly enough that the blood runs out of my fingertips and creeps into my palms. My cheeks sting, the cold gnawing on exposed flesh like flies. I toss the empty bag of McDonald's.

"Lauretta!" I call.

She glances over her shoulder.

I run up to her and hold out my hands. She releases the groceries into them. The bags are lighter than I expected, each filled less than half-way with vanilla yogurts, Entenmann's doughnuts, and navel oranges. I follow Lauretta up to her apartment.

"I had it on my own, you know," she says.

While she fumbles for a key, the skin sags on her forearm as if it's about to slip off the bone. Her apartment turns out to have the same layout as mine—but hers reeks of smoke. I hold in a cough. I'm surprised that her yellow furniture hasn't turned gray from the ash in its pores. Her decor has the feel of a quaint bed-and-breakfast: thin cushions on old chairs, lacy details, and a blush-colored carpet. It's homier than I would've expected for someone so rough. She points to the kitchen, where I set the bags.

"So, you gonna take my advice?" She eyes my outfit.

Before I can find an excuse to leave, she picks a photo off her bookshelf.

"That's my daughter, Zoe," she says, tapping a broad-shouldered woman in Disney World. Lauretta hasn't told me much about her family, only that she has a daughter living in Garden City and a son in Massapequa. Her husband died twenty years ago of cancer. "And that's Zoe's husband. He goes by 'Caveman.'" She gives me a look that suggests she does not like the nickname. "I wrote him off when we met, but he makes her happy. And their kids are damned cute." Lauretta taps the glass between their two little faces. "Those rug rats almost make me want to quit smoking. Almost." She sets the frame down, then picks up another, sliding the photo out before I see it. "And this"—she shows me the frame—"is you."

"Me?"

It's empty.

"It will be," she explains. "Once you quit this double life of yours, I'll put a photo of you right here." She puts the frame back on the shelf. "Look, I know there's a lot of pressure to keep up with the Joneses. Especially out East. And I know everyone's got a few white lies. Even me. But you're taking it too far. You shouldn't be one person *here* and someone else out *there*." She nods toward the Hamptons. "You're cutting your soul in half."

～

Late that night, I eat dinner with my laptop.

My elbow dodges plastic bowls of spicy lamb dumplings and hand-ripped noodles from Xi'an Famous Foods. My lips prickle with chili oil. The slick ends of my chopsticks are red. The Reddit page in front of me is r/ClaireRoss, a three-hundred-thousand-user community. There are fourteen hundred online now, according to the sidebar. Are they all Starlites? I picture them typing away across the world, tuned into bright screens in every time zone. I can almost hear the website buzz like static electricity, feel it vibrating through the keyboard.

It felt like millions of them were in love with her.

Well, here they are.

What are they saying?

On every page, the banner headline shows three vignetted photos of Claire. They're connected with shadowy glue, blending their dark edges together. In each one, part of her face is hidden. She's covering one eye with her book; she's in profile; and on the far right, she holds hands over her mouth. These might've been pleasantly enigmatic before she disappeared. Now, they seem to be in poor taste, glamorizing the mystery. Both sides of the graphic wink with constellations taken from the cover of her book.

I scroll through FINDING CLAIRE.

The thread is disturbing.

Stalking framed as detective work.

The only impressive part of their search is the number of people involved. Starlites have stepped forward from around the world; some posts punctuated with British slang, others with references to hometowns in Australia. But they haven't found her either. After months of festering here like gnats over rotting fruit, their hands are just as empty as everyone else's. So whatever's in these posts, picked over by fanatics, won't lead me to her. Still, I keep reading, theory after failed theory. Maybe the Starlites did find something: every single dead end. All the roads that lead nowhere. All the doors that open to walls.

I have to open the one door they didn't.

The later it gets, the more users log on.

Scrolling feels like sinking.

Every so often, the thread spontaneously changes its mission, becoming a support group for fans who are suffering without her. A Starlite will interject with a bleat of longing. Mournful, lonely. A non sequitur nestled into a serious discussion. Others will pile on in the comments, moving as a pack. They'll talk about Claire as if they shared a deep, romantic partnership with her—as if they split a pan of eggs every morning, held each other every night. And then, the pursuit will resume, continuing right around the pain. They'll go back to comparing notes on her natural hair color, shoe size.

I click my way to ENCOUNTERS.

☆☆✳ THE WORLD'S FAVORITE INTROVERT. FAMOUS FOR WHAT SHE DID ALONE.
BUT WHO IS SHE IN PERSON?
DID YOU MEET CLAIRE? ☆☆✳
UPDATE: PLEASE SHARE ALL NEW ENCOUNTERS ON FINDING CLAIRE.

The fans have been obedient: no new posts in eighty-nine days.

speakV0LUMES has the last comment. Her post hangs like an awning over a deserted store. Two weeks before the wedding, she saw Claire walk across East Sixty-Eighth Street, drinking Starbucks. After Claire threw out her coffee, speakV0LUMES actually removed Claire's cup from the trash and posted a photo of it. The name scrawled across the side is FINCH. speakV0LUMES ends the post, "Am I totally weird if I keep this forever??" I picture the cup in her bedroom, its top crushed into the shape of an eye.

Three weeks before the wedding, DES10NYY saw Claire shopping in Bloomingdale's. Claire was apparently trying on sporty leggings. DES10NYY included a photo from inside the empty dressing room, where two pairs were left behind on a wicker chair. They're both dark green, the color of drenched moss, something lush and private. The photographer's shadow slants over them. Her left arm is idle, the silhouette of her fingers eerily elongated. Des10Nyy doesn't admit that she bought the leggings, but it's too easy to imagine her paying full price for them, especially if they were still warm.

Six months before the wedding, Romantic_Ally1 saw Claire in Central Park. She happened to be reading *The Starlit Ballet* on a bench when she saw its creator stroll by with Roger. Her tone is awestruck, as if this isn't *a* creator, but *the* Creator. Romantic_Ally1 had wanted Claire's autograph, but apparently, her watch cracked when Claire got close. She shared photos of it: an Apple Watch with a spiderweb through the Gorilla Glass, so extensive that the clock was covered in its own white dust. It looked snowed on, frosted over—and that's not even the strangest "encounter" on this page. When Petereader found himself walking next to Claire, he reached for his phone to take a photo. His phone turned out to be so hot, it burned his palm. He posted a photo of the red streak.

If Encounters is deviant, then the Photos page is wicked. It's a montage of candids, all taken by Starlites. I scroll through photos of Claire and Roger on the Upper East Side. *Books are famous—authors aren't.* That comment makes this album even more unnerving, because it means that Claire was unaware of every camera, every click.

Maybe this is what happens when an author reaches her stratosphere of popularity. Unlike pop stars, movie stars, or other kinds of celebrities, Claire doesn't perform. There's no way to see her live. She manages to be an icon and a ghost, haunting popular culture. Maybe this leaves her superfans starved, desperate for her. Forced to hunt for her personal scraps. The size of this community is staggering, given how strange it is. Even I have trouble grasping how many obsessive fringe types there must be, how many are answering customer service calls or bagging groceries, then logging on to this site in the dark.

Who?

One of the Starlites.

But I disagree.

I don't think that a fan has her.

If they did, they would've posted about it.

If a Starlite found so much as a knot of her hair in the drain, they would've shared a photo of it here. That's what they've been doing ever since her book came out. They've been posting everything she touched, down to chewing gum, menu doodles, and used Kleenex. Their culture relies on oversharing. They feed a collective mind. If a deranged Starlite had Claire tied up in their garage, they would've admitted something. It could make them the leader of this strange underworld, the one in control of their queen.

I stare at my laptop long enough that it turns gray. I tap a key, reviving its light. My feelings don't change the longer that I sit here, facing their hive. Their buzzing, teeming hive. If Claire Ross was taken, I don't think the one who has her is a fan.

FIVE

"I have memories that don't belong to me."
—*Claire Ross,* The Starlit Ballet

The next morning, I'm up again before my alarm. I shower and make instant coffee, listening to a neighbor's TV. Maybe they just got back from a night shift. It sounds like a football game, the commentary interrupted by whistles and cheers. The rest of the building is quiet, my windows truly black. It's rare that I ever get a view like this, without headlights skittering across the glass. It's as if there's been a general strike—grocery stores locked, ice machines unplugged.

I could be inside *The Handmaid's Tale*.

Curfew in effect.

I first read Margaret Atwood for "The Modern Novel," my third year into stealing class. I always liked the sound of that—stealing *class,* as if I were pickpocketing status or doing something much more impressive than just sitting down. It took me two years to get the hang of it. Until then, I was always stepping on my own feet. It was embarrassing, really, how little it took to defeat me. I'd get soaked to my underwear on a shift and have forgotten a change of clothes. Or I'd bet on the wrong door into a Humanities building, and there'd be no students flowing through it when I needed them. No one holding the door open for me.

By *junior* year, I was a pro.

It helped that, aside from dishwashing, I worked at the Coffee House near Boston. The shop served mostly college kids. They were always talking in study groups. Pinching croissants idly into hundreds of golden flakes. I overheard so many of their conversations, it became easy to cherry-pick from them. *My middle name is Atalanta . . . The back half of* Middlemarch *can lick my dick . . . If I knew the odds of me passing statistics, I'd be passing statistics.* I'd hang up my apron and leave for class, their words in the back of my mind. *Does anyone have the life cycle of a mushroom? . . . Bahamas for Presidents' Day . . . My parents were class of '87.*

They gave me a thousand things to say.

~

I walk toward Miranda, Eliza, and Roger across Miranda's lawn. From this far away, they look like wishbones, dark lines on spread legs. I can't see their faces, but it must be them. The red curve of Eliza's ponytail. Roger's slump. Their huddle turns toward me. If they're saying anything to each other, I can't hear them. This lawn feels even more massive now that I'm trying to cross it. A green ocean right before the gray one. I wave high overhead with wide swipes. Miranda responds with a shadow of my enthusiasm.

I keep walking.

The air tastes like snow.

"Good morning," I greet them at last.

Roger doesn't lift his hands out of his pockets to return the gesture. After he nods hello, he drops his gaze back down to his sneakers. Eliza is the only perky one here, holding a coffee between her mittens. Steam rises in tendrils. Where's Kira? Yesterday, we chose to meet at eight so that she and Roger wouldn't miss work for the tour. I ask if she's here.

"Not yet," Miranda says.

She pulls out her cell phone, looking concerned.

"Has anyone heard from her?" I ask.

Eliza and Roger shake their heads no.

The moment feels too tense for small talk.

Miranda steps aside, appearing to dial and redial the same number without reaching anyone. As we wait, I peer around the lawn. Fifteen-foot-tall hedges surround the property on three sides. The leafy wall has no gaps, no skeletal patches where I could peek through sticks. Over the dunes, the sky is the same dull color as the ocean, blurring where they meet. How many of Claire and Roger's wedding guests were familiar with the area?

I ask Eliza if she has a copy of the guest list. She offers to send it to me, reaching for her phone. As I spell out my email address, Roger glances at our exchange, then looks back down at his feet. He hasn't said a word since I got here. I wonder if he was always this morose, or if he's just mourning Claire. Does he have a brooding side that would've made them more compatible? They must have connected on some level. She wouldn't have been with him for so long if it wasn't real, wasn't deep. When he catches me staring at him, I look away and pretend to inspect broken blades of grass on my sneakers. Exploded little stalks.

Miranda rejoins our group.

"Has Kira called you?" she asks Roger.

He checks his phone, then shakes his head.

"I can't lose *both* my daughters!" She presses three fingers into her forehead.

In Claire's interview with *Vanity Fair*, published on Mother's Day, Claire described her mom as a woman who loves *hard*. "For some people, love loosens them up," she said. "But when my mom cares about something, she takes responsibility for it in a firm, energized way." She explained that Miranda didn't just play bridge with friends. She became a Master in bridge. She competed in—and often won—tennis tournaments at the family's beach club. And apparently, she loved her daughters in the same fierce, productive way. She checked their homework every night until high school.

I've worked for achievers like Miranda before. In my experience, goal-oriented types are the most prone to miss something obvious.

Because they only see one thing at a time. They focus on their current project. The rest can slip past them.

At twenty past, the gates open to reveal Kira in the driver's seat of a matte-black BMW. She parks, then walks toward us without haste. Her yellow leggings stand out in this gray chill. Eventually, she gets close enough that I hear her slow steps test the grass.

"Where were you?" Miranda demands.

"I forgot to set an alarm."

"You scared me to death!" Her tone is sad, overwhelmed.

I imagine similar exchanges when Kira was a teenager—with Kira staying out past her curfew, forcing Miranda to chase her down, while Claire remained the perfect child, tucked into bed. Eyes dutifully shut. *I've spent the past twenty-eight years trying to do things as well as Claire. Trying and failing.* That must have taken its toll.

Miranda takes a deep breath.

"Did you start yet?" Kira looks at Roger, Eliza, and then me for a hint. Her question feels a little callous. It hangs in the air, unanswered. Meanwhile, she shoves both hands into the pockets of her parka. It's the most billowing coat here. The quilted squares are all so stuffed with down, they look taut and hard. Casually bulletproof.

"Of course not," Miranda says.

"I'm sorry," Kira manages.

Miranda gestures with some resignation to the hydrangea bushes at the end of the yard. We make our way there, Miranda at the front. It's an abrupt transition, but she appears to be recovering now that one of her daughters has returned. We spread out as we walk, with Kira at the rear. White clouds hover like sharks stalled against a current. Eventually, we reach the twiggy bushes. They form a wide C curve taller than I am. Rusty flowers color some branches, but most are bare. Miranda stands in the center.

"This is where the altar was going to be," she announces. I picture how the hydrangeas must've looked in season, boiling over with tiny blue flowers. "We were going to have the ceremony here in the backyard—as I'm sure you know—and then the reception at our beach club. By four p.m. on Friday, everything was set up for the next day. All 302 folding chairs were here in rows." She motions like a flight attendant down the intended aisle. I follow its line all the way to Claire's window. If she woke up there on Saturday, she would've seen the skeleton of her own wedding. I wonder what the chairs would've looked like under the moon.

We walk down the imaginary aisle.

The grass whispers.

"Claire was supposed to enter down those stairs"—Miranda points to the outdoor staircase in the distance, which descends from the second floor to the lawn; a hundred people could fit on it—"and then join Roger in the hydrangeas."

I imagine Claire crossing this lawn through a packed crowd, the lacy hem of her dress dragging behind her. It sounds dramatic, especially for a woman who did not particularly enjoy attention. She endured the press tour for her book with grace, but every now and then—when she got blindsided by an unusually personal question, or when the interview went too long—her composure started to melt. In those moments, I saw how complicated her stardom must've been for her. Her tour aside, she kept to herself. She never had any social media. Never posted a selfie. Her personality seemed to suit a career that required an extraordinary amount of time alone. Emily Dickinson, for one, barely left her room, let alone her house, for decades. Walking this long aisle sounds grand, but it doesn't sound like Claire.

"These chairs"—Miranda gestures to the phantom row beside us—"were going to have cones on the back filled with rose petals, ready to throw after they got married. The cones were made of pages from *The Starlit Ballet*."

I picture dozens of them painstakingly assembled, now in a dark corner collecting dust. It must be hard for Miranda to remember personal touches like that when we can't locate even an inch of her daughter. As she wrings her hands, pressing pale fingertips into blue veins,

I can almost see her coiling the pages. Was that detail her idea? The more I think about it, the more it sounds a little too self-promotional for Claire's taste.

"Did Claire have any strong opinions about the ceremony?" I ask. We walk.

The pause continues for too long.

It becomes an answer.

"Did she contribute . . . anything?" I probe.

"She wrote part of the ceremony program," Eliza cuts in. "There was a message 'To Family and Friends' that she put together, where she talked about how much it meant that everyone had traveled to be part of the day."

Roger clears his throat, scraping away a night's worth of debris.

"When we started to talk about getting married, she wanted to elope," he says. "I said that yes, eloping might make *us* happy, but weddings aren't just about the couple. They're a community event. She wrote something to that effect in the program. 'Our wedding is not only a chance to celebrate our relationship, but a chance to celebrate our relationships with all of you.' It was nice." The bottoms of his shoes scuff the lawn as he walks.

"What did you choose for the ceremony?" I ask.

"Not much."

"Anything?"

"My groomsmen's outfits," he says, looking cautiously at Miranda. "Those were bright-navy Bonobos suits. But I mostly wanted whatever Miranda, Eliza, and Claire did." He clears his throat again. "I just wanted Claire to be happy."

Miranda continues the tour around the property, bringing every spot to life with a description of what was there that Friday—lemonade stand, seats for the string trio—awaiting its role in the wedding. The event sounds like it would've been lavish for a backyard ceremony, ornate for a bride who'd written a novel about spiritual love. After Claire and Roger got married, they were going to exit in Miranda's vintage

BMW convertible. It was parked in this driveway on Friday afternoon and still there the next day. The back seat was going to be filled with a small army of flowers, herbs, and greenery. Eliza lists their names as if I can picture them—locally foraged grasses, maidenhair ferns. I don't ask what happened to the bouquets, but I imagine them in trash bags at the bottom of a landfill, asphyxiating in the dark.

As we finish our lap around the house, I walk next to the hedges. Now I have a clear picture of this lawn on September 18. When people started looking for Claire, they would've wandered through her empty wedding. Everything in place except for the life. I scan the base of the hedges—no tracks, nothing glinting in the silvery light. I may be late to this case, but you never know what's been overlooked and frozen into the dirt.

"How was the rehearsal dinner?" I ask.

They exchange glances, as if they're unsure who should answer.

"Did you notice anything unusual?" I prompt.

"I was so focused on everything going smoothly . . . ," Miranda says. "The dinner was at our club's tennis house. Up until the minute it started, I was dropping banana leaves into vases on every table. I was counting the bamboo chairs before and after. I can be kind of hands on." Clearly, she wasn't watching her daughter too closely.

"How was Claire?" I ask Roger.

"At peace."

~

After the tour, we meet inside around the kitchen table. Roger and Kira remain standing and check their phones, already thinking ahead to their workdays. Eliza tosses her drained coffee cup into a trash bag that sounds empty. I remember the Sharpied FINCH on Claire's. In that photo, the Styrofoam rim was the color of a wedding dress dragged through mud. It looked like soiled tulle, dirty lace. I wonder how many people's garbage is interesting to the world at large. How many people produce zero waste, because theirs are collectors' items?

Miranda takes a seat at the head of the table.

"What do you think?" she asks me softly.

She sounds gently desperate for direction.

Roger pockets his phone while Kira continues to type what appears to be a long email. She only glances up once. It looks like a quick up-and-down to check that we're still here. Her light-green eyes are spotted with freckles. The irises are hazy, each one like a slushy grape that's been cut in half. I can't help but compare them to Claire's, which were a saturated green. All that time indoors gave her stare an unbleached intensity.

"I'd like to do a more thorough search of the house," I say, swiveling around to face everyone. "I'm still getting to know you and building out my profile of Claire." I stop to focus on Miranda. "To help with that, I think I should spend a couple of nights here."

"Excuse me?" Kira asks.

Now she's paying attention.

"Kira," Miranda snaps. "Yes, of course."

"That's absurd," Kira says.

Miranda touches her forehead.

"I am under a tremendous amount of pressure," she says firmly. "Abigail said that something like this would happen, but that she would lead us to Claire." Meanwhile, Roger touches Miranda's shoulder, a small but comforting gesture.

"Have you found anything yet?" Kira demands of me.

"Why did you show up if you're going to be like this?" Miranda asks.

"Because you asked me to be here."

Miranda slaps the table.

I'm relieved that the spotlight is off me, that I don't have to admit what I've learned and what I'm still trying to understand. There's a lot about Claire's wedding that surprises me. The author of *The Starlit Ballet* was uninvolved in structuring her own ceremony? In her book, the two soulmates only get married once—in their very last life, when they are fully mature. When Logan and Cady finally do say their vows, with just one witness in Yosemite, he addresses her by every name she's ever had. He speaks to the permanent spark of her in all of them. If *The Starlit Ballet* is a window into Claire, then a scene that moving suggests she valued marriage. It doesn't make sense that in her own, she'd be detached.

Also, the event that Miranda previewed feels eerily unlike her daughter. It's too caught up in the wedding arms race that adds up to billions of dollars every year. I'd imagine that Claire, of all people, would be happier with less. In an interview on the *Today* show, Claire said her favorite thing about a love story between soulmates is that their connection isn't physical. It's about who they are at the core. As the soulmates change races, religions, and genders—and most of these changes aren't even shown, as the book only follows a handful of lives—their love just gets deeper. In a few appearances, Claire described herself as an "old soul."

Then she channeled Palm Beach at her rehearsal dinner? Claire might've come from a fancy family, but she didn't value elite experiences. It's clear that Miranda took charge of the wedding weekend, but I wonder if Claire had any input at all.

"You want to search the house," Miranda repeats. "Any place in particular?"

"Can I tell you more in private?" I ask.

"Not happening," Kira interrupts with an edge.

I face Miranda like an ally, my shoulders square to hers, hands praying with a subtle clasp. My body language asks for her confidence. For a little connection, even. But she's only looking at Kira, studying her daughter as if the pieces aren't quite aligned. As if she's been scrambled like the Picasso in Abigail's empty home.

"So, where do you want to look?" Kira prompts.

"Your room," I admit.

"Excuse me?" she demands. She crosses her arms and glances around, clearly eager for someone to come to her defense. For once,

Eliza is without her grin. She looks older when she's in neutral, with her eyes on the floor. The smile lines framing her mouth are just wrinkles now, unjoyful grooves sloping down from her nose. Roger shoves both hands into his pockets. He straightens the hunch out of his spine.

"I'm going to use the restroom," Kira says, her tone undaunted and provocative. She takes a slow step back. "Am I allowed to do that by myself?"

She lingers for a moment.

Then takes off.

Miranda jumps and follows Kira out of the kitchen. Roger and I speed-walk after them, on the edge of running. A door slams at the end of the hallway. We find Miranda pounding on Kira's. I get close and hold a finger to my lips.

"Listen," I urge.

Miranda falls quiet.

A drawer opens in Kira's room. Something scratches against wood. Miranda kicks the door.

"Kira, you open this *right* now."

It's unnerving to see someone so elegant dissolve. It's like watching wires snap around a beautiful sculpture, and suddenly, the piece of fine art starts to wobble. Miranda kicks the door harder and harder. The wood cracks under her foot and splinters more every second, as if its destruction has a pulse. Miranda's crying now, but she continues to pound. Force this intense can't be typical for her. Her slim figure doesn't look like it's used to more than the occasional tennis match. She has a body shaped by culture, not sports.

The door swings open.

Kira steps toward me.

My hands fly up to guard my face, but I don't feel anything. I blink and notice that her arm is extended. She's holding a black Moleskine journal.

r/ClaireRoss posted by u/B3LI3V3M3 2 mos ago

FINDING CLAIRE: MEGATHREAD

MEGATHREAD

☆☆✳ PLEASE SHARE INFORMATION RELEVANT TO HER CASE. ☆☆✳
We know her better than anyone.
We should be able to find her. ☆☆✳

Current Megathreads:

ENCOUNTERS
PHOTOS

Reincarnival13 · 1 mo ago

I JUST WANT A GOOD LIFE WITH CADY

What else do we know about her family?

avatarAmour · 1 mo ago

Claire's mom Miranda Blake Ross was in the audience for every book tour event that Claire ever did. (That meant Miranda once flew from NYC to Chicago to L.A. to Houston in less than five days.) There was a **thread** about it last year, which the OG Starlites will remember. Some thought it was sweet. Some thought it was a red flag, overbearing. The truth is usually somewhere in the middle.

My take: actually look at the clips and photos of Miranda at those events. Before you make up your mind about her: go do that. Because whenever the camera panned her way, she looked genuinely happy. (And filthy rich, but I digress.) She wasn't mouthing cues like your run-of-the-mill stage mom. She wasn't trying to control Claire or keep her daughter from saying something (like some of you were suggesting). She looked more like a Taylor Swift Mom, like an advocate. A fan.

Plenty of you will disagree with me (and do it persuasively). Like I said, the truth is usually somewhere in the middle.

SoulM8_Me · 1 mo ago

The real Starlites ☆ **do** ☆ remember that thread. Not like all you new accounts, snouts on a blood trail.

B3LI3V3M3 · 1 mo ago

The Miranda Tour was our first clue that something bad was going to happen to Claire. Miranda was trying to protect her daughter.

Reincarnival1 · 1 mo ago

I JUST WANT A GOOD LIFE WITH CADY

From what?

SeveringSnape · 1 mo ago

RED FLAG. Claire was a HOSTAGE in her own life. I don't know how they kept her locked up and writing, but think about it. This woman was never seen alone. She had a uniform. And the *messages* she sent us. She said that she loved *The Goldfinch*. Her Starbucks name was *Finch*. Do you know what a *finch* is? It's a ☆ *caged bird.* ☆ She was a prisoner—a creative prisoner—asking for help, and we failed her. Now, we might never get her back.

readMeRoss · 1 mo ago

How can you force someone to be creative?

theSixthStark · 1 mo ago

Kira's socials are private, but I made a fake account with her college sorority in my bio. She accepted my request . . . I'll save you the (mind-numbing) details, but after looking at everything she posted for the past ten years—every uncreative Italian vacation, every standard-issue boyfriend—I can say with 100-percent certainty that if Kira was involved in what happened, she wasn't the mastermind.

sweeter-sour_ · 1 mo ago

I was Kira's year at ADPi (Roll Wave), and what I can't get over is that she never mentioned her sister. Not once in four years, including one living together in the house. I thought she was an only child.

newsoulhalp · 1 mo ago

How do you know she "wasn't the mastermind?"

PageByPaige91 · 1 mo ago

Kira seems smart.

theSixthStark · 1 mo ago

Smart, yes. But was she the *brain* behind this?
She wasn't weird enough. I mean, she wore the obvious brands. In the obvious places. Her trips and captions were all recycled and familiar. Nothing about her life was *discovered*. Whoever drew up this plot against Claire had to be more . . . inventive. Deviant. Right?

sadeyes-soulful · 1 mo ago

DIED OF A HEART ATTACK DURING THE DANCING PLAGUE

What about her dad Andrew Ross?

u-cant-pickle-that · 1 mo ago

What about him? He's dead lol

sadeyes-soulful · 1 mo ago

DIED OF A HEART ATTACK DURING THE DANCING PLAGUE

Maybe he had enemies. Maybe he was involved in something that's still affecting the family. Things can be multi-generational

hha2003 · 1 mo ago

I worked for Andrew for 15 years at Ardent (they make the bottles/tubes for most of your toiletries). Great boss. Overpaid everyone.

History lesson: Andrew's granddad started Ardent, then passed the business down to Andrew's dad, who passed it to Andrew. There were photos of the three Ross men together all over the headquarters. There were quotes painted on the walls about legacy, stewardship. It could've felt like propaganda, but the way they did it, it came off wholesome. Honestly. Andrew really seemed to believe that stuff. He always wanted Ardent to feel like a family business, even as it grew.

From what I remember, he was straight-laced. He looked like a politician during an election year. Very crisp. Not a snob. Growing up, he spent his summers working in one of the factories, making the bottles for hair gel. He always remembered my kids' names. Good man, and I like to think I have a nose for this.

We were all shaken up when he died.

SolemnlyVowel · 1 mo ago

Don't ask me how I got this . . . The official cause of
death for Andrew Ross was cardiac arrest, brought
on by CAD (coronary artery disease). No chance of
foul play there. He died at home in East Hampton.
(Yes, the same house where Claire was last seen.)

rhyme-crime · 1 mo ago

the house has moods ☆☆✳
the house ☆☆✳
has dark moods ☆☆✳
the h
o
u
s
e ☆☆✳

MrsLoganCallahan · 1 mo ago

I WAS BORN HERE A COUPLE OF TIMES

Kira doesn't look like Claire?

SIX

"'Dying there is one of my darkest memories.'

'You know what it's like to die?'"
—*Claire Ross,* The Starlit Ballet

"Where did you get that?" Miranda fixates on the journal.

Kira shakes it in my direction.

I take it from her and open to the middle.

Claire described her own handwriting once. What did she say? It was on a literary podcast that waded into some obscure topics, including the penmanship of famous authors. Lewis Carroll, known for *Alice in Wonderland*, wrote in mirror script. Oscar Wilde wrote with gaping spaces between his words. Claire called herself Wilde's opposite, leaving just a crack between hers. The block of text in front of me is almost all ink. The end of every word almost grazes the start of the next. This journal belongs to Claire.

"Kira!" Miranda shouts.

I look up, but she's already gone.

~

I drive home with Claire's journal in the passenger seat. It starts to snow on the highway, blurring the cars ahead and whiting out the horizon. I wonder how Logan would see snow like this in Yosemite, what memories it might stir. In my purse, every now and then, Claire's Moleskine slaps gently against *The Starlit Ballet*.

I debated reading her journal in East Hampton. I stared at the all-black binding, even darker than the cover of her novel. In the end, I had more self-control than I expected and decided to drive home first. I'll pack a bag for my stay at Miranda's tomorrow and then read it alone tonight. I'm now in the fast lane, closing the gap with the car in front of me. Every time Claire's journal rattles, I picture the game from *Jumanji*. It shook before releasing terrors from the jungle: vines, spiders, and, eventually, a whole stampede.

As I was leaving Miranda's, she promised to get one of the guest rooms ready for me. I'm relieved that she trusts me. Then again, the longer a crisis drags on, the more eager people are to try something new. My methods *are* unusual, but maybe they're related to my love of great books. In both, there's a preference for depth, for getting to know a place down to the nicks in the wallpaper. Roger, too, was open to the idea. As we said goodbye, he agreed to stay one more day for a conversation—just between us.

Claire's journal shakes.

What's inside?

I have a view, of course, on who she is.

She spent seven years on a story about soulmates. It's only because I work steeped in broken vows that I understand how unusual that is. Claire devoted herself to the idea that everyone is the star of a multi-generational love story. That everyone has someone, an all-forgiving and permanent home for their soul. Even more fantastically, she thought other people might care about this idea too. People with urgent, real-world problems. She thought they might want 120,000 words of her fantasy.

If Claire has a superpower, it's belief.

Or a sense of purpose.

In the Hamptons I know, where people can afford their every temptation, that sense of *being on a mission* is rare. Most of my clients have a palpable emptiness. For some, that shows up as a low-grade medicated stupor. For others, it's towering stacks of boxes from Net-a-Porter, too many to open, filling redundant rooms. It's affairs with people who don't make them happy. It's getting plastic surgery and then getting it reversed. Most of my clients have every pleasure and no satisfaction, but Claire was the opposite.

She poured herself into *The Starlit Ballet* without any recognition or pay. It'd be easy to downplay the challenge of that by saying that she didn't need to make money—but she did. Her parents didn't leave her with a trust fund. She was clear about that in several interviews, correcting snarky hosts who assumed that she'd been coasting off her family's wealth. *I'm glad to see heiresses these days aiming higher than* The Simple Life. After college, she worked freelance jobs to make rent. Still, she wrote when it was unprofitable, maybe even unwise, at the expense of almost everything else. She followed this story like a religion, like she knew something about it that no one else did.

That's what I expect to see in her diary.

I pull into the parking lot for my building to find Lauretta smoking on her porch. In this weather, it looks like she's exhaling snow. She waves at me. I step out of my car, feeling in her gaze like the empty space in her picture frame. Why am I letting her intimidate me? Maybe it's because she sees me more often than anyone else. As distant as we are, and as involuntary as our relationship may be, there are days when she's my everyone.

"The one-woman show!"

"Thanks, Lauretta."

I enter our building.

Lauretta might be three times my age, but she acts invincible—smoking in snowstorms, cozying up to confrontations. It's so bold it's almost admirable. Maybe that's why I let her torment me. Maybe that's why I *do* want to give her a photo, some proof that I've hit my stride. That I'm no longer sneaking around Riverhead and the Hamptons, living in both places and belonging to neither. At the end of this case, maybe I could gift her a photo of Claire and me together.

Then I'd have nothing left to prove.

~

I finish the last sentence on the last page of Claire's journal. Before I can even wonder what time it is, I reach for my phone and text Kira.

SEVEN

"Last weekend is what happens when I get stuck in a *good* memory. The bad ones? Those are worse than nightmares because I know my memories are real."
—*Claire Ross,* The Starlit Ballet

I wake up to my alarm a few hours later, facing my bookshelves. They're a checkerboard of spines and pages—books shelved in reverse. I don't need titles to identify them. I can tell by the thin, black stripes that I'm staring at *Night Film,* by Marisha Pessl, which includes plenty of dark mode screenshots. I can tell by the nested pen in another that it's *One Hundred Years of Solitude,* which I'm always rereading and re-underlining, finding new sentences to love. And I can tell by the long row of pocket-size pages that it's the mass-market version of Dan Brown's Robert Langdon series. I know all of these inside out.

I turn to my window and face the parking lot. A low sunrise yellows the asphalt. An old Chevy Equinox keeps going past the wet brick edges of town.

I reach for my phone.

Kira texted me back.

I sit up straight.

Last night, I asked her to coffee. I didn't expect her to answer—at least, not right away. Why would she, after everything I just read?

Kira: 8:30 at the Starbucks in town?

~

I stop at a red light in Bridgehampton, behind an empty school bus. Ten minutes from Kira. I tap the wheel across from Candy Kitchen Ice Cream Parlour, a fifties-style shop sealed for the season. Blue-and-white-striped awning, dark windows. Ahead of me, birds' nests are visible in leafless trees, dark clots in their branches.

People on my left wait for the jitney, the bus that runs between Manhattan and the tip of Long Island. A clown sits on the bench in full makeup: one blue diamond around each eye, white face, and a jam-red smile. The makeup is cracking, his skin running through it like pink veins. His checkered blazer has a wilting sunflower corsage on the lapel. His carrot-orange vest and pants stand out in the darker crowd. He stares vacantly. Maybe he performed at a birthday party yesterday. Then, maybe he stayed up late enough to catch an early jitney back to the city. That would sidestep the hitch of paying for a room.

Someone honks.

The clown looks straight at me.

I drive, still seeing him until the next red light.

His lips a tired dash through the fake smile.

~

I sit next to the window at Starbucks, the Moleskine in my purse. Yesterday's snow didn't linger. It only melted into a slick coat, leaving the roads and sidewalks a few shades darker. BookHampton next door is dim. One copy of *The Starlit Ballet* is visible in the window display. It appears to float on a black shelf, emerging from the shadows. The constellations on its cover are connected with glittering lines: long horns, the bones of a lion, and the swirling tail of a scorpion. Zodiac signs carved into midnight. Meanwhile, a dozen strangers flow through the Starbucks. One man gets a Puppuccino for his vizsla.

Where's Kira?

It's almost nine.

I bounce my knee.

Two chatty women pass my window, both carrying Hermès-orange Birkin bags. In another job, maybe I'd feel insecure working out here. But as an investigator, most days, I don't have to report to anyone. No one can *really* tell me what to do—not even my clients. Because they don't know what to do. They only know what's wrong. Besides, being able to see what people are hiding levels the playing field a bit.

Kira walks into Starbucks wearing a fur-lined hoodie over red leggings. She beelines to me, waving in a horizontal line. She sits without making any excuse for being late. Without saying anything at all. I lean back in my chair. Thankfully, dealing with difficult people is easier at work. Because Nina Travers, the elegant detective, is an image. She doesn't get wounded. She doesn't get flustered. She just gets the job done and disappears.

"I can see why you hid it." I get to the point.

"And why's that?"

"Well, it starts right after Roger proposed, and then most of what Claire writes about is how much you tortured her over the past twelve months."

"Right. 'Tortured.'" She smirks.

"No?" I press.

Her amusement persists.

"In the middle of wedding dress shopping with your sister, you told her that you barely knew her," I remind Kira. "She was standing there in her favorite dress, asking what you thought. And *that's* when you decide to say . . ." I try to remember the exact words. "'We're not close'?" I pause, half expecting Kira to offer an explanation. Her smirk fades until she's looking at me strangely. As if this chain of thought isn't funny anymore. "Even if that's true, even if you feel that way, to say it at a moment like that is . . ."

"What?" she demands.

"Spiteful. It's the kind of thing you say when you want to draw blood." She crosses her legs, becoming more compact with time. "Then—"

"What exactly are you asking me?"

"Claire's diary was a detailed account of how much you tormented her last year." I'm still stunned at how much of Claire's energy was sucked into conflicts with her sister. After all, *The Starlit Ballet* was a roaring success during this time. She was planning a wedding. But she used her diary to process the pain that Kira caused, all during what could've been the best year of her life. "These weren't ordinary moments you destroyed. They were milestones: her engagement party, bridal lunch. You dominated every one by starting a fight with her or someone else in the family. It was so consistent, it was like you were doing it on purpose. And some of the things you came up with . . . You can really gut someone."

"Don't lecture me about her journal."

"Why not?"

"Because I read it long before you did. So I know for a fact that you have nothing. Even though you desperately wanted to find some *muck*, didn't you? Some *villain*." She keeps her voice low enough that no one glances this way. "That's the problem with hiring someone like you. You *want* victims. Dirty secrets. Bones. The worse, the better. Because the bigger the conspiracy, the smarter you'll look when you crack it. The weaker Claire is when you find her, the more heroic you'll seem, saving the day."

"I'm just here for the truth."

"Well, the truth is *boring*. You saw it yourself, right there in her journal. No one was threatening her. No one was breaking into her apartment. She wasn't handcuffed to her desk, forced to write like some kind of creative prisoner. All you have are a few fights from months ago, and you're trying to spin them into something more."

Creative prisoner.

"You read r/ClaireRoss?" I ask.

"Don't you?"

"As a chore."

"Right," she scoffs. "Put *me* under a microscope and ignore the maniacs who sleep with her headshot. Is that really wise, *Detective?*"

"First of all," I say with composure, "they haven't found her. No one on that thread knows where she is. And second, the Starlites behind that theory—framing her as an artistic slave—are missing something important. The life of an author *always* looks miserable. To everyone but them. Claire might've behaved like a prisoner, but so do most great writers, if we're being honest. Their worlds are in their minds. So to answer your question, no, I don't think there's anything on r/ClaireRoss worth reading, especially not that theory." Cars honk on Main Street. "Now we're off track. Which serves you well, doesn't it?"

"Excuse me?"

"Let me rephrase."

"Please."

Kira takes a second to scan the Starbucks. A handful of people wait in line with their backs to us. A woman enters with an infant on her chest, the word ELOISE in golden cursive on her necklace. Meanwhile, something's happening behind Kira's eyes. It looks like her defenses are melting in the pause. I wait a few more seconds, letting her own internal dialogue wear her down. Maybe the one way through her armor is with silence.

"Hello?" she prompts.

"How would you describe your relationship with your sister?" I ask.

"She was my best friend."

Kira tears up.

"Are you an only child?" she asks.

"Two older brothers."

She nods. "You don't understand sisters."

"What should I understand?"

"That you fight about everything except what matters."

I almost laugh. "Now, you're sentimental."

"What's that supposed to mean?"

"It means you hid evidence, Kira—evidence that you liked to hurt the woman who's missing." Her light-green stare is glassy. "You can pretend that her journal was 'boring.' But if it was, then you wouldn't have hidden it. Was it jealousy? Did you not like the attention she got? Was it hard growing up in her shadow, having to act out to get anyone to notice you?" I'm being cruel, but I want her to crack, to say what she's not saying. "And then, when she goes missing, when she's finally out of the spotlight, she becomes even more famous. That must hurt, that her absence is more noteworthy than your entire life." Kira's eyes are melting into her lashes. "If I were you, I would've gotten sick of it too. I'd want to be seen. Sometimes, that means moving someone out of the way, doesn't it?"

She stands up.

"Do you know where your sister is?" I ask.

"*Fuck* you."

~

I'm waiting for Roger on the beach outside Miranda's. The waves sound like white noise on a pendulum. The coast appears to be empty except for a few gulls by the waterline. They peck at clamshells and skitter away from creeping foam.

I don't know how far Kira might have gone against her own sister. But she's hiding something. Her whole body this morning was too tightly wound, too closed off. It looked like she was using muscular force to keep something to herself. *She was my best friend.* Were they really that close? I've seen hundreds of clients come to grips with loss. It's always visible, palpable. As if they're carrying an anchor, hands under the barbed flukes, metal chain dragging behind them. It's clear that grief is still working its way through Miranda and Roger, but there's not a speck of it in Kira. *She* was *my best friend.* Still, no grief.

Roger approaches on the boardwalk. The collar of his Barbour jacket is up, protecting his neck from the wind. His lips are the only pop of color in sight, a pale-red line in the midst of neutrals and grays. He waves quickly, then pockets his hand.

I thank him for coming.

"Are you sure you want to talk outside?" he asks, a rush of wind smearing his words together. He seems more concerned with my well-being than his.

The day we met, I ran a quick background check on him—Miranda, Kira, and Eliza too. It was easy enough to pay ninety-five dollars each and wait twenty-four hours for results. I know from Roger's that his parents are from Arkansas. Jack and Sheryl Galvin met at the University of the Ozarks in Clarksville, where they both studied sculptural art. Roger's parents appear to be even humbler, even more painfully shy versions of him. His dad may have red hair and a heavier frame, but the southern gentleman in them both is the same.

"Miranda's in the house now," I explain.

We tread over pebbles in scalloped curves.

They trace the edges of old waves.

"Have you found anything yet?" he asks.

"I'm still getting up to speed. To be honest, I'm having a hard time visualizing Claire in this environment." I watch him carefully. "I was in town today, and I couldn't imagine her there, thinking about *The Starlit Ballet* outside Loro Piana." They were selling delicate cashmere about a mile from the ocean. As if the beach is a stage for commerce, not a place of striking natural beauty. "So, I was hoping to get a clearer picture of her, hear some things you might not feel comfortable saying in front of her mom." We pass a knot of black seaweed. "Things only you knew. That might not match up with what Miranda wanted to see."

"I think you're onto something," he admits.

I move an inch closer.

"A lot of people have the wrong idea about Claire," he says slowly. "She wrote a book about love, but she wasn't as—loving as you might expect." He looks sideways at me, wincing as if the sentence hurts him. "Don't get me wrong. I always loved her, and she loved me, but she loved her work—more. She was passionate about it, crazy for it. All she wanted to do was write. If she'd been working on a suspense novel, you know, about a wife secretly plotting to kill her husband, that would've made more sense."

"What do you mean?"

"She devoted her life to the book. It's just odd that she was writing about—true love and companionship, about characters who prioritized time together above everything else. Because that wasn't how she lived." We part around driftwood. It looks like a single, twisted antler. "I'm sure you know this, but she dedicated the book to me. 'For the one I'll find in every life.' That's the phrase she had engraved inside my wedding band too. But that never felt right. Her *book* wasn't dedicated to *me*. *I* was dedicated to her *book*. In our relationship, *The Starlit Ballet* always came first." He looks down at dull sand. "If I had a nickel for every time she chose writing alone over doing something with me . . . she wouldn't have been the breadwinner."

"That must've been frustrating."

"What?"

"To love someone and feel them push you away."

My tone is more emotional than usual. It sounds like a break in character, a rippling glitch through the elegant detective. I glance at Roger. His profile is steady in front of swishing dunes. Staring ahead as if nothing's changed.

"No, it wasn't like that," he says. "I always knew she was special. I knew that I was lucky to be with her, that she was on a rocket ship. I read a lot of self-help books. You could say that I have a strong, academic grasp of what it takes to be great, and I could see Claire on that path. She was putting in the time. She was taking the risk. She cared. I knew that book was going to take off because I saw how much she bled into it."

"I can't see Claire reading self-help books."

"You're right. She was too busy." He sounds heartbroken.

When Roger suggests we turn around, two gulls screech overhead. Soaring past, they look like white crows. As we retrace our steps, I ask some less emotional questions. He tells me he's been staying at a local bed-and-breakfast. Kira's been at a friend's, one street over from Miranda. Neither one of them has wanted to spend much time in the house since September. He plans to drive back to the city tomorrow, but he'll return the second I ask. Everyone at his firm has been understanding, giving him the option to work remotely.

"She wasn't always like that, by the way." He interrupts himself, returning to an earlier topic. "When we met, she was more open. We went to baseball games. We took dance classes. We traveled. But the closer she got to finishing that book, the more it took her away from me until . . ."

It's haunting to think that *The Starlit Ballet* is somehow responsible for what happened. That even when she was done with it, it wasn't done with her.

Miranda's boardwalk comes into view.

"I had a question about the guest list," I say. Eliza's master spreadsheet is divided into four tabs—*Claire, Roger, Galvin,* and *Ross*—organizing all guests by the individual or family who'd invited them. "It looks like Claire only invited nineteen of the 302 guests?"

"That sounds right."

I grab my phone and find the spreadsheet that Eliza sent.

"It'd be helpful to go through her guests together." I hand my phone to him, open to Claire's tab. "I'd love to know more about them."

He shakes his head. "I didn't know any of them well."

"How is that possible?"

"When we started dating, we spent most of our time with my friends. It wasn't on purpose. My friends just got together more often. Over time, we got more comfortable with each other, and she got further along in her story. So, she spent more and more of her time alone." He shrugs. "Writers can be happy by themselves."

"She had a small circle."

"Even those people"—he hands my phone back—"I bet she didn't know them that well either. They might've gotten pregnant, moved, or who knows since they last spoke."

I pocket my phone.

"For most people, relationships grow as a function of time spent together," he explains. I hear his training as an accountant come through in his choice of words. "Claire wasn't like that. Her friends were people who she had these flashbulb connections with. One intense conversation. One memorable night. She built whole relationships out of . . . spare change, really. She could've connected with someone decades ago, barely talked to them since, and then still considered them a good friend." He shrugs again. "That's very different from me. I have my group of guys, and we see each other all the time. We wouldn't be close if we didn't. Just a few years apart, and something important would be lost."

We turn left and walk toward Miranda's lawn.

"Was she always . . . ?" A loner?

"Always what?"

"That way?"

Our footsteps crunch sand.

"Did Miranda tell you about the last time Claire went missing?" I shake my head no. "In first grade?" I shake more vigorously. "When Claire was six, there was a day she didn't make it home from school." Roger steps around a whelk. "Miranda and Andrew were up all night. Apparently, Claire couldn't even really talk yet. She said things like 'aminal,' 'pasghetti.' People didn't find her until the next day. She was locked in one of the wooden supply bins in her school gym. Those were usually stuffed with basketballs, plastic cones. But that one was stuffed with her." I imagine her at forty-five pounds, folded in a tight zigzag.

"Apparently, Claire had bloody knuckles. Black wrists. Splinters in her back. She'd spent most of the night fighting to get out. Fighting five inches of solid wood." He winces. "Claire didn't open her mouth for the next week. Didn't turn anyone in, didn't say a word. Instead of eating her cereal in the morning, she'd just stir it for ten minutes or crush the flakes with the back of her spoon." A clamshell cracks under my foot. "Miranda only told me about it recently. She's been having dreams of six-year-old Claire, locked in that box."

"Who was behind it?"

"A couple of mean girls."

"*Very* mean girls."

"Claire told me she was bullied. She said that one time, a couple kids locked her in something at school. But she said it with so little feeling. I had no idea she was there *overnight*. That she needed hospital staff to remove the wood from under her nails." Waves drench the beach, slide back into their foam. "Miranda's convinced that night did something to Claire. Pushed her inward. Claire recovered, of course. She blossomed, took over the world. But Miranda said a part of her daughter never came back."

Kira did describe Claire as aloof. *That meant she wasn't eating the sandbox with the rest of us idiots. Then, she wasn't skipping class to smoke under the bleachers.* Maybe Claire was protecting herself. Because she'd seen kids be cruel. I don't think an incident like that would've changed Claire completely, converted her from an extrovert into a recluse. But maybe it encouraged tendencies that she already had.

"What happened next?"

"Claire went back to school. For a few weeks, she wore a long-sleeve shirt. To hide the . . ." I imagine her soft blue hands. "She went on field trips. For a long time, Miranda checked Claire for bruises every night. For cuts. Missing hair. But Claire was pristine. Nothing like that ever happened again." He exhales against the wind. "I remember asking Claire about the box, why they did it. What did she say?" He squints as if he's peering through time. "'There's no creature more vicious than young girls.'"

"So maybe they did it for fun."

We stride across grass. Miranda waves to us from inside the kitchen.

"But like I said, she got past it. More or less. It didn't *maim* her ability to trust anyone. I like to think she trusted me." His voice cracks.

"Who was Claire's closest friend?"

"Kira."

"Aside from Kira."

He takes a few steps, thinking about it.

"Sofia Gonzalez, from Exeter."

We reach the patio.

"Was Claire having any problems with her sister that she mentioned to you?" I ask.

He nods yes.

"It wasn't Kira who did this." He comes to a gentle stop, giving us more time alone before heading inside. "Yes, they fought, and yes, it tore Claire apart. But their fights always had . . . low stakes. Claire wouldn't like it if I said that, but it's true. Kira would derail some of the wedding events. She'd grab the spotlight, but it wasn't anything deeper than that. It was just . . . Kira, wrestling for attention. They were sisters first. That was the permanent thing. Everything else was just—" He gestures to the choppy waves. "Surface."

~

Miranda opens the door to a guest room the size of my apartment. Twin beds under princess canopies are separated by a wide nightstand. In the middle, a coral centerpiece has a hundred frozen arms, all pointing in different directions. It looks like petrified lightning. Another framed piece of coral hangs above it on the wall: a white cross-section that reveals every bubble and branch in the skeleton. On either side, tall windows and bookcases replace wallpaper. I notice a few classics and a whole row of Nancy Drew mysteries.

The transition back to Riverhead is going to be steep. This room might have a teenage feel, but my windows face the ocean. Natural light shines in every corner. Even the wastebasket is beautiful. It's a sea glass mosaic, fusing melon greens and powder blues. I can't imagine throwing anything out in there. It's not even lined.

"Do you have plans for dinner?" Miranda asks.

"Tonight?"

"Yes, we could . . ." She touches her forehead lightly.

Does she feel the need to play host now that I'm staying in her home? I picture facing her at a table for two. One carnation in a thin glass vase. The necessary small talk. *Were you always a private eye?* Miranda doesn't need to hear about my time washing dishes. And I don't particularly want to relive it. I worked on a team with four men who barely spoke all day long. When they did, it was to argue over whether or not you could pay a prostitute to orgasm. They took sous vide plastic bags and pretended they were condoms. The day before two of them quit, they poured everything from the chemical rack into one of the industrial dishwashers. It leaked white foam all night, until the tile floor looked like snow.

"I'll probably work late," I say to excuse myself.

She nods, twisting her hands.

"Let me know if you need anything else," she adds.

She retreats down the hall, past Claire's room.

Alone, I sit at a desk with legs made of seashells. Bleached scallops and tiny conchs, stacked like vertebrae. No wonder Miranda's been acting tense, if she's been dreaming of her daughter in that elementary school coffin. Tiny fingers. Stale air. I wonder if there's anything more terrifying than what kids project onto the dark. Maybe Miranda wakes up every morning asking, *How many times can I lose her before it's my fault?*

I look up Sofia Gonzalez on my phone.

After Exeter, she went to Columbia for undergrad and then medical school. She's now an internist with her own practice in Connecticut. I find her email address at the practice and write her a note, explaining the situation and asking if she has a moment to talk. I add that I'd be able to visit her in person.

Send.

I walk over to a bookcase and stand at eye level with one copy of *The Starlit Ballet.* It's interesting that the public version of Claire was so different from the private one. Claire was the face of love and connection to millions. In real life, though, she barely kept up with her closest friends. Even at home with Roger, she was reserved. *Her* book *wasn't dedicated to* me. I *was dedicated to her* book. *In our relationship,* The Starlit Ballet *always came first.* I wonder what was so alive about this story that it gave Claire complete companionship for years.

Is there something about it I'm missing?

Starlites, the police—everyone looking at this case, really—have all been hyperfocused on *Claire.* On her monochromatic sweatpants, Starbucks name, and the shapes of her walks through the Upper East Side. Some have even traced them like crop circles, as if they have hidden meanings. Maybe they've spent too much time looking directly at her. Maybe I'm doing the same thing, asking about her journals, her wedding, and her childhood traumas. Maybe everyone should pan left, zoom out. I touch one edge of her book. The joints in a constellation under my thumb continue onto the cover. Millions have pored over this story, but how many have pored over it—*as evidence?* How many have considered that her writing itself might be part of the case?

EIGHT

"With so much in flux, there's something holy about what stays the same. Whenever I find something that won't move, won't die, I fixate on it as if it will save me."
—*Claire Ross,* The Starlit Ballet

I jolt awake to my phone's alarm. Sitting up in bed sends *The Starlit Ballet* rolling down my chest, pages turning on their own.

Seven a.m.

Silver light.

I grab the book and look for where I stopped, the last word I read before falling asleep. Last night, I made it through part one, the first soul's perspective across thousands of years. Flipping through it now, I catch glimpses of Logan in Yosemite. It's my favorite literary setting, up there with Manderley and Middle Earth. The sheer cliffs, distant peaks, and pine groves. Yosemite Falls like a spewing cloud, a thick white stream misting into nothing at the sides. The whole park conjured with atmospheric vastness.

I find part two and mark my page.

On my way to shower, I feel cautiously optimistic. As if her book really is an enormous, overlooked clue. A bloodstain, an intimate leak. Yes, her journal was honest and revealing, because those were words she never intended to share. But diary entries are quick. A novel is something that a writer lives with, something that receives their full attention for thousands of hours. The amount of thought and care that goes into a novel makes it just as revealing as a diary, even if it isn't as direct—which is part of why I've always connected with them. A close read of her book is a lot like an interview with her constant companion. Somehow, maybe I can ask the pages, Where in the world did she go?

~

I return from my shower to find a missed call from Eliza. I sit at the seashell desk in a towel and call her back. As the phone rings, I lower my gaze to the blue rug. The tight grid of stitches looks neat and clean, not a fiber out of place. I lift one corner and look underneath, only to find a mesh pad stretching to the other side of the floor.

Eliza answers.

I apologize for missing her call.

"I have something to tell you, Nina." It sounds like she's in a busy coffee shop, a place that grinds its own beans. Conversations blend into a wordless hum. Ice cubes collide with audible friction. Someone shouts, "Tony, americano for Tony."

"Hold on, I'm stepping outside now." The commotion fades behind her. "Can you hear me?"

I tell her that I can.

"I should've mentioned this to someone months ago, but . . ." She interrupts herself to exhale heavily. "On September eighteenth, there was a man who showed up to the wedding." I reach for a pen and monogrammed notepad. "The only reason I'm remembering this *now* is because I just saw his doppelgänger. He was ahead of me in line for coffee. It wasn't *him*, but . . . And before anyone lectures me, I know this is *beyond* forgetful. It's inexcusable."

I ask what happened.

"The day of the wedding, he got to the beach club around four." She sounds less frantic as she gets into the details. "That's when the shuttles were supposed to start bringing people over to Miranda's. He was wearing a tuxedo and waiting in the parking lot. When the buses didn't show, he went inside the clubhouse and asked about the shuttles to the Ross wedding. I was breaking down tables in the ballroom when I overheard him.

"So, I walked over and introduced myself as the wedding planner. He said his name was Pearce . . . *K* something—Kendrick. I'm almost positive that's what he said. But I knew that guest list upside down and backward, and he wasn't on it."

I ask Eliza if she can give a physical description of him. She tells me he was handsome. Pale with a square jaw. Dark-brown hair gelled in place. A little shorter than she was. He didn't have any tattoos, any discernible accent. "He seemed suave." She lowers her voice to add, "It's eerie, isn't it? Someone so debonair shows up uninvited?"

"How did he react when you told him that the wedding was off?"

"He was surprised and then . . ."

Silence.

"He smiled."

I draw one, two dots for eyes.

"Is there anything else you remember?" I ask, retracing the blue lips. They get denser, darker. "Anything else he might've done? Said?"

"I'm sorry. That day, I was scattershot. Looking for Claire every-where at once. And at the same time, calling every vendor and explaining what happened. Making three different contingency plans in case she showed up. And then, realizing something terrible had happened. Folding all 302 chairs. Putting everything back in its box. I've never forgotten anything so important. Not in a hundred weddings. Not in my whole damn life." She snorts once with some despair. "Well, not that I can remember."

~

I get dressed in the guest bathroom, facing an enormous mirror. It's wider than my wingspan, covering everything above the his-and-hers sinks. Steam still clings to glass, blurring my reflection. I wipe one hand across the middle, revealing my nose.

I'm about to swipe up when I pause. Fingers starfished. Maybe I'm sentimental for my mirror at home. Because I want to leave some of the mist where it is. I swipe down instead, over my chin, shoulders. It's enough of a view that I can finish getting ready. Miranda will be drifting through the house all day, which means I can't afford to look sloppy. Not even when I think I'm alone.

Dressed, I head to my laptop.

Order a background check on Pearce.

It's hard to trust a memory that spontaneously returns after months in the dark. Memories are like photographs. They fade with time until eventually, familiar faces become unrecognizable. Clear details become clouds to interpret. Still, Eliza's tip is worth checking. Maybe this Pearce knows something. Or maybe he was a random Starlite. Someone who just wanted to be close to Claire. Who was hoping to grab an aisle seat and finger her veil as she passed. I'm still facing my laptop when a new email arrives from Sofia.

> From: Dr. Sofia Gonzalez <<Sgonz . . . >>
> To: Nina Travers <<NinaT . . . >>
>
> Hi Nina,
>
> I will make time for you at any point.
>
> Before you make the trip, though, I'm not sure how helpful I can be. Claire and I had been growing apart. We were close in high school, but I don't know much about her life more recently. We hadn't seen each other face-to-face in over a year.

If you would still like to talk, how about later this week? Mornings are best for me.

Sofia

I suggest this Friday, two days from now, then sit up straighter. The police probably never talked to Sofia.

~

I read more, tearing through part two in the guest room.

This finishes each story from part one, now told by the soulmate.

Then a new chapter opens, set in 1999. This thread wasn't started in part one, which signals that something important is about to change. Enter Chloe Reed and Luke Olsen in New York City. Chloe is a poet with a bright-blue pixie cut. Luke is a rough-around-the-edges comedian known for his dark style of humor. They meet at the Comedy Cellar. Halfway into their story, one sentence commands my attention. I have an idea—and it's so brand new, so entirely possible, that my fingers feel electric on the page.

r/ClaireRoss posted by u/B3LI3V3M3 2 mos ago

FINDING CLAIRE: MEGATHREAD
MEGATHREAD

☆☆✻ PLEASE SHARE INFORMATION RELEVANT TO HER CASE. ☆☆✻

We know her better than anyone.

We should be able to find her. ☆☆✻

Current Megathreads:

ENCOUNTERS

PHOTOS

ihave100shadows · 3 wks ago

East Hampton Town Police: "After a thorough investigation, we did not find any evidence of foul play or suspicious circumstances."

Translation: Everything's fine. Claire Ross just ran away.

I could scream!

My husband's a cop here in Red Springs, OH, where he works with REAL runaways! You think the "East Hampton Town Police" is used to dealing with them? Let me break it down for you: kids don't run away from trust funds! They don't run away from silver spoons and golden superyachts! You get what I'm saying? No one with two brain cells to rub together has ever run FROM the Hamptons—unless it was for one of their triathlons!

REAL runaways are a type. (Trust me, we see them all the time in Red Springs. You can watch them here like a parade.) Think: bad home life, no job, no s/o, and living in a dead-end area, where there's NO HOPE of things getting better. Kids run when it MAKES SENSE to run. And the better off they are, the less likely they are to bolt.

Hampton Police. Oxymoron!

accomplit · 3 wks ago

Christopher McCandless ran away. He was well off

sen1orspr1ng · 3 wks ago

Okay, one in a billion

holdenDedalus · 3 wks ago

Claire was always one ☆ in a billion

scar-tissue6 · 2 mos ago

she still is
i s n ' t s h e

underc0verl0ver · 3 wks ago

Oxymoron LMAO! What's their specialty, then? Missing *souls*? *Hi, Mr. Police Officer Sir, I lost my soul . . . Can you help me find it?*

NotWithoutLuke · 3 wks ago

Proving foul play **without a body** is incredibly difficult. Without blood or any sign of physical trauma, then it's . . . virtually impossible.

JaxxonL · 3 wks ago

Why doesn't everyone just call foul play *murder*? That's what it is, isn't it?

DeathDoesntPart · 3 wks ago

I SEE EVERY PERSON HE'S EVER BEEN

Hello from Ontario . . . Hope everyone is staying sane.

Have we considered if Claire was involved in any kind of criminal activity? Just spitballing, but maybe she had a . . . shady dealer? Got in with the wrong crowd that way? I wouldn't be surprised if she was on Ritalin or amphetamines or something . . . She wasn't jittery on TV, but my ex once called *The Starlit Ballet* "the term paper from hell" . . . Made me think that maybe Claire got some help writing the book, some off-label help.

editionallyy · 3 wks ago

I live down the hall from Roger and Claire in NYC. (It's a newer building, smaller, only nine floors and four apartments on each. Makes sense they'd want the privacy.) I work from home, so I was 50-100 ft away from her for 40+ hours a week. Trust me: she wasn't getting any sketchy visitors. No one on our floor was. It was like a cemetery out there, a carpeted cemetery. The only person I ever heard in the hallway was our maintenance guy collecting the recycling or vacuuming the rug.

skidreams12 · 3 wks ago

Stop it, her FLOOR??

editionallyy · 3 wks ago

Exactly. And I'm pretty sure our landlord knows because he raised my rent 20% y-o-y. One month before I was going to renew. Of course, the *law* says I need 90 days notice in writing, but . . . worth it. ☆

CLOSER3ADER · 3 wks ago

You're sick. You're all sick.
Worms inside a wound.

xxjjkk66 · 3 wks ago

☆☆✶☆☆✶☆☆✶ WHAT DOES HER DOOR FEEL LIKE PLEASE JUST TOUCH I NEED TO KNOW IF ITS

WARM ☆☆✲☆☆✲☆☆✲☆☆✲ PLEASE JUST TOUCH☆
HER☆DOOR ☆☆✲☆☆✲

rhyme-crime · 3 wks ago

i've ☆✲☆☆✲ been ☆✲☆☆✲ in
your ☆✲☆☆✲lobby

sevenyears_ · 3 wks ago

I CAN'T REMEMBER THE LAST TIME I MET HIM THIS YOUNG.

I don't think Claire had time for *crime*. She invented three dozen major characters across thousands of years of history. You can't shortcut that kind of work. She must've been nose-deep in whaling ship manifests from the 1700s. In fine print on WANTED posters from the Great Depression . . . The only things on her record are probably late library books. She was too busy to break the law.

NINE

"I hold Luke's hand, remembering the Bering Land Bridge . . . I squeeze him tighter and remember the Great Depression . . . I never wanted to leave him. Not today, not in any life."
—*Claire Ross,* The Starlit Ballet

That afternoon, Miranda and I face each other at the kitchen table. She's in a turtleneck sweater that doesn't hug an inch of her figure. It's more of an aura than a garment. Air painted down to her wrists. Meanwhile, I'm in a thin V-neck, wool imitating a cashmere blend. The windows ahead frame pale sky over coastline. The horizon is smeared with winter rain. *The Starlit Ballet* waits between us, next to a printout of the wedding guest list.

"What's all this?" she asks.

She points to the exhibit on the table.

I watch her hand.

The more time I spend with her, the more I see how much she and Claire have in common. It's not just their cheekbones or the way that their chins almost vanish under their lips. It's not just the intent way they listen, as if they care about the *gaps* between your words. Apparently, they both point *under*handed. Showing their palms.

"I was thinking more about Claire's book," I say, "and wondering—"

Gravel crunches in the driveway.

"Oh, that must be Kira," Miranda says. "I'm sorry, she insisted on coming. I trust you, of course, but Kira's been so protective recently."

I turn around to face the front door.

Kira enters the foyer with her high ponytail swishing. She's in skin-tight jeans and knee-high suede boots. Those are a reckless choice in this weather. Her leather jacket is snug around the shoulders, giving her rounded corners. Her sleeves are full of silver zip details, diagonal slashes down her arms. Metal teeth interlocked.

I give her a pleasant hello.

She doesn't wave.

"Can you please be polite?" Miranda asks.

"Hi, Nina," she says dryly.

Kira takes the seat next to her mom. I face them both, wishing the room were half as crowded. Kira's wearing false eyelashes today, evident in the white specks of glue along her lash line. She must've only just put them on, dove right into the beautiful mask. I wonder if she ever goes without makeup, or if she wears concealer to sleep. If she just paints and repaints. Maybe she won't remove the eyelashes at all. She'll just let them fall out on their own. Land on her sweaters all week, curled up like spider legs.

"Nina was just asking me—what was it?" Miranda starts.

"Did you ever think that Claire's book was inspired by her personal life?" I ask.

"Didn't she write about pirates?" Kira asks skeptically.

"It's a little complicated, because she wrote about two souls who become different people over time," I explain. "But what I mean is: Did it ever occur to you that she might've based the souls on particular people?"

Miranda puzzles.

"I think she based one of them on herself," I say.

I open the book and point to the lines:

"You reached the highest spiritual level as Chloe Reed. You, Chloe, spent your whole life detached . . . You are free to move on."

They look at me for an explanation.

"Chloe is the character who made me realize what's happening here—Chloe is one of the two soulmates." The aside is for Kira. "Anyway, she has a different name in every life: Cassia, Carine, Charlotte, Chloe, and then Cady. What do all those names have in common?" I give them a second. "The name Chloe Reed sounds a lot like Claire Ross, doesn't it?"

They don't react.

I understand that each piece of the puzzle is tenuous on its own.

"Chloe is a lot like Claire," I go on. "Chloe's a poet, finishing an anthology in New York City. The more I look for similarities between the two women, the more I find them. They're both writers, of course. But they write the same way—shutting out the rest of the world. They hole up in lonely corners of Manhattan, devoted to their ideas. Typing all day, just emptying themselves out through their fingers. As if their work is a religious mission, or a military order, or something. Writing aside, they both went to New England prep schools. They both went to Harvard. They both spend an uncommon, almost unbearable amount of time alone. They even have the same features, down to the pixie haircut."

"So?" Kira asks.

"In interviews, Claire described herself as an 'old soul,'" I say. "That's literally what Chloe is." I face Kira to add, "Chloe's had thousands of lifetimes on Earth by this point in the story." I swivel back to address them both. "As if that isn't enough, Claire was asked all the time to give advice to other writers. She had a few different answers, but one of them was, 'You need to rip your story out of real life.'"

"She said that?" Kira asks.

"So, I've looked at everything that Chloe and Claire have in common, down to the sounds of their names," I say. "Claire admitted that she ripped this story out of her life." I leave the conclusion unspoken, ready for them to draw it themselves. Kira remains defiantly blank, but Miranda is furrowing her brow, trying to piece it together.

"So what if she based Chloe on herself?" Miranda asks.

"Well, *The Starlit Ballet* is about a deep connection between two souls and all the obstacles they overcome in order to have just one peaceful life together," I explain. "They only get that life at the end of the book in Yosemite."

Kira crosses her arms.

"What if Claire felt that way about someone real?" I wait for an answer that doesn't arrive. "I think that's what happened. I think Claire viewed herself as an old soul with one true love—and I don't think that person is Roger."

Miranda opens and closes her mouth.

"That's insane," Kira says. "Mom, you don't believe that, right?"

"I—I don't know."

"You think Claire spent seven years writing some sort of love letter? For someone who isn't her fiancé?" Kira asks.

"What's more believable," I interject. "That she wrote this book—this heartfelt, titanic book—about people she made up? Or about someone she loved?"

"*Not* Roger?" Miranda asks.

"Well, she started the book two years before they met," I say. "Besides, I'd ask you to take an honest look at their relationship. When I spoke to him alone, I was surprised at how much distance there was between them. The longer they dated, the less time they spent together. Roger said she always chose her book over him. As if they were just . . . roommates. Isn't that strange? Claire writes something *that* romantic, and she was closed off from her own fiancé?"

Miranda is too shocked and Kira too ferocious to agree.

"We've all read her journal by now," I go on. "Roger was barely in it. He was . . . a minor character. That baffled me. How could someone so emotional have such a shallow relationship with her partner? How could she write about a connection that deep, make it feel real, and not have it at home?" *Unless she had it with someone else?*

No one speaks.

"I'm just asking you to consider if that makes sense. I looked around Claire's room, and I heard about the wedding that was planned for her, and I don't see any sign that this was the direction she wanted to go." My tone is as gentle as possible. "I think her book was earnest. If you want to know what she really wanted: look at what Logan and Cady do. That's the life they choose with fifteen thousand years of wisdom."

I point out that when Logan and Cady get married, they don't do it in front of hundreds of her parents' friends. They don't follow it with a meal of lobster and filet with béarnaise sauce, as Claire and Roger were slated to do. Instead, they elope. They spend the rest of their days in a national park. If Claire's book is a window into her mind, she didn't have an appetite for luxury. Building her wedding registry—asking herself which porcelain terrine, which silver tea tray—must've felt like the beginning of a life meant for someone else.

"I'm curious," I add, "if Claire and Roger had any real chemistry together? I know you said that Claire was happier, but I'm asking about them *together*—the way she looked at him, the way they talked to each other." Meanwhile, Miranda fidgets with her left diamond stud. She drags her thumbnail across the backing, making a series of muted clicks. It sounds like a metronome slowing down, losing its beat. Once I've said my piece, she drops her hands to the table. She lifts her chin slowly, drawing our attention like gravity.

"I'll admit I didn't see it at first," she says.

"Mom!" Kira snaps.

"It's true. Claire was different—in a good way—and then the man she finally brings home is . . . completely normal?" She barely inflects the remark, leaving it somewhere between a question and a dull statement of fact. "Claire was an original. You know, she never just agreed with anyone else? She might agree with you generally, but there was always a nuance that was her own. Every one of her opinions was *hers*."

Kira leans back in her chair.

"Then why was she so happy?" Miranda asks.

I clear my throat.

"Well, it's clear from talking to Roger that he really did love *her*," I say. "I don't think Claire took that for granted—especially after growing up without many friends. Kira, you said yourself that she was an adult as a child and a child as an adult. She was always in her own world. Enter Roger. Suddenly, there's someone who cares about how her day went. Who treats her like a queen, looks at her like a modern Cleopatra. As if she's taking a break from Julius Caesar and Roman politics just to have dinner with him. Of course that would make her happy." Miranda listens palpably. "She must've felt something for him. They wouldn't have lasted for so long if she didn't. But I don't think he was the one in her heart."

Kira rolls her eyes.

"Don't take my word for it," I say. "Ask yourself."

The wind changes direction outside, whipping lean branches back and forth. Some of them snap at the joints, shedding twigs on the lawn. Miranda and Kira keep their backs to the view. I can almost see the tension in the glass behind them, withstanding gusts and straddling temperatures, as if it might crack at any second.

"*The Starlit Ballet* was a love letter," Miranda says.

I nod yes.

"So, where is she now?" Miranda asks.

I push the guest list an inch toward her.

"To answer that, I'll need your help," I say. "This might be uncomfortable, but I'd appreciate knowing more about the people Claire dated before Roger. Who were they? Was there anyone she kept thinking about? Or . . . invited to the wedding?"

Miranda glances at the list.

"None of them were invited," she says, now much calmer than when we sat down. A new perspective on an old case must be comforting. She leans forward and picks up the pen. She turns the guest list over so the blank back side faces the ceiling.

"You're treating this like an English class," Kira snaps at me.

"My job is to tell you what I think."

"Not for long," she says.

"And your job—"

"Oh, what's *our* job?" she asks.

"—is to decide if I'm right."

Kira forces a short, dark laugh. For someone who rarely smiles, she has perfect teeth. Like straight, white bones. The color of a skinned apple. Meanwhile, Miranda forges ahead and jots down a name. I ask her for anything else she can remember about them—school, hometown, random facts. She writes a second name, along with two scribbles of detail. I try to read the words upside down, but her looping cursive is too elaborate. Every capital letter has a swirling head or foot. Her grocery lists must look like formal invitations.

"That's the best I can do," she says, leaning back from her list and puzzling at it. "But neither one of these really lasted. No one had any staying power, except for Roger." She looks at her daughter. "What do you think?"

Kira stares straight ahead.

Miranda slides the list around to face me.

"Claire dated the first man, Brett Harris, for a couple months in high school," she says, looking unconvinced that he's a promising lead. "They never got very far. Claire kept breaking up with him. He kept convincing her to get back together. I think she didn't want to hurt his feelings. He was a day student from New Hampshire, maybe a hundred pounds soaking wet. They took all the same math classes, and she was the only girl in them. She had a hard time telling him to move on, really, because he was so nice."

Miranda points to the second name, *Pearce K.*

"Kendrick?" I ask.

"You know him?" Kira asks.

She acts so surprised, I worry that I might've said something wrong. Given something away. Because right now, Kira looks as if she finally sees the cheap wool in my sweater. Finally knows that I've spent most of my career slipping into bedrooms, filming strangers thump out affairs.

That I haven't earned my seat at this table as much as I've stolen it, convinced the Rosses to give me a chance. But it's only a false alarm.

"No," I clarify, my heartbeat slowing. "But apparently, he tried to sneak into Claire's wedding on September eighteenth." Their eyes widen. "I'm looking into it. Eliza told me this morning that he showed up in a tuxedo, asking for shuttles to the ceremony."

"Pearce?" Miranda asks in disbelief.

Her fingertips graze her lips.

"How long were they together?" I ask.

"A couple months. But Claire didn't spend a second on him after that. I think she liked his confidence, but he turned out to be an egomaniac. He's one of those New York City prep school kids, if you know what I mean. They wake up on third and think they hit a triple." Her cool eyes express subtle disdain. It's a glimpse into why she hasn't left her daughters with trust funds. "Anyway, it was a clean break. No one's said his name since."

I stare at Miranda's list.

Just two names.

"There was no one else?" I ask, tapping the white space with my fingers. I expected to find a relationship with legs. Sometimes, though, rephrasing a question changes the answer. "Did Claire ever fall for someone before Roger? Not necessarily a boyfriend, but—"

Kira stands abruptly.

"I'm sorry, I can't stay for any more of this," she says. "Mom, I know we all miss Claire, but this woman is taking advantage of your situation. She is taking your money to read tea leaves and auras as if that will bring Claire back."

"Kira—" Miranda starts.

"It's ridiculous," Kira says, plowing ahead. "Treating metaphors like real evidence, like actual clues? I can come up with wild theories, too, Mom. I can circle different letters in the book until they spell out a random location. That doesn't mean Claire is there. It's just a book, Mom, and this fraud is trying to convince you it's more."

"Stop it!" Miranda interjects. "If we knew what she was going to say, then what would be the point of hiring her?" She gestures to me. "Abigail said this would happen. Stop making this more difficult than it is. I just need to find my Claire." Her voice cracks. "I don't care if Claire didn't want to marry Roger. I just want her home."

Kira looks like she's on the verge of talking back.

Miranda looks like she's expecting it.

They stare at each other, neither one budging.

Eventually, Kira turns on her heel, forcing a high-pitched squeak out of the wooden floor. She walks out the front door without saying goodbye. When it slams, Miranda jumps in her seat. Kira's car retreats on gravel, and I imagine the pebbles flattening into coins. Soon, the only noises are creaks throughout the house. Wind rolls through dark grass, blurring the tips. Miranda glances at my copy of *The Starlit Ballet*. Her gaze lingers as if she's trying to read it through the cover, see things in the story she's never noticed before.

I ask if she's all right.

She nods faintly.

I follow her line of sight.

In some lights, the cover is haunting. The constellations can look like bones in the dirt. Elbows, knees. A broken spine. It can be an image as gruesome as the soulmates' early lives. Maybe it's a warning that this book will kill its main characters a hundred times. That this will be a heavy read, that it might change you. In other lights, the cover looks mathematical. Like a yellow equation across a blackboard, sprawling and intricate. Now, the constellations look like threads in a spiderweb. I can almost see it between branches in the dark. Each constellation part of a broader wheel shape, a hundred silky lines glinting.

"The news about Claire spread fast for a lot of reasons, but I think one of them was the setup," I say. "Her wedding was supposed to be the most romantic moment in this romantic woman's life—but what if it still was? Some people call this"—I hold up my copy—"the best love story of all time, but what if it's even more loving than we expected?

What if it's a gesture of love too? To someone she knew? Authors are thoughtful and strange people. I wouldn't underestimate how thoughtful, how strange."

Miranda leans back.

"Most people have strong feelings, then let them go," she says. "It's part of becoming an adult. Learning how to—lose. Bad ideas. Friendships that ran their course. Goals that aren't worth it in the end. Growing up is *giving up* on the right things." Her tone sounds defeated. "But Claire never learned how to do that. She held on." She stares at me, her green eyes the average of Claire's and Kira's. More softly, she adds, "Are you going to find my daughter?" She looks so shattered that I almost reach for her hand.

~

For dinner that night, I insist again on eating alone. I buy a turkey sandwich on a roll from Goldberg's Famous Bagels for $6.29 and bring it back to a dark house. Miranda's out with another couple at Cove Hollow, a restaurant on the edge of town.

I flip on lights in the foyer.

I pause outside Claire's room with my sandwich. This is where the glow from the foyer ends. The curve of her door handle catches some faint light, but the hallway ahead of me is black. This is the kind of detail that Claire would've noticed, the exact place in the hallway where the light stops. Her green stare felt that perceptive.

While eating, I read the background check for Pearce Kendrick. Since Harvard—Claire's year—he's had a long series of short-lived jobs. He pivots every ten to twelve months, always landing at a shiny new start-up. I double-check the history against his LinkedIn and find his profile photo exactly as Eliza described: pale with a square jaw. Dark-brown hair gelled in place. Suave. The rest of his online presence consists of photos at black-tie events. In each one, he's the center of attention, doing something to draw the eye. It seems like he's always chasing the spotlight—and often gets it—but doesn't have the substance to keep it for long.

Eventually, I go back to his LinkedIn, find his email address, and start to compose a message. I ask politely if he wouldn't mind a chat at his earliest convenience. He seems like the kind to respond to attention, any validation of his importance.

Send.

When I'm done with my sandwich, I turn to *The Starlit Ballet*. This time, I flip all the way to the end and read the acknowledgments. It's short, just a couple of pages. Claire spends the first two paragraphs thanking teachers at Exeter—which is unusual, now that I think about it. Most authors start by thanking their editor or agent, the ones who were in the trenches with them throughout the long, uncertain process. But Claire thanks an English teacher, several history teachers. She must've had a strong connection to the school.

Is that where she met her true love?

I can't let my theory go just yet. Miranda only named one boyfriend from high school, but what if Claire never dated the person who stuck with her? What if she only imagined what could've been? Or what if this was a relationship no one knew anything about? Someone she sneaked into her life, only saw at night? I look outside and imagine their private affair on a silver corner of the lawn. Their own secret, starlit ballet.

TEN

"Losing him doesn't get any easier, no matter how many times I've watched him die."
—*Claire Ross,* The Starlit Ballet

Miranda's lawn is misty this morning, right outside my window. A bird hops through it, teacup-size, hyperactive. We don't get many winter birds here. The ones we do are all gray brown, in the same leaden palette as the rest of the island.

Mary Oliver would've liked this view.

I read her my *senior* year.

By then, I didn't even think of myself as Nina anymore, with that nasal *i* in the middle, that off-key pinch of sound. On campus, my alter ego was Alice Henley. I imagined that she grew up riding horses, playing the flute. I was in character whenever I waltzed into class. The key was to relax, just like everyone else. I had to slouch. I had to nod off once or twice every semester. As if I had somewhere more exciting to be, maybe Jackson Hole or my parents' Park Avenue apartment. As if paying tuition made me a customer, and the school owed me a luxury product. I had to *dare* the professor to be exciting, almost taunt them into it with my palpable boredom. And I did have to take some notes because I took myself seriously. My mind was worth hundreds of thousands of dollars, wasn't it?

At my bravest, I went to a student party. I remember leaving work late one Saturday, walking across campus when I saw three red windows.

They glowed on the fourth floor of a dorm. Iggy Azalea's "Fancy" floated across the quad. I got close enough that a group heading inside the building held the door open for me. Alice took over, grinning and following them upstairs. Luckily, it was September. Everyone was still getting to know each other. I remember the garbage cans on every floor, full of cardboard skeletons left over from six-packs. I'd imagined these stairs a hundred times, never pictured the trash.

The red suite was loud, chaotic. I avoided the bar and took the last seat on the futon. The woman next to me had long, dark hair. It looked like oil dripping over her shoulders. She wore a cashmere twinset and Mary Jane shoes. The Solo cup in her hand was slanted, fizzy drink skirting the brim. She introduced herself as *Siobhan, premed.* I felt more confident than usual with the lights so dim, with everyone else a little bit poisoned. I told her that I was *Alice, English major.* Siobhan told me that she'd wanted to take English, but she was too practical. I liked that. For once, I was the dreamy, indulgent one. Of course, it made sense. Alice didn't need to build a nest egg. Her life could be about beauty, art.

I'd never had sex with a woman before, definitely not with anyone as elegant as Siobhan. Siobhan, who was from Connecticut but who'd gone to middle school in London. Siobhan, who wore pearl studs, played squash, and had two Tibetan mastiffs at home, Valentine and Watson. Her privilege was like a perfume. We had sex standing up. She leaned back against her door, pushing her pelvis toward me. Her back arched like syrup dripping off a spoon. Afterward, we lay on her bed, drenched in moonlight. She fell asleep with one hand on my breast, one smooth leg crooked over my thighs.

I slipped out of her place before she woke up. Back at my apartment, the spell was broken. I couldn't believe I'd been so impulsive. The only reason I managed to sit in on so many classes was because I *haunted* them. I was barely there, a pale ghost in the corner. I couldn't get to know any of the students, not really. So I put my head back down. I walked right past colored windows, tempting music. Every now and then, at work, I did wonder if I was washing Siobhan's dishes—if this was *her* spoon, *her* untouched bowl of white yogurt and oaty granola. I thought of her elongated body, wearing nothing but a braided head-band. I'm still not sure if I was the one who missed her, or if that was Alice.

I roll over and check my phone to find an unread email from Pearce. I sit up and read the time stamp before anything else: 2:03 a.m.

From: Pearce Stanley Kendrick <<Kendr . . . >>
To: Nina Travers <<NinaT . . . >>

Dear Nina,

How are you?

It's a pleasure to hear from you, though I am sorry to meet in these most unfortunate circumstances. I do admit that I've been expecting to hear from someone in your position for some time.

How is 10 am this morning for a Zoom? Please let me know what works best for you. I have more flexibility than usual these days.

I look forward to it,

Pearce

~

I prepare my background for a Zoom with Pearce, still thinking about his email. It was overly formal, almost syrupy with affection. By the time I got to his signature, I half expected him to sign it *Fondly* or something else as familiar. It isn't hard to imagine him schmoozing at those black-tie parties, stirring martinis with an olive-studded stick.

I sit at the desk in front of my Zoom portal, checking the view. The blinds are drawn, preventing a backlit disaster. My suitcase is out of the frame. My pen and notepad are ready, off-screen, where Pearce won't be able to read my notes. I position my face off-center, downplaying the crooked bend in my nose. While I've never been pretty, I know how to look presentable, how to showcase my better side to make clients feel at ease.

Pearce is on time.

"Good morning, Detective," he says, greeting me with a smooth smile.

He's sitting with elegant posture, shoulders back, chest proud. He looks broad and strong, but there's something young in his eyes. He seems more self-assured than adults usually are. I don't want to read him too fast, but it's almost as if he's managed to get this far without failing or losing anyone, and he thinks that life will always be a breeze. His pink oxford is striped like a candy cane. It's aggressively vibrant. Dark hair curls in the V-shaped gap between his top buttons. Behind him, tall shelves hold art books, painted urns with looping handles, and a crystal vase. Windows soak an armchair in light.

"Thanks for joining me from—where are you?" I ask.

"New York City," he says.

"Is that your apartment?"

"My parents' town house. They're in Florida for the winter."

I ask where in Florida. It's a question that makes wealthy people feel comfortable—it suggests that I might be familiar with the area, that we might know the same people.

"Coral Gables." His smile gleams. "They asked me to join, but you know what they say, 'Florida's where people make a fire to escape the heat.'" He laughs with enthusiasm. Most people are compliant enough to answer a few questions for a case, but this is an unexpected level of friendliness. He's treating the interrogation lamp like a spotlight.

"That's a good one," I say, playing along. "So, I actually wanted to start by asking about a line in your email. You knew someone like me would get in touch?"

"I did."

"Why is that?"

"Because Claire never got over me. Not that I blame her."

He winks at me.

"How did you and Claire know each other?" I ask.

He half rolls his eyes, as if the answer is obvious.

"Softball," he says. "I thought you were going to be tough on me."

There's a hint of playful teasing in his tone. I can't remember the last time a stranger flirted with me, which makes me think that he's like this with everyone. I imagine him hitting on baristas, keeping his gaze below their name tags.

I wait politely for an answer.

"We met in college," he concedes. I draw an H inside a shield. "We'd seen each other around, but it wasn't until junior year that we introduced ourselves. On spring break, we crossed paths on the Upper East Side, right between our parents' places—Miranda has a town house in the Seventies, near us. We just started talking." I imagine him extending a slimy hand on the sidewalk, laying it on thick, and laughing at his own jokes. "That night, I took her to my favorite dim sum spot, and then . . ." He smiles as if the rest is famous history.

"How long were you together?" I ask.

He shakes his head.

"You don't understand," he says.

"Help me."

"We had a connection. It's not about how long it lasted."

I draw a heart with an arrow through it.

"How did you spend your time together?" I probe for specifics.

"I'm too polite to answer that," he says.

I hide my distaste. Darken the arrow.

"If you *must* know, I was in the Society of Explorers at Harvard." He speaks with great authority. "It was a very exclusive club. We discovered and maintained hidden places around campus—access to rooftops, an underground fountain. I showed Claire every secret spot. She liked the privacy." His smile becomes a smirk again. "We went to talks about cave diving. We almost went on a guided hike through old subway tunnels in the city."

I tell him that sounds special.

"It was. She was curious, sharp. She had more passion in her fingernails than most people ever do." I pretend to take a note, even though Claire's hallmark trait was never passion. Passion is just . . . energy. Fuel for something else. If Pearce knew her well, he would've said something about her imagination. That was always her gift. She could see what wasn't there. "And she liked that I challenged her. Most people are predictable because they care about being liked. Claire and I don't need to be liked. We care more about being original, being ourselves."

I resist the urge to roll my eyes.

"So, why did this perfect relationship end?"

"I was too young."

"Meaning . . . ?"

"I broke up with her. But she never forgot about me."

I ask how he knows.

"She invited one of my ex-girlfriends to her wedding." He raises a triumphant eyebrow, as if this is checkmate. "Lauren Gregory. That was Claire's way of asking me to show up. She knew the news would get back to me." Lauren Gregory does sound familiar—she was on the *Roger* tab in the guest list. They work together at the same accounting firm. Her email address in the master spreadsheet was her professional one, hosted by their shared company. I already doubted Pearce's theory, but now, I know that he's wrong.

"Did you stay in touch with Claire?" I ask.

"You could say that."

I ask what he means.

"Do you know what her book was really about?"

"Soulmates who reincarnate?" I hazard.

"The book is about me. Well—us."

He believes what he's saying.

"It's about what we had."

"Right, the connection," I say, humoring him. "So then, why didn't she reach out to you?" His expression falls. "Ten years is a long time to go without talking, isn't it?"

"She was afraid of how much we felt for each other."

I nod as if that makes sense.

But Pearce's self-importance is unsettling. Confidence is one thing. *This* is projecting obsession onto Claire after she ignored him for a decade and then got engaged to someone else. The only communication between them was a guest list coincidence, which he interpreted as a message of love. It's such distorted vision it's almost unsafe. Maybe this is why he has trouble holding down jobs. He doesn't see the same world everyone else does. He might walk straight into people who dislike him, unable to believe they exist.

"So, I'm just asking this because of your connection—where is she?"

"I don't know yet."

"'Yet'?"

"She'll come back." He glances sideways, as if she might be turning the doorknob now. "People always come back to their first love, don't they?"

~

After the Zoom with Pearce, I walk down Further Lane. It's hard to see the houses on this road behind their hedges. Even when I can glimpse one, it's behind gates or at the end of a mile-long driveway. People in this part of the world love their moats. I don't know if it comes from a love of privacy or a fear of something. Either way, it's amusing to see layers of defense in a town that's already so hard to access.

I think through what Pearce said about his alleged connection with Claire. I suspect he only felt this way *after* she got famous—and he's not the only one. Claire was asked in a *60 Minutes* special about her devoted Starlites. *"What does it feel like to be at the center of this global community?"* She shyly deflected the question, claiming that popularity is fragile. Then, she went on a tangent about readers in general. Apparently, there's an equivalent term for "bookworm" in a dozen languages, which Claire happened to know. In Indonesian, it's "book flea"; in Chinese, "book insect"; and in Korean, "book bug." She asked why so many cultures thought of readers as insects, dazzling everyone until they'd forgotten the original question.

~

Back in the guest bedroom, I pick up *The Starlit Ballet* and have a seat at the desk. If Claire wrote this as a love letter, did she leave clues in the story about the person it's meant for? Maybe she winks in a semicolon whenever she drops a hint. Or maybe there's one break into second person, just one moment when Claire writes "you" and then leaves a message for him. A tell-all clause in her fiction. After spending so much time with this book, I should be able to pick it apart and find anything hidden inside.

I flip to where I left off, the first scene set in the future.

In 2150, she's still at her soulmate's side, waiting for him to mature.

In this life, he's Liam Hayes, a Formula One driver for Mercedes. She's Candice Kelly, his performance coach. Their chapter opens at the Singapore Grand Prix, where Liam holds the lead at over two hundred miles per hour. The track is fluorescent at 10:00 p.m., a spotlighted and psychedelic white. Checkered with ads for Singapore Airlines and Heineken. Cars whip past Candice in the Mercedes box, kicking up sparks. Drivers ripple with G forces around tight corners. When Liam passes Candice, though, she's withdrawn.

He isn't growing.

At the next turn, Liam's car skids straight through the barrier. It flips over sand, twice, three times. Fire leaps up like a geyser, burning a streak into the night. His team crowds the corner of his box. Their principal is the last one over, repeating *Liam* into his headset. The marshal waves a red flag at the lap line, commanding all drivers off the track. An ambulance speeds toward the crash. A crew starts to hose down the flames, but it's taking too long to put them out. A whole minute passes before the car is damp and smoking.

Liam emerges on a stretcher, dead still.

I read the chapter forward and backward, dwelling in Formula One for so long that I can almost taste the burning rubber, almost feel the pages heat up with the fastest cars in the world, racing in games where a fraction of a second means a difference worth hundreds of millions of dollars. *Liam Hayes.* I say the name out loud a few times in a row, as if it will lure hidden pages out of the spine that will tell the real story under the fictional one. *Liam.* If Claire gave one soulmate the first letter of her name, did she do the same for him? His name starts with *L* in every life. But does his real name start with *L* too?

http://www.reddit.com/r/ClaireRoss

FINDING CLAIRE: MEGATHREAD

MEGATHREAD

☆☆✲ PLEASE SHARE INFORMATION RELEVANT TO HER CASE. ☆☆✲
We know her better than anyone.
We should be able to find her. ☆☆✲

Current Megathreads:

ENCOUNTERS
PHOTOS

i-play-favorites · 2 wks ago

Unpopular opinion, so brace yourself. I think we need to acknowledge the possibility that Claire u n a l i v e d herself.

Before you downvote, think about it.

What are the odds she was depressed? Bipolar? (Or had schizophrenia, PTSD, or another kind of psychosis . . . ?) Personally, I keep coming back to depression. I mean, Claire wore the same outfit to every appearance—black turtleneck, black pants. She wore the same sweatpants almost every time we saw her around NYC. She didn't seem to have many (any?) close friends. Other than Roger, that is. And staying inside all the time, in one silent room . . . Hearing nothing but the vacuum cleaner outside . . . If she wasn't depressed *before* she got in deep, maybe that life did something to her mind.

hermioneDanger · 2 wks ago

If she unalived herself, she would've left a note. Claire was a deeply empathetic person—look at the way her soulmates treat each other. You can only write depth if you have it. She wouldn't leave Roger and her family empty-handed.

pixieparamour · 2 wks ago

If she did, there would've been a body by now. If she dr0wn3d herself in the ocean outside her mom's house, she would've washed up on the beach. Claire was talented. But even she couldn't bury herself.

NoPlaceLikeTome · 2 wks ago

ANCIENT HISTORY. I REMEMBER IT

If she was depressed, Roger would've known. You can't hide depression from your partner, not if you live together.

justin-oldsoul · 2 wks ago

You're onto something. Does anyone know who her doctors were?

CLOSER3ADER · 2 wks ago

Worms in a wound.

dark-angelwing · 2 wks ago

I DIED IN A HUNDRED DIFFERENT NORDIC RAIDS

Stop looking for her.

dark-witcher · 2 wks ago

WHOLE KIDNEY IN THE PALM OF MY HAND

She doesn't want to be found. She doesn't want to
be found. She doesn't want to be found. She doesn't
want to be found. She doesn't want to be found. She
doesn't want to be found. She doesn't want to be
found. She doesn't want to be ☆☆✳︎☆☆✳︎☆☆✳︎☆✳︎☆
☆✳︎☆☆✳︎☆☆✳︎☆☆✳︎☆☆✳︎☆☆✳︎☆☆✳︎☆☆✳︎☆☆✳︎☆
☆✳︎☆☆✳︎☆☆✳︎☆☆✳︎☆☆✳︎☆☆✳︎☆☆✳︎☆☆✳︎☆☆✳︎☆
☆✳︎☆☆✳︎

mbd1089 · 2 wks ago

Hey I remember you.

patentpendingg · 2 wks ago

They don't know anything.

mbd1089 · 2 wks ago

No one knows anything, but they like it that way. Until Claire went missing, Darkwitcher posted nothing but gore in **ENCOUNTERS**. They were all *imagined* encounters, and every single one was torture porn. I kept flagging them to the moderator.

patentpendingg · 2 wks ago

Ignore them. They just want you to twist

dark-witcher · 2 wks ago

WHOLE KIDNEY IN THE PALM OF MY HAND

like a finger on a fish hook

luminoushadow · 2 wks ago

If we all find her together *
can we each * take a piece of her home ? *

RossBoss_ · 2 wks ago

This page is going to eat itself alive.

ELEVEN

"I can only imagine how fiercely he wrestled death itself, how he fought against the smoke in his throat, and how lonely that short struggle was."
—*Claire Ross,* The Starlit Ballet

It's a three-and-a-half-hour drive to Sofia's the next morning.

I leave while it's starry.

She agreed to meet at eight thirty, before her first appointment at nine. We could've Zoomed, but I have a feeling that she's important. She's one of the few people Claire counted as a friend, and their relationship dates back to high school. She may be the only one who could name Claire's love interests from that time and shortly after—not someone she dated, maybe, but someone she paid attention to, someone who got to her.

The sky brightens slowly without looking like morning, only changing the color of the night. Emily Dickinson had the perfect line for moments like this. "Not knowing when the dawn will come, I open every door." That's exactly how I feel. Hopeful in the dark. Eventually, stars fade into the sunrise. I buy an Egg McMuffin, eat it one handed.

At 8:24 a.m., I pull up to Sofia's practice. My legs are stiff as I step outside, onto the empty sidewalk. The town feels sleepy, with nothing open except a lonely coffee shop. Its paper newspapers wait on outdoor racks, their front pages floating up in the wind. The Book Nook next door has every light turned off. Still, it doesn't take long to spot *The*

Starlit Ballet in the window, where one copy is front and center. Today, its constellations look like fireflies, burning streaks into night. The cover can feel like a mood ring. I assume that *I'm* the one who's changing, of course, and it's not the other way around. Some Starlites would beg to differ. A few of the more unhinged users on r/ClaireRoss have claimed to see it breathe.

Outside Sofia's practice, I ring the doorbell.

A woman emerges in a white coat, waving with a firm wrist. She's tall, with sleek brown hair in a low ponytail. Her middle part is a neat line, paler than her face. It glows over her crown like a glimpse of her skull. Her eyebrows are straight, arching only slightly toward the ends. No jewelry. No makeup. Not even a glint of moisturizer. When I get ready for work, I put everything on. It appears that she takes everything off.

She unlocks the door with a smile.

"You must be Nina," she says.

Her Spanish accent is faint.

I greet Sofia and thank her for the time.

She guides me through the waiting room, past two examining rooms, and back to her office. She manages to walk next to me while leading us forward. It exudes some warmth, having a light touch with her authority. If I ever saw a specialist, I'd be in good hands here. She offers me a seat, shuts the door, and sits at her desk.

We small talk while I look around.

Her desk faces a bulletin board covered in photos of her and her husband: smiling in a wedding portrait, their shoulders back and proud; hugging with a diploma in her hands, Sofia in a powder-blue cap and gown, hints of red velvet rope around them; dancing salsa somewhere dim, their bodies blurred; and popping champagne in an empty apartment. There are so many photos, the cork background only peaks through in tiny slivers, beige commas between the memories. At the far corner of her desk, *The Starlit Ballet* is open, face down.

I point to the book.

"Let me guess . . ." I think about where she might've stopped, judging by how many pages she has left. If she's three-quarters of the way through, she may be reading the section I did last night. Right after Liam dies in Singapore, he's reincarnated as Lars, a professional cyclist in Sweden. "Are you at the part with Lars and Christina?"

She looks from the book to me.

"Yes." She laughs once in shock.

"I've read it a couple times," I explain.

"Me too. I started reading it again after Claire . . ."

I nod, knowing what she means.

"In my opinion, that's the saddest chapter," I add.

She nods but seems less moved than I am.

"Because of how much he loses," I explain. We meet Lars in the Tour de France, undertaking two *thousand* miles in three weeks. He's spending up to six hours a day on his bike. A half dozen personal trainers, nutritionists, and massage therapists keep him in shape to spar with the most elite athletes in the world. Until he suffers a paralyzing crash. "One minute, he's speeding through the Alps, leading the pack at seventy miles per hour. The next, he has a breathing tube and a catheter. He can't stand up without a team to help him."

Christina escorts Lars back home. It's tough to see her walk into his pantry for the first time since his accident. The place still looks like it belongs to a professional athlete, full of caffeinated gels and electrolyte powders. His diet used to be edited to a tee. Two pounds of water weight used to mean the difference between victory and anonymity. Now, it doesn't really matter what he eats for dinner. Because he won't race in the morning.

"He loses almost everything," I say.

"But he's still him."

"Exactly. He'd been making some progress in previous lives, but he kept chasing power and prestige. As Lars, finally, the change he endures is so drastic, it snaps him out of his trance. Now, for the first time, he can find a purpose bigger than himself. And finally, he matures." My voice is more impassioned than I expected.

"Were you an English major?" she asks.

"No."

"No . . . ?"

I wear a smile like a shield and change the subject to Exeter. The transition feels smooth, natural. Sofia doesn't seem to notice any ulterior motive.

I ask what Claire was like.

"Successfully impractical," she says thoughtfully. "You know she never wore a winter coat? New Hampshire had these subzero Januaries. Five-foot-tall snowdrifts. And she'd walk to class six days a week without one." Her eyes bulge slightly, the whites stretching. "She tried to justify it, saying that she never walked very far. Fifty yards at most, going from one warm room to another. But still. It took me a while to realize that she was always—inside herself, if that makes sense. She was always swept up in some idea, some fantasy. No matter where she went, she was in her own mind. And up there, I guess, it never got cold."

"She was imaginative," I paraphrase.

"Yes, and it made her likable. The same way she didn't care about the weather, she didn't care about the social climate either. She didn't try to impress anyone. It was so—comforting. I was the first one in my family to go to prep school, and being with Claire was magically straightforward. She never made me feel like a fish out of water. Maybe because she was one too."

I reach for my notebook and flip to the first blank page.

Draw a fish without lifting my pen.

"You knew her well."

"In high school, yes. It helped that we were both committed to our work." She gestures with a flat hand, fingers flexed. Even her casual tics look precise. "I was more logical about it, though. I wanted good grades so I could get into med school. And Claire, she just loved her classes. She read history textbooks like novels. She'd disappear into her homework every night, even the math problems."

I dot one fish eye.

"And you kept in touch?"

"Not that often, actually, even though we both ended up in New York. But every few months, we'd Skype or get a meal." Sofia shrugs. "When Claire started writing her book, she changed. It took her over somehow. I mean, she wrote all day, every day for years. It was like a compulsion or a disease—and I'm saying that as an MD." She looks concerned, as if she's never seen anything like it, a condition where people write down everything they imagine. "I don't think she isolated herself on purpose. She just got . . . carried away."

I ask how Sofia heard the news in September.

She says Miranda sent an email that day, announcing Claire was missing and anyone with information should contact her. "I remember reading it out loud to my husband. We were staying in one of Miranda's friend's houses, eating lunch in the kitchen." She shakes her head. "Miranda wrote in all caps. The email was short. It looked like she was already thinking the worst. We put our forks down and just never picked them back up."

I ask Sofia what she thinks happened.

"The police said she ran away?"

I nod yes.

"I hope they're right. Only because it's better than the alternative." She looks down at her Crocs. "Besides, Claire liked to be alone. Especially when she was working." More to herself, she adds, "Maybe it was a clue about who she'd grow up to be."

I puzzle.

"Claire couldn't think with any noise," she explains. "If we were in the library, and someone started to talk, I could see it on her face. It looked like a city was collapsing in her mind. So she ended up doing most of her homework on her own." She glances at *The Starlit Ballet* over her shoulder, the way people check when they feel someone staring.

"As much as I liked Claire, I never got that part of her. The voluntary, solitary confinement. It takes a particular kind of person to love absolute quiet. To me, it sounds too much like . . ."

"Too much like what?"

"I don't know. Death."

Sofia hugs herself with one arm.

I don't want to debate her, so I don't share that plenty of writers need silence to do their best work. Plenty go so far as to show signs of misophonia—extreme discomfort with noise—including Proust, Anton Chekhov, and Franz Kafka. It makes sense, if they're trying to listen inward, hear faint words inside them. If I had a musical inner voice, I wouldn't want it steamrolled by chewing or car horns either.

Sofia looks rattled. She still has one arm draped across her chest, elbow bent like it's in a sling. I force a smile, as if I were *her* well-meaning doctor. As if I had the medical degree and the control. I make a friendly remark about being "on the subject of high school" and reach into my pocket. Sofia appears to soften at my tone. I remove a printed list of everyone in her and Claire's graduating class and place it on her desk.

"It's your senior class," I explain. All 335 students are there in alphabetical order by last name. "I was hoping you might know if anyone on that list was special to Claire." I lean toward her from my chair. "The word 'special' is vague, but I'm looking for anyone she might've talked to you about, anyone she had an unusual connection with."

"You mean other than her boyfriend, Brett?"

"Yes, actually."

Sofia studies the list, column by column. I ask her to please share if anyone older or younger comes to mind too. She flips the page over.

"You know . . . she did talk to me about Leo Williams." She picks up a pen and circles his name. "Claire graduated second in our class. He graduated first. They took a lot of classes together, but I don't know if they ever spoke. Actually . . ." She tilts her head to the side. Her nose casts a small shadow over one cheek, a dark rupture in her honeyed skin. "Now that I think about it, they had at least one conversation. The night before we graduated."

I probe a little deeper.

"Well, there was this end-of-the-year fair in the gym, and I was waiting for her outside. Claire was supposed to meet me there at eight—it's weird that I remember the time—but she never showed up. She told me later in the dorm that she'd met Leo that afternoon at the cum laude ceremony. They started talking, and they just didn't stop."

"Do you know what they talked about?"

She shakes her head no.

"I only know she had this kind of—erotic respect for him? It's hard to explain, but it was a sort-of-competitive, sort-of-romantic thing. She talked about him as if she was *drawn* to him. At the same time, she wanted to *challenge* him. Score higher, test better. Wrestle him in debates. Either way, Leo got to her . . . brain. Whenever he came up, her *mind* was aroused. In a way that made her"—Sofia looks up at the ceiling, searching for the right word; the effort strains her forehead—"intellectually excited. Fluttery. Sharp. I never took it too seriously, though." She hands the paper back to me. "There were a lot of hormones flying around back then."

"Leo is the only one who caught her eye?" I confirm.

She nods yes.

"But what does that have to do with anything?" she asks.

I fold the list in half and slide it in my pocket.

"Turning over every stone," I say vaguely.

~

I pull into Miranda's that afternoon and find her Porsche in the driveway, sparkling under pellets of rain. Inside, I leave my damp sneakers in the foyer. The first floor is navy blue and silent. There's no trace of Miranda, not even a TV on mute—the way she sometimes leaves it near the kitchen, playing for no one. Miranda never sits and watches TV, but she seems to enjoy its closed-captioned company while she fixes herself coffee. It can make the space feel like a waiting room, where she's stuck in limbo.

I call Miranda's name.

No response.

I drift over to the bottom of the stairwell, looking for signs of life. Her room is on the second floor, but I don't want to intrude. Invading her privacy *is* part of my job, but there are subtle boundaries to navigate. I wander through the kitchen and look at the patio outside. Tarps cover their summer furniture, protecting wood from weather. Chairs are reduced to lumps, shaped like people crouching with their arms around their knees.

I don't remember *exactly* when rich people started making sense to me. When terms like "outdoor furniture" and "guest cottage" crossed silently into my lexicon. It must've happened at school, but I can't pick out the exact moment.

I remember leaving a class late junior year, catching another girl eye me on our way out. She had a broad forehead attempting to hide under bangs. Her turtleneck looked like a high collar, grazing her jawline. *Sorry, do I know you?* she asked. Truthfully, she did. She ate in my dining hall every morning at seven, right when hot breakfast opened. *Maybe, where do you ski?* I smiled. Alice Henley was now a skier. Of course she was. *Park City,* the girl replied. *Please convince my parents,* I told her. *They've been taking us to Stowe my whole life. I've never skied out West. Can you believe it?* And she did. So I must've learned their language before then. As if it were just another class on my schedule.

～

In the guest room, I order a background check on Leo Williams and learn everything I can about him. The rain makes it easy to spend the day indoors. Sheets of it drench the lawn and blur the windows right in front of me. I doubt this is what Percy Shelley had in mind when he said rain brought "twinkling grass." The lawn is closer to drowning.

Knock. Knock.

I jump in my chair.

"Hi—oh, sorry to startle you," Miranda says.

I excuse myself. I didn't know she was here.

"Whenever we cross paths in this house, I feel like I scare you half to death." She smiles kindly, as if the fault is her own. I smile, too, trying to convince her that I feel at ease here. That blending into this place isn't an enormous feat of self-control. Most of the time, I do feel like I'm gliding. But there are cracks in the transitions, going from being alone to being seen, when the stakes are instantly raised. "Anyway, I was in the weeds on a new fundraiser upstairs. I just saw your car. Any leads?"

"Getting there," I say. "Actually, I have a favor to ask."

"Anything."

"This is just a hunch," I say, managing expectations. "It might not go anywhere. And trying to explain it might be like . . . hammering mist. But it's worth checking." Miranda hangs on my every word. "Would you mind sharing her high school transcript?"

"Of course."

Her posture lifts.

I could be imagining it, but Miranda seems to be growing a little more optimistic the longer that I'm here. I can still feel her grief, but every now and then, she moves with a bit of hope. Maybe it comforts her to see me working all the time.

She shuts the door on her way out.

I skim through the notes I've been taking.

Leo was born and raised in Sacramento. His parents are both pediatricians. No siblings. After Exeter, he went to Yale, where he won prizes in literature and applied math. He also rowed lightweight crew. After college, he worked just long enough to strike it big trading options. Then he left to start a nonprofit in San Francisco, fundraising for student scholarships in the developing world. He's just returned from a two-year sabbatical, globe-trotting by himself. Now he's back in California, running his nonprofit full time.

Leo has a strong brow. His eyebrows slope down toward the top of his nose. They're thick enough that they almost cast a shadow over his steady, brown stare. His jaw is as wide as his forehead, squaring off his face. In photos of him at regattas, he's always captured off to the side, never quite in the mix of things. He seems to be a rare mix of athlete and brooding intellectual. Someone who uses his body as an exercise in control. Who works his heart like a speed bag. But who enjoys Shakespearian tragedies as much as physical pain. Who keeps *No Exit* in his gym bag and exudes palpable inner torture.

It's easy to imagine how he and Claire might've fallen for each other. They both come from the same rarefied world, went to schools with places on the world stage. They're both serious, sending out down-beat vibrations on more intellectual paths. Plus, they both seem to have strong hearts. Leo left his first career for something more soulful, and Claire devoted herself to *The Starlit Ballet*. What did they talk about the night before they graduated? I imagine them walking to the quiet edge of campus—the stars would be dense up there in New Hampshire, a few zodiacs in the sky—and sharing their dreams or fears.

Did they stay in touch at college?

Then again, how could they have avoided it? When I was in Boston, the Harvard–Yale games dominated Cambridge every few months. Harvard hosted them biennially, but enthusiasm on campus was a permanent fixture—especially in the fall leading up to the annual football showdown. Anti-Yale posters would cover the city with slogans like, "Our Hatred for Yale Outweighs Our Apathy for Football." Every other year, Yale kids would arrive by the busload with serifed *Y*'s stamped on their cheeks. I used to pass the stadium packed with students, half in crimson, half in navy blue. It's not hard to imagine how Claire and Leo's rivalry might've evolved, from high school GPAs to scores in the big games.

Did she stay with him during those weekends?

I picture him showing her the top bunk in his double, his room-mate already on a plane home for Thanksgiving break. The decision would be hers, all hers. I picture her standing there, backpack over one shoulder, deciding whether to climb the ladder. The view outside gothic and clandestine. Maybe they lingered there, teasing each other with lines from their favorite books. *The top bunk, I must warn you, will guarantee that you dream of my roommate . . . I'm afraid that's impossible, Leo. I only dream of Manderley . . .* Maybe she did choose the top. Maybe they didn't sleep together until the day of her wedding.

I know that I'm reaching—but not very far. The groundwork for their chemistry is clear. Sofia observed it herself. With Roger, it was always so hard to picture the fire between them, to understand how they got each other like no one else. But with Leo, I see the makings of a real intellectual connection—more than that, a soulful one.

I pull up a map of San Francisco on my phone.

I've never been to the West Coast, though I've read plenty of books that take place in California. John Steinbeck's *East of Eden*. Jack Kerouac's *On the Road*. Wallace Stegner's *Angle of Repose*. I have a rich but secondhand feel for water crises, Hollywood nightlife, and the Salinas Valley. I *have* always wanted to go.

I zoom out on the map and notice that San Francisco isn't too far from Yosemite. In interviews, Claire said that's where she set the final life in *The Starlit Ballet* because she didn't want to imagine a futuristic world. She said there was a decent chance that this national park would be the same in nine hundred years. But—what if that wasn't the whole truth? What if she set those scenes in Yosemite because they were a short drive away from him? What if that's where she wanted to end up, and what if that's where she is now?

TWELVE

"Milk-and-honey-poached swan; dormice with crushed pearls; and peacock tongues in honey. They lived with their hands in lard, in leopard . . . feeding unmatched Roman appetites."

—*Claire Ross,* The Starlit Ballet

The next morning, I check my phone to find Claire's high school transcript in my inbox. Exeter's red crest stamps the corner, its leafy border like a laurel crown. The school's Latin name is tucked inside, looped as if it's about to eat its own tail. In the center, a red sun rises over a red river. Red bees flap around a red hive. One of the academy's mottos is printed: *Finis Origine Pendet,* or *The End Depends on the Beginning.*

I scroll down.

This photocopy is tilted, both edges shadowy.

I skim Claire's grades: all A's or A-minuses in slanted columns. I'm not sure what I'm looking for exactly until I see a class called "Classical Rome."

I open a new tab and find Exeter's course manual. The breadth is staggering: from "Astronomy" to "Modern India" to "Symbolic Logic." It's a little foreign to imagine fourteen- and fifteen-year-old children walking from one of those classes to another. I picture them in jackets and ties, their frontal lobes still evolving. *The End Depends on the Beginning.* It's a heavy prophecy to impose on kids, to suggest that these are the years that count.

Eventually, I find a course called "Classical Rome" and read the description. Did this class spark her interest in the time period? I navigate back to her transcript, where another class draws my eye: "US History, Colonial Origins to 1861." That might have touched on yellow fever in 1793. I sit up straighter. Claire also took "Imperialism in the Seventeenth Century," which might have covered the trade routes that took sailors past Madagascar.

Claire's high school transcript is stacked full of courses that study the places she wrote about in *The Starlit Ballet*. Maybe the eras she chose for her soulmates weren't random. Maybe they were an ode to her time in high school. But why? *Claire graduated second in our class. He graduated first. They took a lot of classes together . . .*

~

I'm eating breakfast at the kitchen table when I hear Miranda coming downstairs. It's raining again, making her footsteps sound like small claps of thunder. Drops on the windows look like windswept pieces of the ocean. She emerges in a white turtleneck sweater and khakis, her hair swept into a high bun. She walks toward me as I chew my buttered bagel from Goldberg's. I swallow fast and wipe the grease from my lips.

Miranda takes a seat at the head of the table. Up close, her cheeks are flushed. Her damp eyelashes stick together, giving her just a few spokes on each lid. Pitchforks of hair. Every muscle in her face is slack, her forehead drifting into her eyebrows, her cheeks drifting into her jaw. As if she lacks the energy to lift them.

"Just—a bad dream," she says, gesturing to herself.

Splinters in her back.

"Roger mentioned that Claire was bullied," I say delicately.

I watch Miranda, hoping for more. You can never demand uncomfortable answers, not when someone is this fragile. It would be like peeling a bud, expecting a flower. The most you can do is lead someone to a sensitive subject and hope they'll explain. Hope they'll give their account of what happened. I fold my square paper towel in half a few times. It disappears into smaller and smaller triangles. Miranda watches my fingertips.

"That must've been hard for you," I add.

"Harder for her."

My paper towel becomes unbendable.

I tuck it into my empty mug.

"He said that she got locked in storage."

Miranda nods distantly.

"You know," she says after a beat. Her voice is slowed down and quiet, as if she's thinking out loud. "I never know *in the moment* what's going to matter. It's only looking back that I can tell which days counted a little bit more."

I wait patiently.

"For a while after it happened," Miranda explains, "Claire didn't talk. At first, I thought she'd hurt her throat." Miranda touches her own, stretching her neck. "But that was the one place she didn't have a scratch. Little by little, she started to speak up again. She'd ask me to pass a side dish at dinner. Then, the next day, she'd say 'I love you' when I tucked her in." Miranda stares at the hardwood floor. "I gave her a whole month before I asked about that night. I didn't probe too deep. I just asked if she'd been scared." She looks up at me, her eyes watering as if she's back in her nightmare. "Claire said that she *was*—until she started to make things up. Those were her exact words. 'I started to make things up.'"

"She found a way out through her mind."

"If she hadn't, maybe she would've fought all night long. Broken the bones in her hand instead of just getting a hairline fracture." Miranda tucks one thumb into a limp fist. "But I don't think she stopped. I think she *kept* making things up. After that night, she was—different. Dreamier. Whenever she had to write or draw something for school, she didn't focus on anything real anymore. She wasn't sketching Mom and

Dad like she used to. She was drawing people who didn't exist." Wind hisses past the house.

"Andrew passed when they were at Exeter." Miranda grabs one shoulder, letting her elbow hang on her chest. "I had to tell them over the phone. And Kira, she lost it. She went on a tear of self-destructive behavior. Had to get her stomach pumped." The paper towel in my mug has unfolded like a peony. "Claire—she was sad, but she didn't *snap*. She was distant at the funeral. Distant on his birthdays. It felt like part of her was somewhere else. And I just *knew* that she was doing the same thing she'd done when she was six." She lowers her arm and glances at the storm outside. "'I started to make things up.' It's a childish way to put it, but maybe she was onto something. Maybe the rest of us accept reality too soon.

"Anyway." She leans forward, hands on her knees. Her tone is still heavy, as if she's changing topics without changing her mood.

"Just one more question," I say, pulling my mug toward me. The last sip of coffee muddies the edges of the paper towel. "I've been thinking through another hunch. If I try to explain it, I might end up confusing us both." Miranda lifts her eyebrows. It's a slight, hopeful twitch. "Did Claire ever go to the Harvard–Yale games?"

Her chin retreats an inch.

As if the question literally takes her back.

"I think so?" she wonders aloud. Her forehead is alive again, creasing with effort. "Yes, I think that she did," she adds with conviction. "It was strange because she never really enjoyed sports. When Andrew used to put on the Super Bowl, she'd cross her arms and complain using ten-dollar words—'barbaric,' that kind of thing. But when the Harvard–Yale games came around, she couldn't get on that train to New Haven fast enough."

"Do you remember where she stayed?"

"For the Harvard–Yale games?"

"Yes, I know it's ancient history, but . . ."

Miranda's fingertips dance on her chin, rising and falling in a wave that goes nowhere. Eventually, I try again, asking if Claire stayed at a hotel.

"She might've stayed with someone from Exeter? But it was so long ago, I don't trust myself." She rubs one temple, burrowing toward the memory.

I tell her that's helpful.

"Also, did the ex-boyfriend angle pan out?" she asks.

Constant rain fills the pause.

"The love letter?" she probes.

"Right," I say, still thinking about how to respond. "That reminds me, I was going to ask about a possible trip." She nods encouragingly. A beige tendril falls to frame her face. "I think it might be a good idea for me to visit one of them in California." Her mouth opens, but she continues to nod. The gap between her lips looks like a piece of black string. "Face-to-face, I'll get more information—everything they'd push off-screen before a Zoom. Plus, if I strike a nerve, they won't be able to blame technical difficulties and leave early."

Miranda nods for so long that I feel optimistic.

"Where in California?" she asks.

"Los Angeles," I lie.

THIRTEEN

"You've died 1,021 times."
　　　　　　—*Claire Ross,* The Starlit Ballet

"The word 'trauma' comes from the Greek τραύμα, meaning a physical wound," AM radio claims a few days later. Brake lights cast 495 in a red haze, on my way to LaGuardia. Traffic crawls toward a distant accident. "The word's evolved, of course. Sigmund Freud was the one who popularized 'trauma' to describe inner wounds. Psychological wounds . . .

"And now we're finding that trauma isn't just about what happens *to* you. It's about what *doesn't* happen. It's about all the good times that you *didn't* have. All the good people who *weren't* there. It's harder to measure what *never existed,* but that's what we're starting to do. We're measuring what was *missing.* We're taking the dimensions of those holes and their consequences. The results are extraordinary. Tragic and extraordinary. We're finding that the longer people go without certain crucial and nourishing experiences, the deeper the damage. Over a long enough period of time, this could—"

I turn it off.

Cars single-file past the accident. A gray sedan is scrunched against the barrier, its hood skinned off, engine exposed in a black nest of pipes. An airbag hangs from the steering wheel like an empty pillowcase. The blood across it looks black, as if the night is dripping. A news helicopter passes overhead, its channel number painted on the side. I keep checking the accident in my rearview mirror, but I can't see who was hurt.

~

I stop outside a Hudson Booksellers at LaGuardia, an hour and a half before my flight to Chicago. One layover is all that stands between San Francisco and me. I find myself drifting toward the bookstore, when a man collides with my shoulder. It sends me back a step. He lifts his arms in outrage—as if *I* ran into *him*—and storms off.

I check my purse.

Miranda took my word for the cost of the trip and reimbursed me in cash—plus a travel stipend—in a white security envelope. It's still here in my bag. Of course, I could've told her the truth about where I'm going. I could've said "San Francisco" as easily as I did "Los Angeles." But if this is the end of the search, I want to get there first. Solving this case would be a seismic change in my life. I don't want to give my idea away before I'm standing on Leo's block, looking at Claire through his window.

At Hudson, the table closest to me has two piles of *The Starlit Ballet*. It's a relief from the bestsellers around it: serial killer dramas, divorce fiction, and cheap erotica. Who knew that a book about the best in us—and not the worst—would do so well? Even in New York City, this crowded and impersonal place. This global intersection, teeming with people eager to be somewhere else, steamrolling each other in public.

The book is mind bending on its own, but it's even twistier to think that there's a love letter nested inside it, a message for Leo from Claire. She wrote multiple stories at once. It's more than fiction. It's almost witchcraft. Stephen King did call books a unique kind of magic. That's never felt more accurate than it does right now. *The Starlit Ballet* is possessed. I wonder if Claire sent Leo a copy, or if the story found him on its own. Maybe it drifted toward him on purpose, knowing its role in their relationship.

I touch the nearest cover.

Maybe Leo read it at home in San Francisco. I spent all morning looking at photos of his house on Google Earth and ArchitecturalDigest.

com. It has a sleek and neutral facade. Its indoor garden, floating wooden staircase, and tall windows effectively bring the outdoors inside. Did he read *The Starlit Ballet* on his roof? I picture him flipping through it, steps from the San Francisco Bay. He would've looked up every once in a while to see the water dotted with full sails and short, white wakes. If their connection was as intense as Claire described, maybe he called her before he finished the book.

Was it Leo's idea to take off without telling a soul?

My gut tells me it was Claire's. A plan to *vanish*, sloughing off every commitment, sounds as wildly idealistic as she was. It's a fantasy that I imagine most people have at some point but are too responsible to indulge—similar to the fantasy of writing a novel. I've worked with dozens of clients who were quietly unsatisfied with their beautiful lives but never quite starry eyed enough to jump into something new. People can succumb to the idea that life is supposed to hurt, but Claire was too romantic for that.

Of course it was her idea.

If I do find her with Leo, and their story gets out, I wonder how people will interpret her choices. I'm sure some will villainize her. They'll call her escape self-indulgent and destructive, an unforgivable terror on her family and fans. Some will empathize with Roger, the perfect gentleman abandoned at the altar, deceived for years about what their relationship was at its core. But plenty of others will probably admire what she did. They'll treasure her book even more when they see her bringing it to life. She is Cady getting one last chance in California, with the one she's loved since the beginning.

I walk to my gate, find a table with outlets.

I read more about Exeter, trying to get a feel for what it was like when Claire and Leo were there. The school is set in a small New Hampshire town. Its campus is old-world beautiful: redbrick buildings, a central clock tower, and symmetrical quads. I swipe through aerial photos, stunning but uninhabited. Maybe everyone's studying. Apparently, Exeter gets twice the national average of snow every year. I picture students in the library, their views outside completely blank. I wonder if that mutes the noise, the way Claire would've liked. If, when kids march through snow to class, anyone can hear their footsteps.

I'm too old to steal college again, definitely too old to steal high school. The desire is there, though. Dormant, thumping. I picture myself ten years younger, stepping through Exeter's gates. Teenagers can get in almost anywhere, if they're carrying a couple of books. I imagine following a dozen kids on their way out of a class on Robert Frost or Kazuo Ishiguro. Rock salt on the paths. Bouncing backpacks. Coughing.

Exeter's website has its red mark in every corner. *The End Depends on the Beginning.* Its classes are taught as roundtable discussions. I swipe through photos of these, live-action shots of fifteen-year-olds opening their mouths. They're all sitting in tight-knit, elliptical huddles. I took some risks when I was Alice—sneaking into a few college libraries, hopping over the turnstile when the guard's back was turned, and then, of course, trespassing on a student party. But I never went so far as to waltz into a twelve-person seminar. Where the teacher would've sat six feet away and asked for my name, the printed roster in his hands.

My phone buzzes—it's Roger.

I answer with my name.

"I just talked to Miranda."

He announces this with great finality.

He breathes loudly on the phone.

"Are you—do you think there's someone else?" he asks.

The truth might rip his heart in half. He already sounds weak, his voice on the edge of cracking. Then again, am I really going to lie to him?

"I'm just trying to be thorough," I dodge.

"But what do you think?"

A gate attendant announces over the speaker system that a flight to Detroit is boarding passengers in Group One. Exeter's website is still bright on my laptop, the screen checkered with student testimonials and photos posing as naturalistic.

"You're at the airport?" he asks.

"Did Claire ever talk to you about high school?" I ask.

"*High* school?" He sounds blindsided.

I try the question one more time.

"She liked Exeter," he admits.

"What did she like about it?"

"Is this guy from high school?"

My phone beeps with a call from Kira.

I reject it.

"I don't believe this," he goes on. "All she did was work on that book. I mean, she barely had time for me. There's no way she was seeing anyone else."

"Roger—"

"She wasn't the type to have an affair." He talks over me, uncharacteristically assertive. "You know she wasn't actually that romantic? In real life? Whenever I tried to plan something for our anniversary, or her birthday, she'd find out and ask if we could just relax at home instead. She didn't want gifts. Didn't give them either. Like I said, she loved that book more than anything, anyone. The idea that she would fall for someone is just . . ."

He trails off.

I check my phone to make sure he's still on the line.

"But even if she did," he continues, sounding suddenly more resigned, "she wouldn't hurt all of us like this. It would be—wrong."

I don't defend her.

"I spent five years with her," he goes on. "We planned our whole lives together. The kids' names. Why would she say all that if she was going to leave me? I just want to know, honestly—is that what you think happened? I can take it," he rushes in before I can answer. "What I *can't* take is worrying about her if she left me for someone else."

"Like I said, I don't know for sure."

155

"Take care of yourself," he says abruptly.

The call ends.

I keep the phone to my ear for a few more seconds, feeling for him. Even if Claire *did* choose Leo, she didn't have to leave Roger like this. It feels cruel to let him writhe around, caught between mourning her, holding on to hope, and grasping at wild theories. As far as he knows, someone from r/ClaireRoss has her zip-tied to a pipe in his garage. And every night, he brushes her hair like a doll's. How's Roger supposed to get on with his life? I'm usually quick to assume the worst in people, but my gut tells me that Claire is different. There has to be a version of this where she's the good guy.

I lower my phone to find one new voice mail from Kira, which I'm not inclined to play. She's done nothing but resist my investigation since I met her. Technically, I don't even work for her. I don't have to answer anyone's calls but Miranda's. So, I pick up where I left off in *The Starlit Ballet* and read the very last part.

http://www.reddit.com/r/ClaireRoss

r/ClaireRoss posted by u/B3Ll3V3M3 3 mos ago

FINDING CLAIRE: MEGATHREAD
MEGATHREAD

☆☆✳ PLEASE SHARE INFORMATION RELEVANT TO HER CASE. ☆☆✳
We know her better than anyone.
We should be able to find her. ☆☆✳
UPDATE: WE HAVE A ZERO-TOLERANCE POLICY FOR ABUSE OF
THIS THREAD. IF YOUR COMMENT IS ANY ATTEMPT TO STOP,
CONFUSE, DILUTE, OR DISTRACT US, YOU WILL BE REMOVED
FROM THIS COMMUNITY BY THE MODERATOR.

Current Megathreads:
ENCOUNTERS
PHOTOS

fictionAfflicted_ · 1 day ago

Public service announcement: I can't believe I have
to say this, but if you aren't here with good inten-
tions, we outnumber you.

I'm here because no one made a bigger difference
in my life than Claire. I was at an all-time low last
year, confiding in a friend, when she said she had
the answer. Something to change my life. She talked
about it like a *drug*. Like a beautiful *psychedelic*.
When she reached into her purse, though, she pulled
out *The Starlit Ballet*. I read it . . . and she was right.

That book changed my whole world. Time, color, sound. It was a *trip*. It was *medical*. But it wasn't just the book that got to me. It was Claire. Her personal story. I mean, *seven years*. Her standards were that high. I was so moved, I started demanding better— from my job, myself, the men I was dating. And little by little, that saved me.

Now, I'm here to save her.

Most of us are.

So for some of you to come here with your *snark*. Calling us worms. Telling us to *leave her alone* . . . If you think you're safe, because you're typing home alone with the door locked, I have news for you. Star-lites hate as hard as we love. ☆

dark-angelwing · 1 day ago

> I DIED IN A HUNDRED DIFFERENT NORDIC RAIDS

How could you find us
if you can't even find her? ☽✳

dark-witcher · 1 day ago

> WHOLE KIDNEY IN THE PALM OF MY HAND

☆☆✳☆☆✳☆☆✳☆☆✳☆☆✳☆☆✳☆☆✳☆☆✳☆☆✳☆✳
☆☆✳☆☆✳☆☆✳☆☆✳☆☆✳☆☆✳☆☆✳☆☆✳☆☆✳☆✳
☆☆✳☆☆✳☆☆✳☆☆✳☆☆✳☆☆✳☆☆✳☆☆✳☆☆✳☆

fictionAfflicted_ · 1 day ago

You were warned.

readMeRoss · 1 day ago

EVERYONE ON HERE IS DATA! DON'T THREATEN MUTE OR REMOVE ANYONE!!!! THEY MIGHT BE THE INFORMATION WE NEED!!

PageByPaige91 · 1 day ago

This thread really could've been helpful. I thought it was going to be the first crowd-sourced mystery. And then all of you had to ruin it.

editionallyy · 1 day ago

Since this thread has gone off the rails . . . I'm just here with a message for whoever has her: **Please, I'm begging you, don't cause her any pain.**

Claire is a person. If you're staring at her right now, and she seems too *porcelain*, **remember everything human about her**. Claire loves New York City, the energy of the place. And she loves her mom. And she's such a messy eater, she finds eating at restaurants embarrassing. And she always had scented candles going in her apartment, burning them down into glasses of milk. And she does her best writing while she's reading, so every book she owns is covered in ink and marginless. She hasn't remembered a dream in years and desperately wants to. I know she seems unbreakable, but please. **She's a person.**

editionallyy · 1 day ago

And she means something to the millions of us who were changed by her book. Because *The Starlit Ballet* isn't just a story. It's the idea that our pain has a purpose. The possibility that this world is good to people. That no one is truly alone. So **you wouldn't just be hurting Claire, you'd be hurting all of us.**

editionallyy · 1 hr ago

Hello?

rhyme-crime · 1 hr ago

all ☆☆✴ the ☆☆✴ great ☆☆✴ roman ☆☆✴
statues ☆☆✴ are ☆☆✴
now ☆☆✴ armless ☆

FOURTEEN

"More and more of my dreams imagine what's on the other side. In some, we drift through every color of light. It feels like wind through peace, if trust moved on its own. We're part of it, and it's part of everything."
—*Claire Ross,* The Starlit Ballet

I read the last chapter in a middle seat, while women on either side of me sleep in eye masks. I'm one of the few awake for the beverage cart. The fizz of my club soda is drowned out by the engine. The bubbles pop in silence, misting my chin as I sip and read. The final pages of *The Starlit Ballet* glow in the precise beam of my overhead light.

Cady and Logan fall asleep on her porch. The next morning, Logan asks her to marry him. On their wedding night, soon after, *The Starlit Ballet* comes to a gentle stop. I love that the book doesn't show their last moment together. There's something romantic about the idea that the greatest love stories never really end. It isn't hard to imagine Cady and Logan having children in Yosemite, blending her dark brows with his wide-set eyes. It isn't hard to picture them living longer than they've ever lived, spending more time together than in any other life. I see them growing old, still looking at each other as their eyes fail, still listening to each other as their hearing goes, and age never dulling their love.

~

I wake up to a lurch in my stomach as we're landing in San Francisco. The woman next to me opens the shade to reveal a sunrise. Our gray wing cuts through it like a knife fileting a fish, leaving pink sprays on the horizon. I'm leaning forward against my seat belt. The thrill of speeding down the runway doesn't stop when the plane does. Even after our layover in Chicago, which dragged on for hours longer than it should've. Even though everyone else looks resentful of the delay. I'm the only one who claps for the pilot, as if this trip were a dream.

I'm so excited it's hard to breathe.

I've always had strong instincts. I was only eight years old when I first suspected that my parents weren't safe with themselves. Maybe my judgments are sharp because they've always had to be, because I was always on my own. And right now, I know that Claire is in this city. The feeling is as firm as the armrest in my hand.

What I love about solving a case is that, for a moment, I'm the only one in the world who knows something important. I don't have many opportunities for power in my line of work. I can't afford expensive things, despite being surrounded by them on the job. My clients always have at least one diamond winking at me, at least one handbag with hardware. I can't flaunt my accomplishments because my work is confidential. I can't surround myself with successful people because the ones I know never want to see me again. All this means is that *catching* someone—figuring them out, digging up their secret—is the most power I can have. It's the power of outsmarting someone. It's walking into a situation and knowing I am the most prepared one there. I'm now in Claire's blind spot. Better than that, I'm in everyone's blind spot. The only one who knows that I'm here, about to stroll into their love nest, is me.

When the seat belt sign goes off, I'm the first to stand.

I speed-walk off the plane.

Get in a taxi.

Drive toward my Zipcar in the city.

I'm fidgeting for the next half hour, until my hands are slick and slipping over each other. I catch my reflection smiling. This is better than finding any Picasso. This is finding the artist herself. She's hiding in her story, and I'm the only one who sees.

I started working in the Hamptons partly for the people. Plenty of them graduated from the schools I worked for, spoke up in the classes I shadowed. They were the ones I admired for belonging to places I never would, the sophisticated and beautiful insiders. Whose aristocratic names commanded respect before they ever opened their mouths. With country club crests on their shirts, polo players on their socks. Casual references to Virgil and tennis. I could never *be* them, but I could get close. As their private eye, I could get inside their heads. From my first job, it was like slipping into one of their black-tie gowns, walking down one of their long hallways, and then watching the train swish and glitter. Housekeepers for the wealthy step inside their mansions, but private eyes live in their minds.

I laugh out loud.

"Something funny?" my driver asks kindly.

"No. Yes."

He leaves me alone.

The Golden Gate Bridge comes into view, and I wonder how Claire would describe it. With just three or four simple words, she'd make you feel like she was reading your mind while elevating it. The road suddenly gets steep—too steep. Almost vertical. The houses on either side sit on an extreme slant, every ground floor tilting sixty or seventy degrees. Cars are parked facing uphill. I rub my eyes, but everything stays on an impossible incline. This doesn't look like the real world. It looks like a flimsy top layer, a tablecloth with a ripple.

There was a thread about this.

ENCOUNTERS.

It was for Starlites who claimed that strange things happened when they got close to Claire. But I never believed them. I thought they were too rabid to think straight. Yes, Claire has a magnetic field—like all charismatic people—but the events they described were too bizarre, too dreamlike. I remember the watch covered in its own white dust. I remember the red burn on someone's hand, like lips in the middle of his palm. I remember the Starlite who claimed she'd had prescient dreams for the next few nights, predicting the near future.

I rub my eyes again.

On the other side of the hill, I look back to see the block curling up toward the sky. We drive through several intersections with no traffic lights. We cruise up another hill and pass Lombard Street, which curves all the way down to the Bay. Cars snake through the zigzag in slow motion. A homeless man crosses the street right in front of us, wearing his comforter like a toga. My driver swerves around him. We speed through a block where every window box is jam-packed with succulents like green roses or pale-blue artichokes. I've never seen any of them before. One plant like giant, purple scallions tosses in the wind.

Eventually, the Golden Gate Bridge comes back into view. A dozen green hills look alive right behind it. Frothy waves crash around the bottom. Alcatraz sits in the center of the Bay. I stare at it for a few seconds before I realize that the best views in this city might be from that old prison. I swallow, and for some reason, I just can't tell myself that San Francisco is always this way. That this has nothing to do with getting closer to Claire.

~

I drive toward Leo's in my rental—a practical, black Honda.

I feel a little calmer, but the city still looks strange. I find myself stopped next to a bright-red trolley. It's an anachronistic thing from the 1800s, surrounded by motor vehicles. There are no walls in the front or back, just open-air benches. People sit on them facing out, snapping photos on smartphones, taking everything in like tourists. A line of five people stares right at me, ogling me as if I'm part of the landscape.

I roll up my window.

Pass them.

Eventually, I pull over for a bite at the Mill, a coffee shop with a handsome brick front. Steel tracks in the road vibrate as cables pull the trolleys forward. It sounds like a hundred old telephones ringing, all handsets rattling at once.

Inside the Mill, hairs prickle up the back of my neck. Is Claire sitting right here, right now? Six brunettes are scattered and hovering over their laptops, bitten apples glowing in the centers. The dark tops of their heads point at me as I pass, but I see just enough of their cheeks and noses to know that Claire isn't here. At the sleek counter, I order an everything croissant, pointing at one behind the glass. It comes to almost six dollars, but the price doesn't bother me today. My mind's too full to react. As I carry the croissant back to a table, I wonder if Claire's ever been here. Did she get the toast with almond butter? Or with halvah spread, toasted pistachios, date syrup, and salt? Claire admitted that she has a "sweet tooth" in a lightweight interview with *Cosmopolitan*. The more I think about it, though, the more I doubt that Claire's gallivanting around town, ordering fancy toast.

I eat with my hands.

Oily fingers, salty lips.

When I'm done, I check my phone to see another missed call and voice mail from Kira. By now, Miranda must have told her where I am and what I'm doing. But—two voice mails? Why does she get more desperate to talk the closer I get to Claire?

~

I drive slowly through Leo's neighborhood.

This place is unusually cozy for somewhere so expensive. On both sides, $15 million estates take up less than an acre each. They sit right on the street, exposed enough that I look straight into the living rooms. I can see every inch of the art hanging in some of the most elite homes in the country. I understand why Claire and Leo would settle down here. Yes, it's prohibitively expensive for most, but there's a small-town atmosphere that does feel welcoming—as deceptive as that may be. I can almost imagine kids going door-to-door, trick-or-treating. Have they talked about raising a family here?

At the end of the street, Leo's home comes into view. After a grave-yard shift in flight, and then a morning on the road, I'm finally here. All things considered, though, it's been even longer than that. His house looks narrower in person—much taller than it is wide—but the view is more spectacular than I expected. The Golden Gate Bridge is a red halo around his home. The towers are so vibrant, I can't help but think of all the wasted, gray opportunities around the Northeast. Why aren't more bridges painted?

I park several houses away.

The only noise comes from a bird feeder. Right across the street from Leo, it hangs from a tree, fanning out into a shallow bowl filled with seed. Half a dozen finches are flapping around it, pecking at the rim and whistling. A few more color Leo's lawn, leaping patches of yellow and brown. One flies past my window, visible for a red second. Otherwise, there are no signs of life, nothing moving except the wind. Leo's garage door is shut. All curtains are drawn except for those on the top floor. Is Claire up there now?

I settle into my seat.

I've done my fair share of stakeouts in Long Island. Most were slow, almost meditative jobs. But now, my blood is quick. The backs of my legs are tensing, too, from my calves to my tailbone. I dig one thumb into a hamstring. A line comes to mind from Jane Austen's *Persuasion*, from the penultimate chapter. I can almost see it on the page, carrying a whole novel's worth of anticipation: "I am half agony, half hope. Tell me that I am not too late."

I check my phone.

My only notifications are Kira's voice mails.

Instead of indulging her, I open Safari and read more about Exeter, where all of this started. Every few seconds, I raise my gaze and scan the long line of pastel homes for anything new. I check every bay window, every balcony, every rooftop, and then pay special attention to Leo's place. Nothing moves except the birds.

Exeter feels rigid, even in glossy slideshows. Five days a week, classes start at eight or nine and end at six. Those are dark times in a New Hampshire winter. I imagine Claire and Leo passing each other on their way to breakfast, the air still gray, the buildings black. Half-day classes take place every other Saturday.

If I'm being honest with myself, the school doesn't sound very romantic. It's not Lake Como. It's not Paris at midnight. But maybe it is a place that binds people together. It's where boys and girls are only allowed in each other's rooms between seven and eight p.m., with faculty permission. During these "visitations," the door must stay open. Maybe Claire and Leo had to pack all their intimacy into the classroom. Maybe that supercharged their discussions, sharpened everything they said to each other across the table. I picture them in "US History," taking opposite sides in a debate on the American Revolution. Maybe they challenged each other in a way no one else did. Maybe they were the only two who did the optional reading, and it gave them their own private language. Maybe they tried to touch each other in class.

My phone rings. Miranda.

I answer with a polite hello.

"Where are you?" Kira demands.

I pull the phone away from my ear.

She used her mom's cell.

"Where in LA?" she demands.

"Excuse me?"

"Tell me."

Her tone is urgent.

Leo's garage opens. A black Tesla pulls out.

I hang up and start my car as soon as the Tesla's out of sight.

I follow, craning forward, but I can't see who's driving. I can't see any details other than the shadowy back of someone's head.

Is that you, Claire?

I squint, getting closer.

I hold the steering wheel with both hands, but it keeps sliding out of my grip. I wipe my fingers on my jeans, leaving four streaks on each thigh. We drive toward town on flat roads, for once, passing a green next to the Bay. A long line of cyclists drifts behind us, not a cloud in the sky to dull the sun on them. In town, leggy palm trees grow along the sidewalk. Fire escapes zigzag up pale buildings between restaurants with al fresco seating. We pass a flower shop so lush, buckets of sunflowers spill onto the sidewalk, blooming for everyone. It looks like a gorgeous landslide.

We stop at a traffic light.

Feeling brave, or excited, I inch closer to the Tesla until my Honda is at risk of touching it. The glare from my hood sparkles onto its trunk. The sheets of metal are so close, I can almost see the light bouncing back and forth between them. My foot is only tentatively on the brake. Part of me wants to release the pedal and end this. If there were any damage, the driver would have to step outside and show their face.

Green light.

The Tesla darts ahead, only to slow down and park in front of Delarosa, a restaurant with orange tables on the sidewalk. I'm forced to pass as the Tesla's front door opens. A tan woman in sunglasses steps outside. She has long, shiny black hair. She's in a tight green tank, leggings, and high-top sneakers. She looks like she spends her weekends hiking with a heavy pack. Her thighs are firm, toned into long strips of muscle.

My heart sinks.

Claire was never athletic. Her body looked like she barely used it, like she didn't lift more than her laptop, didn't run anything but her fingers.

Someone honks behind me.

I drive another two blocks before, magically, someone leaves their spot. I pull into the space, while the next car speeds aggressively past me, proving a point. I cross the street quickly and head back toward Delarosa. Leo himself is seated at one of the tables outside. I slow my pace to a crawl, careful to stay in the shadows. He has the square jaw and strong brow that I expected, but he's even bigger in person. His arms are wide, strength hanging off the bones in heavy bulges. I'm not sure how he ever rowed *light*weight crew. He must have been hungry for years—counting every ounce of beef, every flake of salmon—shrinking steadily into his skeleton. As if his bones were feeding on him.

He smiles and stands when he sees the dark-haired woman. As soon as they're close enough, he puts his hands on both sides of her face. They kiss, and right when I think they're done, he brings her in for a second, more tender one. A chill pricks up my spine as they linger in their two-person world. I sit on a bench in a blue slant of shade and watch them take their seats. Leo faces me. The woman's hair is sleek down her back. They hold on to each other across the table, all four hands in a pile. Underneath, their feet touch.

Leo kisses her again.

They pull apart when a waiter arrives to take their order, but keep their hands and feet together. How long have they been seeing each other, to be this—in love? She's living with him, but she's still going to drive here to have lunch with him, to play footsie? As covertly as possible, I take a couple of photos with my phone. I catch her profile in one and try to zoom in on it, but she's still wearing those sunglasses.

Kira calls—I reject it.

She calls again. I watch it persist, bright and relentless. Maybe she isn't trying to stonewall me. Maybe she does need to talk.

I answer on the final ring.

"Please don't hang up," she says.

Her voice sounds strained.

"Please, did you find her?" she asks.

I don't know.

"Tell me, Nina, did you find her?"

A waiter carries one thin-crust pizza over to their table. Wide circles of mozzarella melt over red sauce. Fat basil freshens up the top. The black-haired woman throws her head back and laughs.

"Does your sister like pizza?" I ask.

"Please," Kira says, sounding more desperate than I've ever heard her. Her edge is gone. "I need to tell you something." Her volume drops precipitously. "Claire told me that she was leaving, all right? She told me the night before. We were in her room, sitting on her bed. She said that she was leaving—for someone else. She said that there'd always been someone else, but he wasn't ready. Then, he reached out to her just a few weeks before the wedding." Her voice cracks. "Claire made me promise not to say anything. Maybe that shouldn't matter, but I gave her my word. She said she just wanted a moment alone with him. A *moment*." She stretches the *o*, giving the letter an even emptier shape. "If I knew she was leaving for months, I would've made her say his *name*. Their *plan*. Something to *use* in case things went wrong. Because—did they? Or is she okay? Please."

The couple does a "Cheers!" with two slices of pizza. The tips are drooping.

"I know I've been giving you a hard time. I'm sorry I've been such a *fist*. Such a *wall*." They take their first bites in unison. "I was just trying to keep Claire's secret. And now, I really just need to know if you found her." Leo laughs with his mouth closed. His slice, colored like the Italian flag. "Please, you have brothers, too, right?"

"No, I don't."

"But—"

Her side of the line is silent.

"Oh, right," I remember.

Sometimes, I tell my clients that I have siblings. Wealthy people tend to have bigger families—dynasties, really. I'm used to working with parents of at least three, so every now and then, I mention brothers to make myself seem relatable.

A moped speeds past me with a dull roar. The man and woman on board both wear white sneakers. They park in front of Super Duper Burgers, where a street sign advertises organic cones with their ice cream. I wonder for a moment if any of the noises making their way back to Kira could reveal where I am. Is there anything in the background that could direct her to this point, to this exact spot on Chestnut Street?

I ask Kira if she's still there.

But her end of the line is dead.

~

After lunch, the woman walks back to her Tesla. Her oversize sunglasses hide everything from her eyebrows to her cheekbones. All I can see is the tanned point of her nose and the small curve of her chin—but I can't even see those well. Her hair is long and layered enough that strands keep blowing across her face.

I get in my car smoothly, then follow her. There's a red Jeep Wrangler between us, with surfboards vibrating in the back. Eventually, the Jeep turns. There's no one left between our cars. I give her a half mile of space, in case she's checking her mirrors. We drive back to Leo's house, where she glides into the garage and shuts the door behind her. I circle the neighborhood and then park in my old spot. There are still no signs of anyone else on the block, as if Leo owns every house in sight.

I wait, replaying clips of her in my mind. Her hair keeps getting in the way. It's like ink spilling across a page, drowning half the words. She does look to be about Claire's height, something that's hard to fake. Everything else is easier to disguise. But if she *is* Claire, her body's changed. Every soft spot looks hard. Her flesh is contoured, knotted. She must've spent the past couple of months hiking or climbing several times a week. That would've been a radical change from her intellectual life. Instead of handling ideas, suddenly, she would've been dealing with physical resistance. Real soreness and pain.

I'm going to need a better look.

Eventually, the sun starts to descend.

Light dims.

New birds arrive, surrounding the feeder with flashes of color. Some peck along the sidewalk, moving headfirst, their teacup bodies following on stick legs. A few of them jump so fast, they disappear for a split second.

I get hungry enough that in time, I have to address it. I drive back into town and buy snacks from CVS: a giant bag of Flamin' Hot Cheetos, jumbo tins of salted peanuts, and a two-liter bottle of club soda—things that won't disappear overnight under a layer of green fur. After checking out, I stop in the bathroom to find it covered in every color of graffiti. Some of the declarations are more intelligent than others. My eyes linger on the words SOME SAY THE WORLD WILL END IN FIRE, scribbled across gray tiles. It's a line from Robert Frost's poem "Fire and Ice." I continue the poem in my head on my way out of the store, "From what I've tasted of desire I hold with those who favor fire." I eat a handful of Cheetos on the drive back to Leo's and park where I can keep an eye on his home.

FIFTEEN

"Fifteen years old in this life, and I've spent all of them looking for him."

—*Claire Ross,* The Starlit Ballet

The next morning, headlights wake me. I jolt in the driver's seat, heart pounding. The black Tesla passes, moving fast enough to shed its edges. It's one bright smear. I think there were two people in the car—that woman and Leo. What time is it?

Five a.m. on a Saturday.

Where are they going?

I face the steering wheel, caught between wanting to follow them and wanting to stay with their house. Eventually, the white glow of their headlights fades to gray, then disappears. I release the wheel. They'd spot me, trailing them at a time like this. There aren't going to be many people on the road. Besides, chances are that I'd lose them. They're at least a mile ahead of me already. Considering the shape they're in, they're probably on their way to hike. I couldn't follow them up a mountain in my old sneakers.

I eye the house.

It's barely visible, a denser shadow than the rest of the night. I eat two handfuls of Cheetos and follow them with a long swig of flat seltzer. When my tongue is revived, drenched in warm pricks of CO_2, I wipe my hand on the passenger seat. If I left any orange film on the leather—any neon swirl—it's hidden in the dark.

Outside, the air is surprisingly brisk. In my mind, the West Coast was always warmer than this. Didn't Steinbeck promise good weather out here in *The Grapes of Wrath*? Now, I'm rubbing my bare arms, as if I can smooth the goose bumps. I feel invisible gliding through the night, slipping past palm trees that hide thin stars behind their leaves. I make it across the street and face the long staircase that leads up to their front door.

I climb, looking for cameras.

Try the front door—locked.

I crouch in front of the welcome mat and rub underneath it, seeing with my fingertips. The wooden planks are smooth as ice. Eventually, I feel dull metal teeth, and my heart rate spikes when I realize what I'm holding. They left it here, right here where anyone could find it. If this is the key to Claire's new home, she must believe that her secret is safe. That even with everyone looking for her, they are completely alone.

I slide it into the keyhole. The door opens.

My next steps are slow and steady as I listen for an alarm. But the only noises are coming from me. I move deeper into the shadows. Soon, there's no starlight, no difference when I blink. I consider using the flashlight on my phone, but what if Leo's neighbors see the light and get suspicious? Chances are, though, that no one else is awake.

No one is going to see.

I turn my flashlight on.

I'm standing in the living room, staring at the floating wooden staircase. This place feels more spacious than it looked from the street: sky-high ceilings, minimalist design, and barely any furniture. The couple's clothes from yesterday are strewn across the sleek, gray sofa in the center of the room. The same leggings, tank, and high-top sneakers that fit her so precisely are now discarded in wrinkly piles. Leo's polo is on the arm of the sofa, its collar a frozen black wave. The gray pillows look like they took a beating and held on to the impressions. It's not hard to imagine the two of them right here, leaving this mess. Did they have sex as soon as he came home?

I walk up to the sofa. My shins touch the edge.

So, they stole away for lunch and then fucked that night in the living room? This is the kind of thing that people do when they're new to each other—or maybe, when they've been reunited after a long time. Suddenly I'm even more awake, buzzing despite the sleepless chain of flights, followed by the night in my car. This is something that Claire and Leo would do. I pick up the tank on the edge of the sofa and lift it to my nose.

It smells faintly sour.

I turn around to face the fireplace. It's only knee high, long and low in the wall. Photos embellish the mantel. In the first one, teenage Leo poses with his parents in the redwoods. Giant red thighs twist out of the ground. His mom stands behind him, hugging his waist. The next one shows the three Williamses in Big Sur. And then, they're at a kiwi farm. It's vineyard-like, kiwis hanging like engorged grapes. Leo bites one through the skin. The family shots are followed by a few photos of Leo alone. Smiling in a Jeep behind wild lions. Crouching next to the pyramids in Cairo. And then—standing on Half Dome.

I lean toward the photo.

Pick it up.

Leo has a wide stance on the granite, his arms raised in a triumphant V shape. I've never been to Yosemite, but I feel like I have after spending so much time with Claire's book. From his vantage point, Leo could probably see the whole park.

I return the frame.

My flashlight brightens a bookcase in the corner. Vases filled with smooth white stones act as bookends. The titles are interspersed with wabi-sabi ceramic bowls. As always, I see one black-and-yellow book before the rest. At eye level, there are two copies of *The Starlit Ballet*. Millions of people own one. How many own two?

My breaths feel shallow.

I pull one off the shelf.

It looks weathered, like someone brought it to the beach, maybe, or around the world. I open it to the middle, where a few sentences are underlined in blue pen. I flip ahead. This copy is underlined all the way to the end. *"I remember every name he's ever had. Every face, every flaw."* And, *"Are you finally ready to go home?"* Every two or three pages, someone found a phrase so important, they drew it a pedestal. How many people mark up a book they read for fun? Unless they have a special connection to it or to the author? Several corners hang on to creases where they've been dog-eared—but there are so many, they can't all be from the same reading. Someone read this story multiple times.

I slide the book back into place.

Remove the second copy.

This one looks new, its cover unbleached by the sun. The spine crackles as I open it. There's something written in black Sharpie before chapter one. I can see its blur from a few pages away. I flip to the dedication. Usually, this reads, *For the one I will find in every life*. But here, someone wrote a comma over the period and continued:

For the one I will find in every life,

For Leo.

Claire

I sit on the floor. Reread it.

This has to mean what I think it does.

For Leo. I touch the script. The two words are connected, as if she wrote them without lifting the pen. The end of the *r* becomes the smooth start of the *L*.

For Leo.

I was right. They really did have a connection so intense, Claire spent years writing about it. Then, as if that wasn't romantic enough, she left everything—her fiancé, her family, her whole career—to be right here with him. And now, I'm here too. I'm the only one who's figured it out. I made it all the way across the country, following the map inside her story. This feels like waking up in someone else's dream—or even better, stepping into *The Starlit Ballet*. I'm now with Cady and Logan, where they chose to spend their final life.

For Leo.

I take a photo of the dedication page. Did he get this autographed at one of her signing events? She appeared for a dozen of those right after *The Starlit Ballet* came out. I vaguely remember the schedule. All took place in bookstores, mostly on the East Coast, but with some exceptions: Magic City Books in Oklahoma, Blue Willow Bookshop in Texas, Bookends & Beginnings in Illinois, and Pages in Los Angeles.

I stand up and return the book.

Claire was here. Right here.

I pass their clothes on my way to the kitchen, where none of the cabinets or drawers have handles. It makes the place look smooth. I open the refrigerator and face a bakery box. Its pink seal is ripped in half. I feel the jagged edges of the sticker. Its glue still has enough bite to latch on to my finger. Inside, I find two half-eaten slices of cake: a white piece on the left, topped with cottony meringue and toasted coconut flakes; Funfetti on the right, finished with a neat half inch of frosting and a dense coat of rainbow sprinkles. I imagine Claire and Leo sharing these, their arms crossing and uncrossing as they chipped off bites with their spoons. I plunge a finger into the polka-dot sponge and bring a taste up to my mouth.

I walk upstairs and find myself stepping into the primary. A blackout shade hides the windows on all sides. Their king bed is a mess but in a way that looks familiar. Their comforter forms a scrunched C shape at the end of the mattress, as if they just kicked it off, lifted the window, and ran away from everything—with nothing. Two pillows lie on the carpet. I tread carefully around the bed, one hand dragging on the sheets, the other holding my phone like a torch. It lifts the black veil from their room.

I step into their closet, where I'm surrounded by men's clothes. They're sorted into garment racks on one side, shelves on the other. I face hanging oxfords and sport coats right over hanging pants. They look like flattened people. Two shopping bags are almost hidden under the hems. I crouch down and fish into the first one. It's full of new leggings and tops just like the outfit downstairs. Tags dangle from plastic spokes. I run my fingers over the leggings—frictionless. The second bag is translucent, stuffed with something dark. It almost looks like a crow, its neck bent and tail folded. Wings crumpled in order to fit. I reach inside to find a long, layered black wig. It's soft—so soft, I'm hardly breathing.

I can almost feel her in here.

I head back to the bed, sit down. Their mattress sinks beautifully beneath me. I turn my flashlight off and lean back until I'm staring at the ceiling. I stretch my arms into a T shape and feel the urge to make a snow angel in the sheets, do something to savor this moment as much as I can. I've figured it out. Her book was a cipher written in plain English. It was a puzzle with over half a million pieces, so gorgeously laid out that no one ever thought to rearrange them, to unscramble them and read the truth.

My phone vibrates. Kira.

I answer, sounding more than a little preoccupied.

"Hi, it's Kira and my mom on speaker."

"Miranda, how are you?"

It must be close to six a.m. here, nine on their coast.

"I don't know." Miranda sounds brittle. "I'm sorry, but Kira just brought some things to my attention. I wanted to check in with you?"

"Happy to."

"You worked for Abigail Waters," Miranda says.

"Yes, I did."

"Well, Abigail's back from the Maldives," Miranda continues. "Kira was driving by her house this morning when she saw the lights on. She probably left skid marks on the road, with how fast she turned. The two of them talked, and—I didn't believe Kira at first. So I called Abigail myself." A short pause. "She said that your methods made her nervous—which isn't exactly what her gardener told us. He said they were 'unusual.' And it became clear that he didn't give us the right message at all. Maybe her phone cut out during their call. I don't really know what went wrong. But Abigail gave me the full story.

"Things she never told him.

"She said you slept in her guest room for two whole months. She'd come downstairs at six every morning to find you in the kitchen, sipping coffee, reading. She was willing to trust you, though, because you seemed to be making progress. And you said that was how you'd get to know her, get to know the case. But—" A longer pause. "She said you always had Claire's book. Even when she walked in on you at dawn, the book was next to you on the banquette. She said it looked like you'd wrestled with it, read it to shreds. The pages were all kinked, underlined within an inch of their lives. The jacket was covered in handwritten notes."

"It's one of my favorites."

"And you asked her about Claire?"

"I ask a lot of questions."

"But Abigail said you had a real focus on Claire specifically. You asked what Claire was like when she was growing up? When people knew she was 'gifted'? And if Roger made her happy? Abigail even drove you to our house. You asked her to park on the street and tell you stories about us? And then, no matter what, you always had that book?"

"I was reading it."

"But it wasn't the first time?" Miranda continues, her pitch rising. "She said you referenced the book so often, you might've memorized it." Meanwhile, I stare at the ceiling, too dark for details. I lift my free hand and can't see a single finger, not even a flicker as I wave to no one. "Did you ask Abigail if she had any photos of Claire?"

"I'm afraid I can't talk about past clients."

For once, an NDA works in my favor.

And discretion protects me.

"You didn't find her painting," Kira cuts in.

"Kira," Miranda says.

Silence.

"Abigail did tell us," Miranda goes on, "that the *police* found her Picasso in connection with another art theft. After two months of work, she said you hadn't gotten anywhere. You'd just been living in her house, rearranging her books, and asking so much about Claire, Abigail thought *Claire* was a suspect." Miranda pauses, as if she's letting that sink in, as if I don't already know this. "Then, when Claire's case was going stale, Abigail decided to say something. Her gardener said you'd lead us to Claire, but he made it sound like a referral. Abigail *meant* you'd lead us to Claire—because she thought you might be involved."

Something rustles on their side of the line—quieter than whispers, as if the Rosses are mouthing words to each other. I picture the ocean coloring glass windows behind them, while their jaws open and close. The longer I hold the scene in my mind—their lips wrapping around a series of *O*'s—the more it looks like an aquarium.

"Do you have anything to say about that, Nina?" Miranda asks at last.

"I'm afraid I can't talk about past clients."

"Excuse me?" Kira demands.

Her tone is rough.

Does she expect me to fold—on the phone? It's hard to be scared when I'm hidden on the other side of the country. I have a twenty-five-hundred-mile head start.

Besides, with Miranda in charge, this has been the most polite gotcha moment I've ever heard. It's so courteously long winded that Miranda hasn't even said what she really thinks yet. She hasn't gotten to the point and asked me where her daughter is, asked me how long I'm going to keep her to myself. Instead, Miranda's been painstakingly transparent and considerate. She broke down why she doubts me in exhaustive detail. It doesn't make much sense, though, telling someone untrustworthy the evidence against them.

"Are you . . ." Miranda appears to struggle with her own question.

. . . a Starlite?

A rabid Starlite?

No, I'd tell her. *Of course not.* Starlites care more about their own community than they ever did about Claire. Yes, they love her book. Some are even saved by it. But they regurgitate everything they learn about her, keeping nothing to themselves. r/ClaireRoss is still humming, even without her around. *No, of course not, Miranda.* They're all too adolescent with their obsession. Impressionable. Desperate for validation. And, ultimately, unable to find her. *No, I'm not one of them.* I am the real thing.

"Where are you?" Kira asks.

"I'm right here, listening to every word," I say with absolute calm. Smooth as a black pond in the dead of night. "And I'm sorry to hear that Abigail found me . . . inelegant. I wish I could share more, but I'm working right now—on your case. I'm close." I fondle her sheets. "At this point, I'd strongly advise you to trust me because in a few days, I'm going to give you an update you won't want to miss. And then, all of this will make sense. All of this will make perfect sense." My tone is confident, as if I really am planning to report to them. Instead of just pushing them into the wings, somewhere I can't hear them.

"You owe us this," Kira snaps. "Where is she?"

I pull the phone away from my ear and watch the clock that's recording the length of our call. It ticks on, second after second, climbing into a new minute. When the screen turns black, I tap the glass, bringing it back to life.

What are they saying?

It's nice not to care. Freeing, light.

I hang up, then roll back and forth in the comforter. I imagine how Claire and Leo might fall asleep, the exact positions of their limbs. It's not long before I'm sliding my ankles under their sheets, rubbing my cheek against a pillow. I've never been more comfortable than here in the epilogue of my favorite book, Claire's real-life happily ever after.

SIXTEEN

"He felt as familiar as my own hands."
—*Claire Ross,* The Starlit Ballet

I wake up to the sound of birds. A dozen different songs overlap, all of them high pitched and fleeting. I'm in a king bed I don't recognize, with a puffy comforter pulled up to my chin. Shadows hide most of the details. A blackout shade snakes around the whole room, even behind the headboard—I'm in Claire and Leo's bed.

I jump out when I remember.

How did I let myself fall asleep? I'm never this careless. I never celebrate too soon. I haven't even seen Claire face-to-face yet, not really. I creep toward the door—open just a crack—and listen for anyone downstairs.

Are they here?

I swallow.

Nothing.

It's just after nine a.m.

If Claire and Leo were back, they'd be making noise, right? I'd hear *something*? I push the door open all the way and wince as it creaks. No one starts shouting at the sound. No one runs in this direction, now that I've given myself away. I peek down the floating staircase. The banister is a tall sheet of glass, invisible except for one glittering edge. The first floor looks exactly as I left it: clothes abandoned, curtains drawn.

No one's turned on a light.

I walk downstairs, feeling more relieved with every step. My shoes squeak on the smooth wood. Eventually, I sit on the sofa, between Leo's polo and Claire's tank. Her top is coiled in a green swirl. I pinch a tent into the fabric and watch it stay erect. *Are you at Yosemite right now?* I imagine them stopping in the valley for a view of Bridalveil Fall. Maybe Leo's running a finger up and down her back, then pulling her in for a kiss. Maybe she's pushing him behind a tree, somewhere no one can see them. Lifting his shirt over his head, while he does the same for her. I imagine what it's like for two cerebral people to go mindless.

There are no sex scenes in *The Starlit Ballet*, not one in thousands of years. The book is so modest, I assumed she might be too.

But is she?

What's it like to kiss Claire Ross?

I stretch her tank with my fingers, feeling every thread. I should get moving—stand up and get on with it—but the truth is that I'm in awe.

First, she wrote my favorite book, one so alive that I've spoken to it, slept next to it—and I'm not the only one. It's spellbound people in every language. Her wildest dream came true. And then, in another fantasy, she threw it away. She cut ties with all her obligations, all her people, and ran off to be with her true love. No one gets to start over as an adult—no one except Claire. And the love that she ran off to—if it's like the one she wrote about, it could survive every death, disease, and war. It could grow even during the most brutal periods in history, through famines and massacres. It made her feel so intensely, she spent her adulthood writing about it and then traded everything for it. What's it like to kiss someone like her?

~

I make a quick trip back to my car.

Outside, it's brighter than I expected. The whole block is pale orange, bleached yellow. The light barely hangs on to its colors. I'm blinking as I cross the street, adapting from the shadows. I open my car door, still doing the mental math. If Claire and Leo left at five, they probably didn't plan to reach their destination before sunrise, two hours later. That gives them at least four hours of travel, round trip, plus at least an hour wherever they decided to stop. So they won't be home until ten at the earliest, still an hour from now.

I hop into the driver's seat.

Another car approaches from behind.

As soon as I hear it, I lean onto the passenger side and bury my face. All I needed to do was grab the toiletry bag out of my suitcase, but I stay put, inventing tasks for my hands. The hum of the engine gets louder and louder, then softer until it fades into nothing. When it feels safe enough, I sit up again. The whole block is empty except for the birds and a few sturdy trees. Their trunks are as dark as if they're soaking wet.

I walk back to Leo's alone.

In his living room, I feel comfortable enough to turn on the lights, unzip my bag on their sofa, and remove two battery-powered cameras. Each fits in the palm of my hand. I search for a spot to hide the first one, scanning the mantel, bookshelf, and then the potted plant at the base of the stairs. It looks tropical, with tall stalks and leaves wider than my face. I touch one of them. It feels synthetic. My gaze drifts to the planter.

They won't be watering this.

I dig into the fake soil, making just enough room for the camera. Slivers of dirt creep under my nails, black crescents at the ends of my fingers. Ten open parentheses. I plant the device. It doesn't take long to bury everything except its uninvited eye. From a foot away, it's invisible. But the lens will capture most of this floor.

And just like that, I've moved into their home.

I carry the second camera upstairs.

In their bedroom, I drag one finger along the mattress. My heart's beating faster, and whether that's from the stairs or from the thrill of what I might tape in here, I can't say that I know. I scan for hiding places. The seamless floor-to-ceiling windows don't offer much. In

Claire's closet, the options aren't better. The camera *might* stay buried under a pile of clothes, but it's too risky. My best shot is the small gap right under their headboard. The camera won't film much, but I'll hear every sound in this room.

I wedge it in there.

And disappear.

SEVENTEEN

"Then again, after this many fashion eras, every outfit feels theatrical."

—*Claire Ross,* The Starlit Ballet

That night, I watch Leo's house. The live streams are playing on my phone, in room six at the Safe Journey Motel. Both feeds are dead black. Two graves, separated by a thin green line. They show nothing except my reflection, up to the tip of my nose.

Are they really not home yet?

There's one window in my room, between iron bars and a gauzy curtain. A shadow passes on the other side. I glance up, then return to my phone. It's hard to tear my eyes from the screen, even though it's been dark for hours. Another plane rips through the sky, descending into San Francisco airport. Staying under a flight path doesn't bother me. With rates like this, I didn't expect to be comfortable. A few reviews for this place also warned that after paying by credit card, fraudulent charges showed up for chain restaurants in Pennsylvania. But I'll be using twenties from my white envelope, straight from Miranda's hand.

I have enough cash to last one week. If I need more time than that, I'll have to dip into my savings, and those don't run deep. Not to mention that the longer I'm here without that update for the Rosses, the more I put my whole career at risk. Not many people can run off with someone's money and continue to get jobs in the same area. The Hamptons aren't a small town, but they are tightly knit. If I were more clearheaded, I'd do something to soothe Miranda and Kira. But all I want to focus on is Claire. I'm so close, and I just want to see her in person, have one private minute with her. She's every thought I have.

The microwave next to me warms my elbow. Inside, my macaroni and cheese spins on a glass wheel, thawing in yellow light. The footage on my phone still won't even flicker, as if the cameras are sinking in tar and taping their way down.

Suddenly, Leo's hallway brightens.

He enters with Claire, their arms around each other. They look spent and satisfied. Her head's leaning against his shoulder. She's still wearing that wig and a cropped hoodie over leggings. I've never seen her belly button before—an innie, like a tiny eye turned on its side. My heart rate picks up. Are they saying anything? I try to turn up the volume, but it's already at its max. Leo stops them by the sofa. She sits on the arm and looks up at him, rounding her neck. It's an inviting posture, open. Her hair drips down her back in a long ponytail. He leans forward, one hand on each of her thighs.

My microwave beeps.

I open and slam it shut.

They kiss slowly, rushing nothing. I've seen plenty of people kiss in this line of work—and do plenty more—but never this carefully. I check if my camera's lagging, but it's not. It's working in real time, sending me every frame.

She pulls his shirt off over his head, then drops it on the floor. His torso is sculpted, all the muscles as hard as the rib cage striping them. Every breath slides through him with precision. Claire rubs her hands up his chest, her fingers spread wide. I sigh hard against my teeth, impatient. I didn't come all this way to see *him*. When Claire lies down, the sofa swallows her whole. Leo climbs forward, straight over the arm, then straight over her, on his hands and knees. When he takes her hoodie off, I only see her fingers in the air. Soon, they're both out of sight, except for two knobs of his spine.

"Shit," I say out loud.

One of them is murmuring.

I can't make out the words.

"Fuck!" I shout.

I hit the side of my phone, as if that will do something.

A whole minute passes before someone's foot emerges—and it's not even hers. I remember my pasta and open the microwave, releasing cheesy steam. I carry the warm paper dish over to my bed, where I sit cross-legged and watch the live feed. Leo starts to groan. The sounds are low and rhythmic, as if he's purring. Now, I can barely hear her enjoy it. Her voice is still there, leaping high above his every once in a while. But for the most part, it's buried. My spoon hovers over my food, twisting back and forth between my fingers. Here I am, watching Claire make love, and I still don't know how she does it.

I eat my pasta.

One soft bite after another.

I stockpiled more Stouffer's in the mini fridge. Baked Ziti, Creamed Chipped Beef, and Lasagna wait in the cold for their turn. I remember Miranda's freezer was full of home-cooked meals: cauliflower gratin, carrot-ginger soup, and lamb shanks. Each box had its own label with the date it had been packed. Abigail loved to cook, too, but she had more food sensitivities, all probably invented to disguise her general fear of eating. She couldn't eat eggs, gluten, or dairy, to name a few. The reasons changed like the weather.

I'd never slept over at a client's before I met Abigail. But when she mentioned how well she knew the Rosses, who lived just down the road, of course I had to stay. It wasn't even a conscious decision. The words left my mouth before they ever crossed my mind. My smile didn't so much as flicker when I invited myself over, inventing reasons why it made sense. To my surprise, Abigail reacted just as smoothly as I had. The next day, I moved into one of her guest rooms, started drinking from her tap.

Did you ask Abigail if she had any photos of Claire? I remember waiting for the answer. I was sitting in Abigail's Range Rover, staring at her in the driver's seat. The Rosses' black gates were framed in her window. Her lean eyebrows pinched together. She didn't seem to understand why I was asking for photos of someone so famous. Didn't seem to grasp that I wanted the candids, the unguarded and intimate shots of Claire at a birthday party or Fourth of July cookout. Abigail said she didn't have any—and she was telling the truth. I searched her house for them, for any sign of Claire's green stare in the back of a Waters family moment.

I stab my pasta with a spoon.

Check the feed.

Eventually, Claire and Leo stand and head for the stairs. He's in the foreground, blocking most of her body. She only peeks through in the tip of her nose, her swinging arms, kneecaps. They're out of sight too quickly. I watch the other half of the split screen, listening hard as I scrape burned cheese off the bottom of my dish.

A soft, feminine noise.

Is he still touching her?

". . . or Rwanda with you," he says.

"Why Rwanda?"

"Gorilla trekking."

The sound of a kiss.

"You'd love it." Him again. ". . . right in the rainforest." More softly, he adds, "You gave us thousands of years, and you never let us meet any gorillas?"

"You had to read between the lines."

I can hear him smirking.

"We could turn it into a longer trip and see Southeast Asia. You've never been?"

"Never," she says.

I hear Roger in that word.

"Everything there is so far apart, but we could take a whole year," he says. "I'd love to show you Vietnam. The rice paddies . . ." I lose the end of it. They must be in the closet now. Leo's still talking, his voice low, but every sentence sounds like he's chewing it. ". . . they grow in staircases. People call them Vietnam's pyramids." The mattress heaves under them. "And if we do take a year, we could hike in Nepal."

"Then, the moon."

He laughs.

"I know," he says. "I just feel like—we lost so much time."

He adds something too quiet for me to hear.

I try to picture them in bed. Is she lying with her knee crooked over him? Or are they both sitting up against the headboard? How would I lie with her, if I got the chance? A shouting match erupts above me. I drop my spoon but hang on to the question. If I were to lie down with Claire, at the end of a long day, more than anything else, I'd want to see her face. After all, it's her mind I love the most. I'd want to see it in her eyes. Both live streams go black. But I don't think I'd ever turn off the lights, not even when we went to sleep.

~

I wake up the next morning, heart racing.

In the bathroom, I splash cool water on my face. It drips off my jawbone into the sink, as if my skin is melting. Without a stopper, the drain looks endless. I splash a few more handfuls onto myself, then wipe it off with wet fingers. I'm still rattled enough to check the mirror for anything strange behind me. Nothing moves, not the yellow curtains, the chain lock on the front door, or the lump of sheets I've just abandoned.

I dreamed that Claire was standing on Leo's street. She looked like her old self—pink hair, clear glasses, and pale skin—but something wasn't right. Even in the wind, her hair stayed in place. Her green stare was deadened, like eyes on a peacock tail staring lifelessly ahead. I got as close to her as I could. The sun was right over us, turning a few of Claire's stray hairs white. She didn't move. I couldn't hear her breathe.

I just wanted to make sure she was real.

I pressed my thumbs into her cheeks, felt my way down her neck. She was warm and firm—even more so than Chloe, Candice, Cady, and everyone else she brought to life. I squeezed her shoulder, then reached for her hand. I was going to take her home when something cracked inside her. The noise didn't sound right. It was too loud, too devastating, like a whole wall of glass shattering. She doubled over, clutching her arm. It was bleeding at the joint, pouring onto the asphalt. I reached for her again. But every time I touched her, it sounded like her skeleton had snapped in a hundred places. Her bones splintered and cracked, as if I were killing her from the inside out. Still, I couldn't stop. I wanted to help. I kept reaching for her until she was unable to stand, every hard part of her soft, every piece altered until she didn't even look human anymore. She was just skin in my hands.

I get dressed, haunted by the idea.

I comb my hair with my fingers, then braid it. I catch glimpses of my jagged part in the mirror, the brown strands like zipper teeth down my scalp. Of course I'm not going to hurt Claire. No one wants to take better care of her than me.

For some reason, I repeat this to myself as I tune in to the live stream on my phone, as I cook a Creamed Chipped Beef. The microwave beeps only once before an airplane swoops low enough to drown out the alarm. For a few seconds, the loudest noise is a droning rumble, as turbines shred clouds into a million pieces. It sounds more violent than usual. I carry the hot meal back to bed and eat while watching my phone.

Wait for Claire and Leo to wake up too.

Bite after bite, the taste of salt dulls.

I feel calmer and find myself drifting down the headboard. My neck bends at a deep angle. In this position, my toes point up on both sides of my phone, pricked like ears. I drop my empty dish on the rug and sit back up, hearing my spine click inside me. The screen still won't flicker. The thin green line runs through empty space. Of course I'm not going to hurt Claire. No one wants to take better care of her than me.

At five to eight, Leo groans with pleasure. Then, again. And again. Their headboard brushes against the camera, as if they're wiping the microphone with a dishrag. Eventually, the rocking stops. Their heavy breaths fade. A brief silence gives way to murmurs. I hold the phone up to my ear, turn the volume to its max. They're still barely audible.

". . . ten a.m.," Leo says. "But not today."

"Leo," she chides.

"I'd rather stay with you."

Silence.

What's at ten?

"I wanted to write today," she says.

Their voices trail off.

Write about what?

Claire was asked in plenty of interviews for a preview of her next project. The most she revealed was that her writing might take a new form. This raised the natural follow-up, *Are you saying it might not be a novel?* Several interviewers pressed her on this, but she kept her lips sealed with a smile. I always thought that after mastering one type of story, she was looking for the next mountain. This time, what would it be?

~

That night, Leo cooks them dinner.

He does it like he's seducing her: oysters, *cacio e pepe*, and tomato salad with torn basil. He goes so far as to roast the oysters and mix them with butter. He grates the pecorino for their pasta himself. As he cooks, he waxes about what else he wants to make this week, including lobster pomodoro and burrata lasagna. I can't see much when they're in the kitchen. But every once in a while, Claire's black ponytail swishes into the frame.

Why is she wearing that at home?

Over oysters, it sounds like they're planning an extended trip. They toy with different destinations in South America. Leo's Spanish accent is smooth, trilling every double *r*. They keep coming back to the Uyuni Salt Flats. Leo calls them "the world's biggest mirror," more than four thousand square miles of glass. Next, they consider the Annapurna Circuit, a twenty-day trek through the Himalayas in Nepal. Then, as they swirl cacio e pepe around their forks, Leo suggests skiing in Japan. For an hour, they talk about globe-trotting with the freedom of two people who have no obligations and no desire other than to be together—just like Logan and Cady.

After dinner, they help each other with the dishes.

They move to the sofa and read.

I listen to them turn the pages. Their ankles overlap on the arm of the sofa. It's such a peaceful moment—so easy and perfect—I almost wouldn't change a thing.

EIGHTEEN

"I'm laughing as he squeezes, like it's all coming back to him now, and he feels the connection that's kept us together for thousands of years. When he sets me down, my knees wobble, but he catches me—the way he's always caught me."

—*Claire Ross,* The Starlit Ballet

The next day, I park a few houses from Leo's. It's almost noon on a Monday, and the block is empty except for some yellow-throats on the feeder. They whistle and squeak in a call-and-response. I keep my eyes on Leo's garage.

It's my first break from the footage since yesterday. I watched it even when they were asleep, when I could no longer hear them breathe. I hadn't pored over videos of her like that—my whole body curled around my phone, fogging up the screen—since her book tour. Back then, there were new clips of her every day. I'd watch every one several times in a row, just luxuriate in it, as if I could take a bath in her details.

She was fascinating for a hundred thousand reasons, but one was the number of choices available to her. Most people don't get that many. My clothes, apartment, people, even what I say: I have a tight band of options. There's only so much I can afford. There's only so much eccentricity I can risk, as someone whose income depends on looking trustworthy. But Claire was unusually free. She had license to be one of a kind. She worked on her own dreams—no clients, no schedule, no boss. I studied her every inch, because she could edit every one. On tour, she wasn't just answering questions about her book, but something deeper: What does a woman who can say, wear, *do* anything become?

Any minute now, I expect her to head into town and meet him for lunch. I find myself pinching my arms, twisting small rolls of skin into tildes. No one else ventures into the street. Maybe this place is full of second homes, only visited by sitters. Birds come and go, all flapping as if they've just escaped a cage, new to the taste of fresh air.

Leo's garage door opens.

The black Tesla emerges.

I tail her all the way to the center of the Marina District, where she swoops into a parking spot. I slow down and watch her walk into Cancha, a Peruvian restaurant on Chestnut Street. Someone honks twice behind me. I slide into an open space two minutes away, farther than I would've liked. Sunlight finds every silver speck in the sidewalk. I check my reflection in a shop window, feeling my pulse in all my fingers. I'm still wearing what I wore on the plane: white tee, off-white pants, and a tan blazer. My hair is tucked into a low braid. I look clean enough. Normal enough. When I get Claire's attention, she'll have no reason to run in the opposite direction—especially when she hears my voice.

Hi, Claire, remember me?

She and Leo will need some time to eat—and hold hands on the table, tie their feet in a knot underneath it. I imagine they'll flirt with a few different destinations, all exotic corners of the world. Hopefully, they'll go their separate ways after lunch. He'll return to his nonprofit, and I'll catch Claire on the way back to her car.

In the meantime, I walk down Chestnut Street and try to breathe evenly. I want my voice to come out steady and confident. I want to look Claire in the eye without my knees buckling. I didn't come all this way, after all these years, to stop here. I don't have a script in mind—don't have the exact words—but I know what I'm going to say.

"Hello," I try to no one.

It sounds too smoky.

I clear my throat.

"Hello," I try again.

Better, but still too alto.

I'm rubbing my brow when I pass a bookstore and head inside without thinking. The shop is one long aisle, with floor-to-ceiling shelves. It smells woody with decay. A few people browse, hips cocked. They glance up when the door opens, then return to skimming inside flaps. Two glossy piles of Claire's book face me on the first table, front and center. But these copies of *The Starlit Ballet* are different: each has a quarter-size sticker on the cover, *Signed by Author*. I pick one up and open to the title page. Sure enough, there it is. Claire signs her name with an enormous, legible *C* at the beginning of Claire and an equally massive *R* at the start of Ross. The rest is a wavy scribble. Did she really sign these—here?

When could that have happened?

A man with a name tag—Dan—appears with a stack of paperbacks. He has white hair and eyebrows, even though he looks to be in his thirties. His wiry frame is fit. He drops the books in a gap on the table, staring curiously at me.

"Did she—sign these?" I ask.

"Every one," Dan says.

"Here?"

"We get them from the publisher."

I nod that I understand, still holding a copy.

"Want me to ring you up?" he asks.

"I've already read it, actually."

"Shame what happened to her."

I play dumb.

"What do you mean?" I ask.

"Claire Ross went missing . . ." He furrows his brow. "You didn't hear?"

I shake my head no.

"I'm not here looking at newspapers," I say, gesturing at the books.

"Fair enough," he says, returning my smile briefly. "Well, I'm sorry to be the one to tell you, but she went missing a few months ago. On her wedding day." He winces. "The police say she ran away, but her family thinks she was kidnapped."

"Some kind of crazy fan?"

The phrase comes out too soon. I hear it at the same time as Dan and watch him closely. His face is relaxed, as if we're talking about the novel supply chain, the routes of container ships that carry new books to America.

"That's the dark side of fame, I guess," he says without missing a beat. "Everybody thinks they know you. In any case, just give me a wave if you want help."

He walks to the front desk.

Some kind of crazy fan?

But of course I didn't give myself away. That theory got plenty of airtime back when Claire disappeared, back when the media was still covering her case. Of course Dan doesn't know what's about to happen. I'm the only one who does.

I put *The Starlit Ballet* down, keeping my fingertips on the smooth front. Today, the constellations look like mesh in a fishing net, dragging through dark ocean. If Claire stays missing, she won't be able to publish— whatever it is that she's writing. Is that her plan? I press a thumb into one corner of her hardcover. When you have a talent like hers, you can't just keep it to yourself. You can't hide from the world and enjoy the salt flats in Bolivia, or the rice paddies in Vietnam, not when we love you this much.

Outside, the sky is acid blue.

I pass an incoming Malin+Goetz shop. It's covered in bright posters for cilantro hair conditioner, eucalyptus body wash, and cannabis perfume oil. The trees on either side have chalky bark. Their leaves are lush, almost spiky, and dotted with white, spherical flowers. A man walks by carrying a skateboard with red wheels.

I find a bench across the street from Cancha.

Today, Claire and Leo are indoors. I can't see their table from here. Maybe they're sitting side by side and sharing every plate. My throat feels like it's getting smaller. Am I excited or terrified? Minutes from a dream or nightmare? I feel like Marlow in *Heart of Darkness*, facing the edge of the jungle. "There it is before you, smiling, frowning, inviting, grand, mean . . . and always mute with an air of whispering, 'Come and find out.'"

My whole body starts to sweat.

I glance at the bookstore, but Dan's nowhere in sight. He's not standing by the window, confirming a dark thought that crept into the back of his mind. Two pigeons land on my block, wobble this way. It's strange, I've read dozens of books that take place in California, and none mentioned the pigeons. Stories about the West Coast always felt grand and lustrous, abundant and golden. But gray birds bum around here too.

What's Claire saying now?

Maybe I could imagine it. I could make a collage, drawing from her interviews. *I . . . love . . . you.* I've seen her say each word. It's not a leap to piece them together, cut and paste clips in my head like I'm assembling a ransom note.

Eventually, she and Leo leave the restaurant together. I lean forward and watch them kiss goodbye. Her all-black outfit makes her body look like a single pen stroke, smooth and inky. Leo tucks one knuckle under her chin. Her arms wrap around his neck. When they finally head in separate directions, I stand and run-walk across the street.

She closes the gap with her car.

Too soon, her Tesla is just twenty paces away.

I should speed up and get her attention.

I *should*, but I'm locked in step behind her.

Am I going to do this or not?

I jog ahead until we're next to each other. She turns to look at me with the face I know so well, down to the small curve of her jaw. Yes, she's changed, but only in the details. I remember her cheeks used to be rounder. Now, they're steeper slopes on her face, cutting down to her chin. She's shaded in her eyebrows too. Brown shadow clings to the hairs like dark snowflakes. The last time I saw those, they were so faint, they were almost invisible.

"Claire," I say.

She looks at me, confused—and her expression is so persuasive, I almost doubt myself. We keep walking without missing a step.

"I'm afraid you have the wrong person," she says.

"Claire, it's me, Nina."

She looks apologetic.

"Nina Travers." I'm adamant, but how can I be frustrated when she's *here*? "I used to work in the dining halls at Harvard—you went there, right? I worked at the Coffee House in Cambridge too. You showed up with your laptop every weekend. Medium cappuccino, almond milk. That's where we met, remember?"

She doesn't stop walking.

"One day, you were crying in the back of the shop," I go on, reso- lute. "It was just the two of us there." I leave out the details—her ruby- red T-shirt, high-waisted shorts, and patent leather loafers. The way she crossed her ankles, widening the gap between her knees. "I asked if you were okay. You told me you'd sent a manuscript out to agents everywhere. It'd been exactly one year, and you hadn't heard anything back. You thought you'd never get published, never make it as a writer. So, I talked you through it, even asked to read your book. You said that *someone* should, so you printed a copy and gave it to me the next day." Finally, she slows down. "I read it in one sitting. I told you to keep writing, that you have a gift.

"You're *Claire Ross*," I insist, sounding attached to the truth of it. "I heard you went missing. Are you okay or are you . . . ?" I pretend to put it together in real time. "Look, I won't say anything you don't want me to say. I'm just so happy to see you again."

Two steps from her car.

"Would you want to get coffee?" I ask.

We reach the Tesla.

"Or dinner?" I press.

She walks to the driver's side.

I find myself stepping between her and the front door. Am I actually going to stop her from getting inside? We stand still, on the brink of escalating this. Neither one of us seems to want to move and test the other. A couple holding hands passes us, absorbed in their own conversation. We wait until they're out of earshot. I feel a prickle of anxiety, even though I shouldn't. Claire can't ignore me now. As far as she knows, I'm a threat to her perfect escape. If she pushes me aside, then I take her secret with me.

"Dinner could work," she concedes.

"Anywhere. Anytime."

She sighs, long and hard.

"How about . . . the Farmer's Daughter?" she asks. "Eight p.m.?"

"I'll be there."

I should move out of her way.

Now that we have a plan, I should step back.

I remember what happened when I touched her in my dream. I'd barely held her hand, but the sound was harsh and catastrophic, as if every one of her joints split, every vertebra was hacked and quartered. She lost her shape in a way that shouldn't scare me in the middle of the day. I hold my own hands, as if I'm restraining myself. Of course I'm not going to hurt Claire. It's her mind that's sensitive, not her bones.

"Can I . . . ?" she asks.

She gestures to her car.

"Right," I say.

I don't want to lose her.

But I won't, right? I have cameras in her house. If she were to travel anywhere, she'd need to use her passport, and she doesn't want to be found. The only way to stay missing—to keep her happily ever after—is to see me tonight.

I step back.

She gets in the car without waving goodbye.

Eight p.m.

The Farmer's Daughter.

It's only when her Tesla disappears that I start to think about what that means. After all the meals that Leo previewed for this week, she's going to eat with me instead? Even if her hands are tied, I can't help but get a thrill out of that.

NINETEEN

"I run my hands through his hair. He hasn't had hair this long since we were Vikings."
—*Claire Ross,* The Starlit Ballet

I'm here first at the Farmer's Daughter, an upscale farm-to-table spot: white brick walls, unvarnished wooden chairs and tables. Most of the other people here are young women, eating in small, quietly chatty groups. At my table for two, I've already read all the blurbs on my menu about the produce, where every leaf was harvested.

It's a minute past eight.

I squeeze my napkin, eyeing the entrance.

I don't know how long I've been in love with her. It must've started when I read her work. Until then, Claire was just another undergrad in a sea of students I admired, in their crimson sweaters, down parkas, and plaid scarves. Claire didn't draw attention to herself, and there were plenty of others who did: people who protested in Harvard Square, who spoke up every week in lectures, or who were already famous at eighteen. Premeds who could draw molecules with precision but who indulged themselves at parties. I was enamored with all of them—until I brought Claire's manuscript home.

Because that story dripped.

I still have it on my bookshelf in Riverhead, a blond inch of under-lined and annotated pages. It follows twenty-eight-year-old Fiona, a line cook at her dad's upscale restaurant in Manhattan. When their place gets slammed in the *Times*, her dad disappears, and Fiona takes control. A week later, she gets to work early and catches her dad stealing wine from the restaurant's cellar. He's several days into a bender and doesn't recognize his own daughter. That's when you learn as a reader that he's a struggling alcoholic. Even though Fiona's been narrating, she's been in denial about it. At the intervention for her dad, the spotlight turns on her—the intervention is also for Fiona, in denial about her own eating disorder.

It's a heart-wrenching book.

About the pain we ignore.

It must've been two in the morning when I read that section. That's when I fell in love with her depth, her empathy. She built such intricate people and cared about them—I could just tell that she cared about them. Claire's style was different back then, more descriptive. She gave her main characters dozens of details, as if everything about them mattered. She made their freckles seem important. Their back teeth were memorable.

When Claire and I met again, on a bench in Harvard Square, of course I raved about her story. I said that it had brought me to tears. But I did more than that—I told her about my parents. Not *Alice's* parents, who'd taken her home from the hospital to a dedicated nursery. Who wore tweed blazers and needlepoint slippers. Who enjoyed fox hunting, grandfather clocks, and an occasional cigar. Not them. *My* parents.

I'd never told anyone the truth.

I asked Claire how she understood it all so well. But really I was asking, How did you understand me? How did you know what I went through in the moments when I was alone? And the sex scenes—I didn't bring those up to Claire, but I noticed them. More than noticed them—I read them out loud until my lips were numb. In the story, Fiona dates another chef, Camila, and they sleep together every few chapters. Through her narrator, Claire describes a woman's body the same way she describes great food—as if she knows it, as if she loves it.

I never asked Claire if she likes women, but I didn't understand how she *couldn't* with paragraphs like that. The evidence was there on the page.

I told her she had to keep writing.

She had to make the premise of her next book so epic, everyone who heard the sound bite would have to at least skim the first few pages. I even suggested something like *Cloud Atlas*, a novel so ambitious, it was destined to succeed.

We talked for so long that eventually, Claire asked where I went to school. I couldn't have imagined a better compliment. I considered telling her that I was at Harvard too. After all, I was taking "Poetry Since 1950" and "Thoreau" that semester, among others. Every day, I wove my way through the Barker Center, under its branching antler chandelier, past the eighteenth-century portraits. *Veritas.* But I couldn't lie to Claire. I didn't even want to. So I told her that I wasn't in college but dropped in on every Harvard class I could. It was easy enough to blend in because no one ever noticed me—and that's when she touched my shoulder.

It wasn't anything more than that.

But it was more than anything I'd ever had.

She graduated that spring and left for New York. I wouldn't say I "followed" her because that word is too intentional. I just had to be around her. If not around *her*, then people like her, people who knew her. Claire mentioned that she spent every summer at her mom's place in East Hampton. So, I took jobs in the area. I kept hoping that we'd run into each other, that I'd get a chance to prove there was something special between us. After all, she heard me when no one else was listening, and I did the same for her. I encouraged her to write when she was at her lowest. I was Claire's real-life guide, the one to tell her who she is.

"Hi, Nina."

I forgot she's a brunette now.

Her oversize oxford looks like it belongs to Leo. It's Yale blue, sleeves rolled up to her wrists in chunks. I can't see an inch of her figure, definitely not the private dent of her navel. Her jeans are wide legged, hanging low on her hips and hiding everything behind them. Her sunglasses are thick, defensive. Thankfully, she takes them off and slides them into her breast pocket. By the time I stand to greet her, she's already in her chair.

I follow, out of sync.

"Thanks for coming," I say.

"I didn't really have a choice."

She looks at me warily.

A waitress arrives and asks if she can get us anything to drink.

Claire shakes her head no. I mirror her.

The waitress leaves.

"It's funny," I say, touching my fork nervously. "You know that question, If you could have dinner with anyone, living or dead, who would you choose?" I feel my pulse beating in my tongue. "I always said you, every single time."

"And here I am."

She's deadpan, toneless.

"So, what exactly do you want?" she asks.

"I just want some of your time," I say, trying to soften things.

She stares at me, her high ponytail tight.

I get the sense that she feels trapped. I don't want it to be that way.

"I'm not going to tell anyone," I say, trying to lighten the mood. And I mean it with every muscle in my smile. Why would I ruin this moment with other people? This once-in-a-lifetime crack of space and time, where I have her almost all to myself? "Besides, I know how much work it took to get here. I understand why you did it."

"You do?" she asks.

I nod eagerly.

"You spell it out in *The Starlit Ballet*," I say. "I know you based it on your relationship with Leo." Her eyes widen. "In your book, one soulmate waits for the other to mature. And in real life, *you* were waiting for Leo to recognize what the two of you have, what you've had since high school. You chose all the time periods based on classes you took with him. Now that you're together, you just want to spend time—"

Our waitress arrives to take our order.

Claire, stunned, opens her menu but doesn't read it. She just stares at the options, her eyes perfectly still. Eventually, she orders the sea bass. I say with a smile that I'll have the same thing. The waitress leaves with our menus.

"Why are you telling me this?" Claire asks.

"To prove that I understand you." I interlace my fingers like I'm praying. "And that I admire you." It takes restraint *not* to say her name now when I enjoy it so much. There's power in that syllable, in the fact that she made it her own. No one thinks *Claire* anymore without thinking *Ross*. "Everything you've done is . . . it's beyond. I don't even know how to describe it, but you would." I hold her stare. "It's aspirational— maybe that's the right word." Meanwhile, Claire picks up her glass of ice water. She plunges her spoon into the drink and stirs it, clinking edges against the sides. Eventually, she picks up an ice cube and lays it on her tongue. It crunches like gravel in her mouth.

"'Aspirational'?" She sounds skeptical as she puts down her drink, leaving three clear fingerprints in the mist. "You know I left my family, right?"

"But—"

"They don't know where I am."

"But they didn't understand you. That's what I'm trying to say. Not Miranda, not Roger, not Kira. Not the Starlites who tracked your every move in New York. Who think they know you just because they know where you live. Because they can quote from just *one* of your books." I picture the ☆-studded raves they wrote for her novel. Forget about five-star reviews. They left her constellations. "Not even Leo. I'm the only one."

"You're the only one who understands me."

"I found you, didn't I?"

"I thought we ran into each other." She states it as a matter of fact. But I hear traces of pleasure at having caught me in a lie.

I prop my elbows on the table.

"The truth is that I wanted to. I've wanted another chance with you for the past ten years. I just—it's your writing. It makes me feel like you know me, and no one knows me. Everyone looks straight through me—everyone except *you*." I hold both hands out as if I'm presenting her. "Your first manuscript, it took everything I ever felt and made it all sound important. Beautiful. I knew we had a connection, something special and—permanent."

We were this close on that bench in Cambridge. It's hard to overstate how enormous that moment still feels. At the time, I was living on my own. I'd spent most of my life with a mom who'd get so drunk at home, she wouldn't even blink when I walked past her. As if I were just noise on the floor. Disembodied scuffs. For Claire to understand me on the page, and then to sit with me and pay attention, was a shock wave. I *know* she felt it too. I understood her as much as she understood me. Her book was our own private telephone line.

"A special connection," she says, still dry.

"I knew you were a writer before anyone else. I helped you become the person you were meant to be." Her stare is blank. "And I tracked you down, didn't I? I found you twenty-five hundred miles from where you were last seen. Has anyone else?" I look rhetorically around the room. Everyone continues to eat without flinching. "It doesn't look like it, which makes me believe, really believe, that I'm the only one who could. That I know you best."

The waitress arrives with a basket of bread.

She leaves it halfway between us.

"Do you want some?" I ask.

"Why don't you tell me, since you know me so well?"

Her cold expression is a challenge. Before I can answer, she takes a roll and rips it in half. Crumbs snow on her plate. She picks up her butter knife.

"Chloe is a writer," I go on. "Because you are too."

She drops her knife.

"What do you want?" she asks more aggressively.

"I want you to believe me."

"Believe what?"

"That I understand you. Because even though you're"—again, I swallow her name—"and I'm me, we are each other's one-in-a-billion."

Her expression doesn't budge.

"Do you remember the manuscript you shared with me?" I ask. "Fiona was dating that woman . . ." My voice comes out shaky. I take a long sip of water. "You said once that when you're writing, 'You need to rip your story out of real life.' Right?" Nothing. "Their love was so . . ." I make a fist. "Hard and *real*. I know you *think* that you love Leo, but I'm asking for the chance to do it better. If you're open to loving me."

Our food arrives.

The white filets steam.

I can't believe I said it all.

As much as I hoped for it, and worked for it, I never imagined that I'd get to tell Claire Ross how I feel. I barely think about my feelings when I'm alone. But I know that I'm drawn to *her*—and I would be in any gender, in any time period.

She picks up her fork and knife.

"Do you think you can manipulate me because you know who I am?" she asks, angling the knife toward me. It's subtle but unmissable.

"No." I blush. "I mean everything I said."

She digs into her food, butchering her fish without any apparent desire to eat. She cuts the meat into shreds and ignores the spinach beside it, as if there isn't a paragraph about it on the front of the menu, as if it isn't the crown jewel of the Farmer's Daughter. I take a bite, but I can't eat more while she's wrecking her meal.

She puts down her silverware.

"'Each other's one-in-a-billion'?" she asks at last, her voice as cold as our drinks. "Do you know how many people tell me they're in love with me? I got the letters every single day, whole bins of them. Most were in languages I couldn't read."

"But how many of them found you?"

She won't answer that.

"Who else knows you like I do?" I go on. "Not even Leo does." Her head scoots back an inch. "You've spent, what, two months together? Total?"

The waitress returns, but I can't tear my eyes from Claire. Everything else is a muted halo around her. I vaguely hear the waitress ask if we need anything. Otherwise, I don't register any of her details—not her hair color, not her expression. She disappears into the hazy frame around the only one I see. Claire's lips are dusty pink, in a firm line.

"Just the check," she urges.

I put my fork down.

How can she not see the proof right in front of her? I'm here, two feet away. Who else followed her halfway across the world? Who else cares this much?

The waitress returns too soon with the bill. Claire pays in cash, dropping the bills with relief, as if they were weighing her down. I scramble for the white envelope I got from Miranda and put money on the table, wincing with each twenty.

Claire has one foot out the door.

"Wait!" I chase after her.

Outside, everything is shades of purple. It feels like we're in the cool shadow of the mountains just barely visible around us. Claire finds her car on the street and opens the door. She slides into the driver's seat before I can stop her. I manage to clamp one hand on the window, preventing her from shutting it.

"I'm sorry," I say.

She keeps her fingers on the handle.

"I'm sorry, but I deserve better than this. I was there when you needed someone. I said you had a gift when no one else would *read* your work, let alone pay for it. And now here I am, promising that your secret is safe, and you don't even thank me. You owe me more—more—" I hear the tortured desperation in my voice and notice that Nina the elegant detective is gone. I don't even know who's left. Someone raw, unnamed. Hell-bent.

"What exactly do I owe you?"

"More time."

She stares at me for so long, it's as if she wants to intimidate me into looking away. But I don't budge. I love her eyes. They're the warmest green I've ever seen. Tight pupils, wide bands of color. Eventually, she releases the handle.

"Do you need a ride somewhere?" she asks reluctantly.

"I'd love one."

"Where are you headed?"

I picture my ground-level room at the motel—the barred window, square meals in the mini fridge. Claire's shoes look cleaner than the carpet.

"I'm staying by the airport," I say vaguely.

"I'll drive you."

I can't move.

"You want more time, so I'll drive you."

The passenger side seems far away.

Part of me is afraid that if I give up her door, she might slam it shut and leave without me. Then again, she'd only be running back to my hidden cameras. She can't have sex or chew cereal without me listening in, much less plan a getaway.

I take a deep breath and let go.

As I walk around the hood, her door shuts. I speed up, yank mine open, and jump in. Wasting no time, she puts the car in reverse and turns toward me to look out the rear window. The top few buttons of her oxford are undone, exposing some of her breastbone. If I leaned forward a few inches, I might be able to hear her heartbeat.

She catches my eyes. I look away.

Before I know it, we're on the freeway, still picking up speed. It's a half-hour drive to the airport, but at this rate, we'll be there in fifteen minutes. The speedometer keeps rising. There are no cars ahead of us in the fast lane.

"You want to share how you knew all that?" she asks.

The car keeps accelerating.

We're hurtling past everyone on our right, now going almost ninety miles an hour. I grip my armrest and watch the median blur. I can't let anything happen to her. My nightmare comes back to me just in my hands, the feeling of her skin without structure. She turns to stare at me, taking her eyes off the road for two excruciating seconds.

"Claire, please," I beg, uncomfortable.

"I asked you a question."

"Your mom hired me to find you," I admit.

Claire faces me again.

"Please, watch the road," I insist.

"My mom?"

"Yes, I'm a private eye. She put me on your case. And I *knew* your book was part of it. Everyone said you disappeared without a trace—but we were surrounded by *The Starlit Ballet*. At all times, on all sides. They were *pieces* of you, weren't they? Six-by-nine-inch chunks. They had to make up a *trail*. Or at least an *arrow*. So I read your book—for the hundredth time—and dug into your time at Exeter. It didn't take me long to put it together." *Because I know you, Claire.* "But I never told Miranda what I found. She doesn't know anything about San Francisco. No one else is going to show up here—if that's what you want."

"What about you?"

"What *about* me?"

It takes me a beat to understand.

"No one knows I'm here either," I say.

Claire looks at me skeptically.

"Please, I wouldn't lie to you. I only want what's best for you."

She seems to consider my words before taking her foot off the pedal. The car slows, dropping to eighty miles an hour, then seventy, and then finally to the speed limit. I release a lungful of air I didn't know I had in me. Claire seems calmer now. She leans back in her seat, letting the leather feel every inch of her spine.

"You only want what's best for me," she repeats.

I swear to her that's the truth.

Watch her drive.

"You know, I do remember you," she says slowly.

The car vibrates over a rougher patch of the highway. My body feels like it's buzzing. On the other side of the median, for some reason, I only see the Teslas. There are more of them here than in New York, all with retractable door handles. Each short stripe looks like a metal stitch holding the car together—sealing off the way in, the way out.

"You look the same," she says.

"Your hair's darker now."

She fights it, and then, she laughs.

We drive in peace for a few miles. The engine sounds like the bass to a perfect song. Eventually, Claire takes one hand off the wheel and lays it on the console. The edge of her pinkie is so close. There's just one smooth stripe of leather between us. I stare at her little finger. It looks like a matchstick compared to mine. I wonder if she uses it at all or if it just glides through her life. We drive another mile, and it stays there, tiny and blind. If I tried to hold it, I'm almost sure I could. But how are you supposed to touch the one you love the most? I don't know if I'd be able to stop—whatever it is I'd start to do.

"How long are you in San Francisco?" she asks.

"That depends. What about you?"

"I'm not sure yet."

A short pause.

"Leo wants to travel." She proceeds to tell me what I already know, listing countries they might see on a trip around the world. When she talks about their plan, though, she starts every sentence with "Leo says . . ." or

"Leo thinks . . . ," as if she's had nothing to do with it. Her hand gets even closer to me as she gesticulates. Apparently, their trip might take longer than a year, but a lot of the details still need to be worked out. "And honestly, I haven't thought that far ahead. Which is a little out of character, isn't it?"

She turns to me as if I'm the expert.

I look away from her hand.

"It's not," I fumble.

"So, you really don't know how long you're in town?"

"I didn't think that far ahead either. Like I said, I just wanted to see you again. And I thought that chance was worth—everything."

A plane flies across the horizon, right through the stars. I'm tempted to ask Claire if she'd consider that "starlit." I have a thousand questions for her, but I don't want to overwhelm her more than I already have. Writers are sensitive people. I've always believed that they feel more intensely. They *must* in order to find a blank page so stimulating, to record infinitesimal details with such precision. I've given Claire a lot to process, and it's going to take time for someone as thoughtful as she is to work through it all.

We drive in silence.

It's wild to share a mundane moment with someone extraordinary—even wilder than talking to her over dinner, because this is something I never imagined. I never pictured Claire just driving from A to B, clipping her toenails, or pumping gas. And here she is, keeping her foot on the pedal and her eyes on the road. The longer we go, the more intimate it feels, speeding through the night. Her profile in the soft glow of head-lights. She doesn't fidget, doesn't move more than she needs to in order to stay in her lane.

Eventually, I ask Claire to drop me off a mile before my motel. After all, I'm competing with Leo and his palace right now, which isn't just full of physical luxuries but intellectual ones—massive bookshelves, photos from around the world. I may be as smart as he is, and even better read, but I don't have the proof.

Claire pulls into a rest stop and parks.

I step out of her car with just one foot.

"When can I see you again?" I ask.

I'm still in the front seat.

I won't move until we make another plan.

"Look, I'm grateful that you helped me in college," she says, her gaze low. "But—"

"There must be something I can do for you. Think about it. I'll do anything." The highway is loud. "Please, Claire. Everybody needs help."

We lock stares.

I'm not just begging. I'm insisting.

Something special happens when we're together. It rearranges us, somehow, and we're no longer the same. Ten years ago, we had just *one* conversation, and it shaped the rest of our lives. How much more powerful could a day be? A whole night? Even right now, it feels like my veins are shifting inside me. She must feel it too. I stare in her eyes. From here, they reflect the sky—a cloudy stripe of the Milky Way, scraps of zodiacs. Her expression is fixed, but the longer we stay like this, the more her resistance appears to melt. She has to work *with* me, doesn't she? I know where she's hiding. I have leverage.

"If you want, you can stop by tomorrow," she concedes.

"Your place?"

She looks weary.

"I thought you could read my mind?"

TWENTY

"In his eyes, I see every person he's ever been. I see the one who's been through everything with me, everything this short, wild life has to offer."
—*Claire Ross,* The Starlit Ballet

I'm parked near their house, eager for Leo to go to work.

I listened to them fuck this morning, as usual. I'm tapping my hands on the steering wheel now, willing him to leave. The live feed of their bedroom is silent. They must be in the closet, getting dressed. I wonder how I'd act in his place, if Claire were stepping into jeans next to me. *How are you?* I'd probably lean on that one simple question, that soft way of getting in her head. I'd save more complicated ones— *Does living in so many characters erode your sense of self?* And, *When you entertain the world, do you feel all powerful or the opposite, like you serve everyone?*—for after her first cup of coffee. But if we were both just reaching for shirts, *How are you?* would be perfect. I wonder what her sleepy, half-dressed answer would be.

They walk to the first floor.

"What time is your meeting today?" she asks.

"It might not work today."

He murmurs something else.

I crane toward my phone on the passenger seat.

"Don't you think it's important?" she asks.

They're in the hallway, steps from the door. Leo looks sharp in a slim-fit oxford and dark slacks. Claire's in a blue maxi dress made of something so silky, she could wear it to bed. It cinches at her waist, strings dangling onto her thighs. With every step, the hem flows around her ankles. It's almost Aphroditic, swirling foam as she emerges from the ocean. Leo drops his hands into his pockets. There's almost a foot of space between the two of them. Did he answer her question or not? I was staring too much at Claire to notice.

He kisses her goodbye on the cheek.

A beat later, he's outside, trotting down to the garage.

As soon as his car passes, I run-walk to the bottom of their stairs. I leap up two at a time and let myself in with the key under their mat. Claire's still standing where he kissed her goodbye. In the flesh, her expression is sadder than I realized. Her whole body language is heavy, as if there's something so dense on her mind, it's physically pinning her down. Only her stare moves to greet me, coloring the corners of her eyes. I wave hello.

She doesn't respond.

"Is everything all right?" I ask.

I'm smiling, even though I'm worried about her. Because here we are, alone together. Here we are, with almost nothing left between us, nothing except her sea-foam. I'm standing right here in the video I've been watching.

"You came back," she says.

I tell her of course.

She rubs her brow.

"You said to stop by," I remind her.

I feel very aware of my hands. I'm squeezing them too hard, but there's nowhere else for this intensity to go. Claire has her own magnetic field.

"In your car last night," I go on. "I said—"

"I remember."

Of course she does.

She glances at the nearest window, shuttered with curtains. The only noises are coming from birds, bright little peeps and squawks. I want to take another step toward her. Standing there in her bare feet, in that thin fabric, where only I can see her—I've never seen her like this. It's a vulnerable view of someone gifted. She's mesmerizingly exposed. Everyone strong and powerful is really only strong and powerful in specific places, under specific conditions. But here she is without a pen, without her family and fans, even without her famous face. She's Claire Ross, but right now, she might as well be Jane Doe.

"You're not going to leave, are you?" she asks.

"There has to be something I can do."

Her stare is green fire.

"Anything," I insist.

We stay perfectly still.

I hold my hands even tighter.

"Ok*ay*," she says eventually. The word feels noncommittal, but of course she has to mean it. I'm part of her secret. I'm part of her San Francisco getaway, as much as the Golden Gate Bridge and steep streets. "I think I have an idea, if you really are just trying to help." Her tone is exceedingly cautious, the words trickling out like slow drips from a faucet. "I don't know what you can do about them, to be honest. But—" She glances again at the window. It's a leading look, showing me something on the other side.

"Do you hear that?" she asks.

Her expression is pained.

I listen hard, but all I hear are birds.

Suddenly, I remember Sofia. Her efficient gestures in that neat office. Her precise descriptions. *It takes a particular kind of person to love absolute quiet.* Of course. If Claire's going to spend the day writing, she needs me to get rid of the noise. I imagine her trying to start a new chapter upstairs, the birds scrambling every idea.

"Leo's neighbors are out of town, but they pay someone to stock the feeder," she says. "I'm not expecting anything. But since you did manage to find me . . . maybe you can figure something out." She takes a step backward. My palm is stinging. I glance down to see the skin dotted with red arcs, thread-thin marks from my nails. When I look back up, Claire is gone.

A door shuts on the second floor.

I stare at the place where she must be, diagonally overhead. The birds make their music. I'm torn between following her upstairs and heading outside. Is she going to try and write up there now? *Claire couldn't think with any noise. If we were in the library, and someone started to talk, I could see it on her face. It looked like a city was collapsing in her mind.* I find myself drifting to the front door, hating to leave but needing to help. I can always come back when it's quiet, when we're truly and completely alone.

Outside, the feeder is popular.

I watch the birds eat from just a few feet away. The feeder hangs at eye level, swinging in a slow loop. I could just take it down, but that wouldn't get rid of the birds who've grown to expect it, who'd sing in this tree and wait for it to come back. I look behind me up at Leo's, to find Claire's face in the glass. She backs out of sight. Did she look concerned? I stand still, wishing she'd come back. *Don't worry,* I want to tell her. *There's no reason to worry. No one will take better care of you than me.*

~

I drive back to Leo's from Walmart. It's later than I would've liked, the light already past its peak. I spent all morning in different stores, looking for the right supplies. At one point, I found myself in the newborn section of T. J. Maxx, oblivious to how I got there. I was just staring at cribs, as if I had a kid in need. At least the people are friendlier here. I met ten different clerks, all sunny and proactive. They treated me like they believed in my cause, like they were Starlites and knew who I was helping. My new tools are next to me now on the passenger seat: one plastic mixing bowl, one box of latex gloves, and one jug of CyKill.

I park near Leo's to find the same curtains drawn. There's no sign of Claire from here, but I watched her come home from lunch not too long ago. I turn to face the box of gloves. A cartoonishly inflated white hand waves at me from one corner. A fine-print note cautions that these may cause allergic reactions. It's a cute warning for a product that will protect me from rat poison. I puncture the cardboard center and peel out a pair. The gloves are translucent, go on easy. They feel like dipping my hands in water.

I carry my CyKill and mixing bowl outside.

The warnings on this jug are bigger, more urgent. I read the whole label back at Walmart. Apparently, most rats eat enough of the green crystals to die within hours. Less frequently, it takes two or more days for the poison to work its way through a body. As I cross the street, I feel like I'm in an Agatha Christie novel. Poison was her weapon of choice. That's because despite killing so many characters, she was a pacifist at heart. She avoided graphic, face-to-face murders and chose death by injection instead.

I walk toward the birds.

The house behind them looks like an Italian villa—whitewashed facade, stone tile roof. Every window has its own terrace. And every one is shuttered.

I stop next to the feeder, where a finch stares at me from the rim. He's a bright mix of red and blood orange. I'm not looking forward to this. Maybe I'm another pacifist, another poisoning pacifist. I unhook the feeder, sending him and a few others into the air. They spray out in a vivid burst, like drops in a Jackson Pollock painting. I empty the seed into my plastic bowl, then mix in the CyKill. When everything's blended, I fill the tube and rehang it.

It swings lazily from side to side.

I toss my gloves and bowl into the nearest trash bin. They land on large black bags, thorny with edges and corners. I store the CyKill in my trunk. On my way to Leo's, I see birds already back on the feeder. They're every color, making every sound. The rosy finch nibbles with high expectations. I don't know if I believe in reincarnation, but I hope the birds get more than this—more than one chance before they disappear.

After climbing the stairs again, I find their front door unlocked. I smile as if it's a private message from Claire, a phrase in her book that only I underlined. The lights are off on the first floor. I walk straight to the kitchen sink and run my hands under hot water. With three pumps of soap, I scrub my knuckles and palms until they're pink and tender. I press so hard my fingers curve into waves, testing the strength of my bones.

Claire's walking downstairs.

"Problem solved," I announce, drying my hands on a paper towel. I can only see her from the knees down. Her dress looks darker in this low light, less like froth, more like the bottom of the ocean. She slows down when she hears me but doesn't stop. Standing on the last stair, she flips on the lights and looks even more beautiful. It doesn't matter that she's in her disguise because her eyes are exactly the same. Her cheekbones, the cartilage in her nose—they're what I remember. She's still Claire in every version.

She glides to a kitchen cabinet and removes a glass, looking more at me than at the cup in her hand. I notice a pen behind her ear, and my heart jumps, as if this is a peek at what she's working on, a few words read off a draft. She approaches the sink. I step aside, hiding my hands so she can't see them—too raw, almost scaly. Birds twitter and peep, as if I haven't done a thing about them, as if I spent all morning glued to my live stream, listening to her breathe.

She fills her cup with water.

"They sound louder," she says.

"I promise. Just give it a day."

She looks at me skeptically, but I'm too thrilled to care. I'm an arm's length away from the pen she's using. I'm one room away from her newest page.

"I promise," I repeat. "Just give it a day."

She takes a sip of water.

"I'm going upstairs now," she says.

She walks away too soon.

"Can I stay?" I ask.

She stops in the living room.

Turns around to face me.

"Please just—" she starts.

"I've seen every interview you've ever given." I make an effort to keep my voice soft. "Every single one." At first, it was an overwhelming amount of material. But even with Claire, someone who feels infinite, there's a limited amount to know.

"Where is this going?" she asks.

"I'd watch you, and you know what struck me? Everything, of course, but you know what *really* struck me? The love for you." I feel more composed than I was last night. *Now*, I can make my point. Make it so coherent, so airtight, she'll have to understand. "I used to wonder what that's like. Sure, pop stars know, but . . . when pop stars talk about their lives, they use plain vanilla words. Obvious and empty clichés. They have their gifts, but they're not as rigorously educated. They're not as intellectually fertile as . . ."

I hold out my palms, gesturing to her.

"But ask a writer what that's like? Ask Claire Ross? Now *there's* hope. *There's* my chance to step inside an exceptional life—or, at least, to hear you describe it. And you did. On Jimmy Kimmel, after his audience finally stopped shrieking for you, he asked, 'How does that feel?' You said, 'Mildly intoxicating but mostly isolating.' *Isolating*. I had to sit with that for a while before I realized one of your secrets."

"I have secrets?" Claire asks.

"Not from me."

"Then from who?"

"Everyone else. And one is that your life is . . . bizarre." My tone is still full of praise. "People know you're different. But unconsciously, they minimize everything strange about you. Because they *want* to like

223

you. So they underestimate how much of a—the word 'freak' has a bad reputation, but it might be the best one for you. It's a paradox, isn't it? Millions relate to your story, but *you're* unrelatable. You rarely go in public. You work all alone. Every sentence you write has to be one that's never been written before. So no matter how relatable you seem, you never will be—which isn't unlike me. I'm a freak too." I put both hands on my chest. "And whether or not you're ready to believe it, the only person you can *click* with is your most devoted fan, because I'm on the fringe with you. We're outliers, Claire. We live at extremes. *That's why* I understand you. *That's why* I'm the only one who can."

Claire doesn't move.

Her water's a contained blur.

"You know me because you watched my interviews?" she dares.

"It's more than that. I . . ." Drank them. Memorized them. "I'll teach you things you didn't know about yourself. I'll give you everything I have." I feel the insides of my empty hands. "We have a window into each other. An unusual window. Don't make the same mistake you made ten years ago, walking away from it. Please, let me stay."

Her hesitation drags on.

I feel more vulnerable than I expected, waiting for her answer. As if I've turned myself inside out. Maybe I should've executed some master plan—full of opportunities for me to be charming, sophisticated—leading her into my arms. But the root of our relationship was that we didn't have to pretend. Our bond was real and deep from the start.

She takes a sip of water.

I watch her neck roll.

"You know what scares me about you?" she asks after a pause.

"What?"

"I'm not afraid of you at all."

Her tone is flat and honest.

She climbs upstairs.

Her door shuts overhead.

I feel myself drift over to the staircase and stand at the bottom. Her last sentence stays with me. It's not exactly Jane Austen's "You pierce my soul" or Emily Brontë's "Whatever our souls are made of, his and mine are the same." But it is something. It's Claire starting to think about how I make her feel. It's Claire starting to wrap her mind around what we are, what we've always been for each other. There's something mundane but perfectly accurate about "I'm not afraid of you at all," because I am her safest place. Maybe that's why I should take her home, keep her safe for the rest of her life.

TWENTY-ONE

"'Sorry, how long have you been together?' Mom asks.

'For as long as I can remember.'"
—*Claire Ross*, The Starlit Ballet

I park near Leo's the next morning in pink light.

There's a soft lump under the feeder. It's red and blood orange, right on the sidewalk. Only two birds perch on the plastic rim. They're brown crumbs, no more than an ounce each. They stay in place, heads bent toward the seed in drowsy arches. Just a few notes peep every now and then, as if the two of them have been here for a while, swallowing green food. Ten feet away, there's a yellow-throated mound on the edge of Leo's lawn. Four more color the end of the block, as if they might've dropped out of midair. If Claire's as sensitive to noise as I think, I wonder if she heard them hit the ground.

I spent most of yesterday afternoon in her living room. She was upstairs for hours right above me, working in that blue dress, feeling her way through a new idea, doing everything I ever wanted to see—and I stayed there on the sofa, staring at the ceiling. I just kept wringing my hands, kept toying with that idea of taking her home. *How* would I do it? The *when* is more straightforward. Miranda's money will only last a few more days. But I kept wondering *how*, imagining my answers. I don't want to take her by force. I don't want to find a secluded place back in New York, somewhere my neighbors couldn't hear everything.

I want her to *want* me.

Deep down, of course, she does.

I watch Claire and Leo on my phone. They're in the hallway, saying their goodbyes. She's wearing a long, white knit dress. It clings to her like another layer of skin. It's hard to see her face with Leo standing between us. For a second, I cover his body with two fingers, so that Claire's edges are the only ones in sight.

"What time's the meeting?" she asks.

He tries to kiss her.

She leans back.

"Are you skipping again?" she asks.

"Claire, please."

"Are you?"

"Getting to Saint Luke's is a nightmare."

"You can't miss another one."

He reaches past her to lean on the wall.

She flinches—did I see that right?

"We can't go through this every day," he says.

"It's important."

"If it's that fucking important . . ."

I lose the end of his sentence as they emerge on the outdoor stairs. Their features are indistinct from here—noseless, mouthless. Leo's words stay with me. He sounded like my mom, resisting Alcoholics Anonymous. She'd say something like that whenever I reminded her of a meeting. *If it's that fucking important, how about you go for me?* Those were always held in churches. What other "meetings" happen there during the day? On my phone, I search for the one he mentioned, but there are so many Saint Luke's within driving distance, it's useless.

Leo's car passes.

Is he—an addict in recovery?

Slipping in recovery?

I almost don't believe it.

I've heard his voice on tape for days now. He never slurred once. Sure, I did miss a few large chunks of time. They went out to dinner last night, and I've been sleeping, myself, tuning out for six hours in a row. Sure, I do pay more attention to Claire when they're together, making everything else seem fuzzier, less important.

Did I miss something?

But I didn't see any signs of it in his past. When people have a debilitating addiction, it shows up somewhere, and Leo's record is too clean. That's why I thought Claire had chosen him. He didn't have any dark cracks. Did I see him all wrong? Now that I think about it, he did leave a desk job and then go awhile without one. He spent two years traveling the world—and what do I know about that time? Only that he was accountable to no one, jumping from place to place. A lot can happen in two years when no one else is watching.

I open my car door.

The red feathers are still there. They look like spilled raspberries on the other side of the street. His face is hidden, beak flat or sideways underneath. I'll get to him later, but now, Claire needs my help with something else. She had this conversation with Leo yesterday too. I remember it in snippets. And the day before that, Leo must've been trying to skip another one. This has been happening since I got here.

I step closer to Leo's, disoriented.

Remembering Mom.

Like I haven't in years.

As if I'm ten years old again, in that apartment. When she sold perfumes, she came home every day smelling like all of them. Aggressively floral, faintly spiced. Her uniform was a black sheath dress with black hose and platform heels. I can see her coming home in that outfit, opening the front door. Mom thin, the uniform tight. When she crossed the threshold, there was graffiti on the stairwell behind her: a smile emoji made to look like it was dripping, an octopus with a crown, and block letters I couldn't read, maybe nonsense.

I remember slipping on that stairwell and coming home with a scraped elbow. I was washing it when Mom walked over to the kitchenette and saw the pink inch of water. Our sink was always slow to drain. She emptied her beer on my cut. The bubbles gave my forearm a thousand eyes. She was too foggy to react when I screamed. As if I were no more real than her movies. She went back to her daybed for the rest of the weekend.

Mom wasn't a good student of the program either. It was only when things got truly terrifying that she ever went to a meeting—after she fought someone stronger, after she woke up on a highway underpass. Those were chilling moments because it was never just her life she was risking. It was mine too. My tiny, little existence.

I find Claire inside on the sofa. She's staring blankly ahead, as if Leo took part of her to work with him. The muscles in her face are slack. She looks at me too deadened or distracted to react. Without thinking, I sit next to her. We're just one gray suede cushion apart. Her hands are shaking on her knees. She hides them under her armpits, hugging herself around the rib cage.

I feel like I've walked into the wrong house.

I thought I'd found their happily ever after. But what if Leo turned out to be different from the man I expected? Different from the man *she* expected? After all, she didn't spend much time with him in high school. For the next decade, he was more a daydream than anything else. When she met him in real life, maybe there were problems she didn't anticipate.

"Claire, I've been honest with you, so I hope you'll be honest with me." I resist the urge to touch her. "Are you having any problems with Leo?"

She holds her neck.

"Problems?" she asks.

"Yes, problems."

No answer.

"I heard you and him . . . ," I start.

"You heard?" Her eyebrows rise.

"Nothing."

"What—*how* did you . . . ?" She scans the room, then turns the intensity of her stare on me. "So, you want to tell me where the bugs are?"

I feel cold.

"It's not a question," she adds.

She sounds so sure of herself, there's no way I could convince her otherwise. She knows I have an eye in this place—but she doesn't know I have two. I stand and lead her past the leafy plant without looking at it, not even seeing green in my periphery. We head upstairs, my stomach sinking. It's never been a point of pride, hiding in other people's private moments. In this case, it's also a breach of Claire's trust—and that's what I want more than anything. That's what I've wanted for the past ten years, ever since her first page one.

Their bedroom is a mess: comforter in a tangled heap, pajamas balled up between the sheets, and pillows strewn across the carpet. The blackout shades are still drawn on every window, rolling the clock in here back a few hours.

"In the bedroom," she says.

She sounds impressed with the audacity.

I reach under the headboard and grab the camera. It looks like a bottomless hole through my palm. I stuff it into my pocket, apologizing.

Claire sits on the bed, looking exhausted. I can feel her pain from here. It's so palpable I don't know how I missed it. It must've been her magnetic field, warping the world around her. I can't help but notice, though, that her pain doesn't make her any less beautiful. It doesn't change the fact that she's on a bed in the shadows, her neck limp, her knees knocking.

She leans back onto her palms. Little bones peek through the middle of her chest. I feel every part of my body heat up. How could I not? I've had a hundred dreams that started just like this. In my mind, I've kissed her more times than I can count. I've wrapped my hands around her waist, felt her pulse in my fingers. I've put my head between her legs and felt her pull me by the hair even closer, giving as much as she got.

Claire hasn't written a sex scene since college. With all the experiences she's had since then—all the ways she's grown up and into herself—how would she describe it now? Maybe she hasn't written about it because no one's loved her softly enough, carefully enough. Leo's probably never touched her the way a woman would, the way only women know how. I want to make her feel so good, she'll have to write it down. I want to touch her until she's scrambling for a pen and scrawling on her arm—or mine. I won't let go until she's inspired.

She stands up too soon and walks past me.

At the end of the hall, she stops next to a doorway. I follow her to the threshold as she steps inside. This is where she's been writing. The room is spare—little more than a chaise longue and an uncluttered desk—but with a breathtaking view of the Golden Gate Bridge. Its red towers poke through a thick cloud. There are dozens of sailboats on the Bay, all gliding across the water as if they aren't already in paradise, as if there's anywhere better to be. Claire sits in front of her laptop, then turns around to face me. Her posture sags.

"There must be something wrong with me," she says.

"There's *nothing* wrong with you."

"Because today, I don't want you to leave."

~

I spend the morning on their block, gathering birds into a trash bag with gloved hands. Most of their bellies are swollen. There's a half teaspoon of blood under every beak, staining the sidewalk. Some lawns have red-tipped patches.

It reminds me of the news Mom watched every night. Missing children found in shallow graves. Brutal murders in a gated community. She consumed so much tragedy, she watched it without flinching. She'd just lie on her daybed, dreary eyed, spooning strawberry Jell-O into her mouth. Her favorite foods were always a poisonous shade of red. I'd be doing my homework, but I looked up whenever I heard the warning for graphic content. It never felt like a caution. It felt like the anchors were asking people to pay attention. Eventually, I wound up like Mom. I watched the news blank faced too. Teen gunmen on killing sprees. An eight-year-old stabbed in an unprovoked attack. I can see a lot without flinching.

Pick up another bird.

Rub my eyes with my forearm.

All morning, I've been seeing her.

She used to have big plans for herself. Her first dream was to be a movie star. I'm not sure she ever let that dream go, even when she did nothing but watch TV. When Mom and Dad fought, he'd needle that soft spot. He'd call her a "diva without a stage," a "diva without a show." It was cruel, but he was a little bit right. I always thought that's why she was so easily offended at work: she felt like she was meant for something more. How *dare* Jenelle tell her where she could smoke? She idolized all the Old Hollywood stars—Grace Kelly, Lauren Bacall. The famous elites. The people who mattered. The people she might've been.

I pick up another sparrow.

This time, I catch a glimpse inside the bag, at the heap of feathers, dull eyes, and scaly feet. I do my best to go numb. Like I'm Mom watching the news.

~

Later that morning, I find myself in the living room, looking upstairs. Every now and then, I hear Claire hit the space bar. It's a quick, mechanical pulse. A sign that her writing's alive. The steps groan quietly under my feet, just a whisper that I'm coming.

On the second floor, Claire's door is cracked open. I watch a thin strip of her from the threshold. She's so wrapped up in whatever she's typing—facing that bright screen, hands leaping across the keyboard—that she doesn't seem to hear me. I want this moment to last—and maybe there's a way that it can. I take out my phone, open the camera. Eventually, Claire's fingers stall. She looks left, clearly wrestling with an idea, and I snap a picture of her profile. When she looks back at her screen, I feel an urge to get a closer shot.

The door creaks as I push it open.

I fumble to hide my phone.

"Nina." She jolts in her chair. "What is it?"

"I—I just wanted to check on you."

She seems to relax.

I take a step forward, feeling my hands. They're getting drier and redder every day that I'm here. Maybe I'm scrubbing too hard, but I have to. If I'm going to touch Claire eventually, I need to be clean. She can't end up like one of my birds, misshapen and floppy.

"Do you want to go for a walk?" I ask.

She glances at her laptop, visibly weighing the options.

"If you want to stay," I cut in, "I understand, but . . ."

"All right," she says, shutting her computer.

She stands and passes me, coming so close that I feel her exhale on the corner of my mouth. It stuns me as she walks downstairs. I follow a few steps behind, touching my lip. She's already on the first floor by the time I pull myself together. As we slip on our shoes, I stare at the knobs in the back of her neck: three in a row, right under her hairline. Round hints of her beautiful spine. She rubs them as if she can feel me watching.

We head outside in sync.

There's no one else on the street with us. Even the trees are mostly empty, mostly quiet. Claire's black ponytail shines in glossy patches, like sunlight on dark water. It's a perfect moment. Our arms swing right next to each other.

"You said my mom hired you."

I tell her that's right.

"How're they doing?" she asks.

They feel like a distant memory.

It takes time to remember.

"Well, Miranda's taking it pretty hard. I stayed with her while I was working on the case. It always seemed like she was on the verge of breaking down. Kira did a better job of coping, but only because she knew you were okay. And Roger . . ." Claire doesn't react to his name. "He's . . . frozen. If you're still alive, he doesn't want to move on."

"He'll meet someone else."

We take a left.

"The older I get, the more I understand the reality of remarriage," she adds. "I used to think it was the most cold-blooded thing in the world. I thought that if my person died, I'd keep my vows, keep their photos up." She shrugs.

"You're also happier alone than most people."

She looks slyly at me.

"I forgot," she says. "You know all my secrets."

I shrug like a guilty woman.

"Anything that would surprise me?" she asks.

"Where to begin?"

I savor the challenge.

"Your interviews . . . ," I start, remembering clips I'd watch in Riverhead. "You know what else struck me?" She shakes her head no. "The physical vulnerability of them. You went on every high-profile show with the whole world knowing you'd be there. Including the unstable. The dark and deranged. People who think they married you in all their past lives. And you still went on TV, not knowing how many threats were in the front row.

"I realized you could only risk your safety because you cared about your work—more. You, Claire Miranda"—I add her middle name as a flourish, blending them to sound like one exotic word—"love your work more than you love yourself." My tone is still marveling. "I don't mean that as a flaw. But most people don't want to see that side of you. Because it feels a little . . . dangerous. Maybe even unholy. For someone to care more about a story than about their own arms, legs." Claire looks more intrigued the longer I go on, as if I'm rearranging: my lips sliding left, eyes sliding right. I can tell that she agrees.

"I know." I'm gentle.

"Enough about me."

She sounds uncomfortable.

Maybe it's easier to be known superficially by millions than it is to be known very well by one. All that love might not add up the way I thought it did.

"Were you always this way?" I press.

I can feel that I'm probing a soft spot.

She takes long steps.

"I was bullied," she admits.

I picture the box in her elementary school gym. Dry blood in the dark. Just how many *mean girls* forced her inside? Now that I'm thinking about it, if there were only *a couple*, Claire probably could've wriggled out of their grasp. She probably could've shouted for help. But maybe there were more kids involved. Maybe Claire was so outnumbered, she didn't even try to fight until they'd locked her inside.

"Let's talk about you," she says.

"Me?"

"Tell me about your family."

I hold my pace, even though her question catches me off guard. We pass a few more narrow mansions. They're crammed together, less than a handful of space between them. The Bay looks like a series of blue dashes on the other side.

"I told you," I say. "On that bench in Cambridge."

"I know."

"My mom and dad divorced when I was eight," I add, refreshing her memory. "They were addicts." Claire doesn't interrupt me, but she must remember. I remember everything about that conversation—the view of the Charles River. Claire's jean shorts. She had freckles on her left thigh, a gappy line of brown spots down to her knee.

"But you still loved them?" she asks.

Hairs prickle up my neck.

The question isn't dangerous.

But my body seems to think it is.

"Nina?"

Mom always insisted that I do my homework. Even when she couldn't get the words out. *Do . . . it.* She'd point at the round table in the living room, next to the hanging laundry. Once I was sitting there with my backpack, she'd return to the TV. It was the brightest thing in our apartment, a cube of the sun. I still don't know why Mom cared about my homework. Maybe she wanted to keep me quiet. Keep me out of trouble she wasn't equipped to handle. Or maybe she did want me to end up in a better place. Regardless, I read the Bill of Rights with the MGM lion roaring. Mom sighing when Debbie Reynolds came on screen.

Loved them?

Even at her best, Mom was never fully there. Her obsessional loop was always right behind her eyes. A lone wheel turning in the back of her mind. Even on her clearest days, she'd change clothes on her daybed with the front door open. If we were both leaving the apartment at the same time, she'd ask me the same question sometimes twice in a row. *You don't listen, do you?* I asked her once. Her reply was incoherent.

"Hello?"

"I'm just . . ." I piece it together. "You know what they were good at?" Claire shakes her head no. "My dad stopped working thirty years ago. That's when he started living off his veteran's checks. He stayed at home . . ." I remember him jogging in place in the living room, his hands in front of his face. *Stray dogs are smarter than pets,* he'd say. Hook, jab. *We fend for ourselves.* Mom would reply, *I guess we're all wild here, aren't we?* "Mom had jobs, but she stuck it to her boss every chance she got. No one ever offended her and got away with it. Even if that meant there was no one left." I shrug. "They knew how to be alone."

"A family of loners," Claire says.

"It made room for their obsessions."

A brief pause.

"When you're addicted, you're never really cured, are you?" she asks.

"No, you're always 'in recovery.'"

I watch her.

Is she going to talk about Leo now?

"It's never just the addict who's at risk," I say carefully, walking under a canopy tree. Its branches spread like black veins overhead, twisting through shades of green. All the way out to craggy and white, sun-bitten edges. I keep my eyes on Claire, her profile marbled with shadow. "It's everyone around him too—that is, if he doesn't take the problem seriously and get help." *You know how this works,* I almost add. *You wrote about it better than anyone.*

"So, what'd you do in Cambridge after I left?" she asks.

I don't want to change the subject.

"Did you hear what I said?" I ask.

"Every word."

We leave the canopy.

"Did you hear what *I* said?" she probes.

Maybe she needs more time.

What was her question?

"I didn't stay long," I admit. "I'd already earned my unofficial degree." She puzzles. "It's thirty-two courses to graduate, right? Well, I'd audited twice as many by then, all big lectures. In a way, I robbed the richest school in the world, and no one noticed."

"*No* one?"

"That's what it felt like."

"Is that liberating? Or . . . ?"

"Or what?"

She shakes her head, ponytail swinging.

"It's impressive," she says. "Not everyone in your shoes would've wanted to . . . go to college *twice*. For absolutely no credit." It's the first time anyone has noticed my invisible student years. All the close reading. The early-morning classes. Taking notes while kids my age slept against the wall. "You're the real *Good Will Hunting*, aren't you?" I feel hyperaware of my swinging arms, my padding feet. I never imagined that Claire, of all people, might compliment me. That she might find something in me to admire.

"Nina?"

"Oh, I didn't go near the math building."

She laughs.

"Did we take any classes together?" she asks, a wry smile.

"Trust me, I would've remembered. You were probably in the advanced seminars, and I never sat in on anything that small." Even though Alice would've been able to hold her own. Gesturing with an annotated *Persuasion*, her neon Post-its effectively doubling the page count. "I stuck with the survey classes—Milton, Thoreau, Faulkner—and read everything for them. I always was a good student, even when I wasn't on the roster."

"Who was your favorite author?" she asks.

She blushes, tells me never mind.

"You already know my answer, and I already know yours." She raises an eyebrow. "You'd say Donna Tartt for her grit. Her literary endurance."

A cyclist waves to us as he passes.

We both pretend we don't see him.

"You really do know my secrets."

She looks at me, her half smile like a snagged skirt, giving me an intimate peek. And I want her the same way I wanted Siobhan. I imagine Claire against her and Leo's bedroom door, her back arching, pelvis pushing toward me. Her eyes two slits, closing when it gets too good. Her bottom lip tucked under teeth, Claire sucking on it like she's thirsty.

"You have that look," she says.

"What look?"

"Like you're holding back."

We walk under a thin pine with little shade.

"I was just thinking . . ." *How good I could make you feel. How much I want to please you.* I drag my fingers across one branch, feeling the needles bend. Claire smiles through the pause. "Thinking how perfect we are for each other."

Her smile fades.

"Maybe we should turn around here." She pivots.

I follow, feeling time run away from me.

"I'm sorry, but are you sure about him?" I ask. "Do you even know him that well? I interview people every day, and you know what that's taught me? Our memories are almost useless after twenty-four hours, let alone after ten whole years. You really think you know Leo *a decade* after you last saw him? You want to bet your life on an impression?"

She stares at the pavement.

"And honestly, does he know you?" I press, thinking of the conversations I've overheard between them. "Does he ask you any questions? Does he have any photos of you in his house?" I picture the array on his mantel, Claire absent in every frame. "I know you *think* you love him, but maybe what you feel says more about you than it does about him." She looks confused. "Meaning, you love him this much because that's who *you* are, and that's how *you* care about someone—not because he's special. And—"

"*What?*"

For once, she has her sister's edge.

"Did he love every version of you?" I ask, already knowing the answer. "It's easy to love someone who's on top of the world. But did he love you, Claire, before you were Claire Ross?" We turn a corner, and

Leo's house comes into view. I feel myself scrambling. "Since you've been here, have you learned anything about him that scares you? Anything that makes you wish you hadn't spent so many years dreaming about him? I've seen the end of the road for addiction. If he's anything like my parents . . ."

She reaches the bottom of the stairs.

I can't lose her now.

I hear myself start to apologize, my tone still urgent. I'm begging Claire to forgive me with the same intensity I was begging her to leave him. She stops and turns around. "Please," I go on, "I'm only thinking about what's best for you."

She stares at me for a few seconds. By now, she's sweat through some of her makeup. The tips of her eyebrows are white blonde. I wonder what color her hair is under the wig, if it's still pink all the way to the roots. I always loved that color, so rich it verged on purple. She took a rock and roll shade and made it intellectual. It was lush and punchy, but smart and interesting. Does she still have the pixie cut, or is it longer, held in place with clips?

"Just don't talk to me about Leo."

~

Any second now, Claire will leave to meet Leo for lunch. I'm by the front window, watching for her car. She gave me the option to stay here—and looked hopeful that I might. Maybe she doesn't feel entirely safe with him. After all, she's alone here in their private corner of the world. No one ever knocks on their door. The phone never rings. Their curtains are always drawn. If things got out of hand at home, only I would know.

The garage opens below me.

I might've said too much on our walk, but I couldn't help it. I felt the momentum shifting my way. She's going to *want* to come with me—soon. I won't even have to lie. I never wanted to tie her wrists when her hands are so valuable, when those nerves feed into my favorite mind. I never wanted to explain that this was for her own good, while she was fighting against zip ties. Every one of her bruises would've hurt me more.

Claire drives to the bright horizon.

I touch her car on the window.

Until it's gone.

I lock the front door, then face the living room. If Leo has a stash here, I'm going to find it. I start with the sofa, removing all cushions and sliding my hand into every crevice. There's nothing stuffed in the seams, not even crumbs. Somehow, my fingers come out cleaner. I put his sofa back together, then head to the kitchen and open every cabinet, every drawer. There are seasonings I don't recognize—furikake, ponzu—but nothing hidden behind them. More than a dozen kinds of olive oil, and rows of vinegar, but nothing sinister.

I don't know what I'm looking for exactly.

But it's not on the first floor.

Upstairs, I check under the mattress and around their bed—nothing.

In the closet, I rummage through folded clothes. I wonder for a moment if Leo actually has an addiction, or if I just *hope* he has demons pushing Claire and him apart. It's hard to think clearly when you're this emotional about the one you're watching. I feel like I'm competing with him, but so what? A few months ago, I was competing with the world.

I remember now just how many Starlites would kill to be in my place. Before she went missing, they used r/ClaireRoss to organize group gifts to her apartment: fan fiction about the soulmates, illustrated editions of her book, and hand-drawn pictures of Claire, photorealistic sketches. Whenever a one-star review for *The Starlit Ballet* hits a major retailer, Starlites still pile on to it in the comments, sometimes with threats. Someone once went so far as to react, PIPE BOMB, with numbers between the letters so AI wouldn't automatically block it. And then, there's everyone who joined r/ClaireRoss in the past few months. Maybe they're Starlites. Maybe they just love a good wound. Either way, they have a dark lust for something.

On the top shelf, there's a black tackle box just barely within reach. I manage to pull it down and place it on the carpet, picturing hooks and lures. Maybe Claire and Leo spent a few weekends fishing. I open the box to find a semiautomatic pistol.

TWENTY-TWO

"I could feel his hand for a thousand years."
—*Claire Ross,* The Starlit Ballet

I'm arranging a bouquet of tulips in the kitchen when the front door opens. Claire's back from lunch—crying. She slams the door, leans against it. I ask what happened, but she doesn't answer. Her eyes stay shut, forehead on the glass. I step close enough that I could touch her shoulder. It's right in front of me, bare, shaking. Looking smooth as bone.

She cries even harder.

I thought I knew all of Claire's noises. She sleeps soundly, she laughs once at all her own dry jokes, and she has sex like she's studying—quietly, then with moments when it all comes together. But I've never heard her sob quite like this. The air straining against her throat. The longer it goes on, the more violent it sounds.

I can't let her ache like this.

My fingertips graze her shoulder, just barely touching the skin. I watch Claire for any resistance, but she doesn't flinch. I slide my whole hand onto her back. The moment is so perfect, I almost forget that she's sad. This feels too good, too electric. It's exactly what her book described, a feeling strong enough to survive thousands of years.

She throws her arms around my neck.

I should be melting, but I'm tight.

Because their gun is here, tucked in the back of my pants. If Claire moved the wrong way, she might brush the metal, get the wrong idea. But of course I wasn't going to leave it upstairs. When Claire nuzzles into my shoulder, I put my other hand on her back. Her ribs are distinct under the thin dress. I feel one under every finger. There's something beautiful about our bones so close, like mirror images of each other. Claire would describe it better. She'd find the phrase so crisp and particular, it would sound mathematically correct.

"What are those?" She points over my shoulder.

She must mean the tulips.

I tell her they're my gift.

"Those are . . ."

"Your favorite flower," I say.

She loves them for their history. When *Glamour* asked what her favorite flower was, Claire turned the most canned question into something substantive. She talked about how, in seventeenth-century Holland, tulip bulbs were a currency. People quit their jobs and left their families to grow them. Claire said that she loves tulips because they're so beautiful, they drove people insane. It wasn't hard to find a dozen while she was out.

"I swear," she says. "Do you know what I'm going to say before I say it?" After a quick, bright burst, her expression sours again. "I'm sorry, Leo and I . . . just had a small fight. It's not a big deal." She swipes one hand through the air, as if she's pushing the problem aside. But her eyes are too wet for me to believe it.

I'm reaching for her when she turns around.

She heads upstairs.

By the time I get to the bottom, she's already out of sight.

I find her in the bathroom, where she's leaning toward the mirror, spritzing something from one ear all the way across her hairline to the other. The travel-size bottle is green, with a stack of olives and avocados on one corner of the label. Claire puts the bottle down. Now, she's massaging the mist hard into her skin with two fingers.

I wait on her bed, not sure if she knows that I'm here, not sure what she's doing until the fleshy edges of something curl up across her forehead. She peels off her wig with excruciating care, then drops it in the sink. Her pink hair is vibrant under an elastic headband—not rose quartz, not subtle blush. It's the color I remember. Almost a short bob now, but she looks more like herself. My heart flops like it's lost its balance. When she turns around, she doesn't startle. She walks over to the bed and plops down as if she's exhausted.

"Do you want a cup of tea?" I ask.

She puzzles.

"You said once that a cup of tea solves everything," I say.

"And you know what my favorite kind is?" I do. Anything with a cinnamon stick. "Sorry. I'm just starting to believe that you know more than the—information. That you know *me*." I do. I really do. "And the ones who I *thought* knew me . . ."

I feel an opportunity.

"You said once that you feel sixty-five years old, because you avoid parties, people, and any and all reasons to leave your apartment. But another time, you said that you're definitely not ready to have kids, definitely not ready to be a 'full-time grown-up.'" Her jaw drops. It's so slight, I'm the only one who could tell. "That's when I realized age isn't useful for someone like you. *Age* is only revealing for people whose lives follow the same general pattern. People who go through the same phases. For you . . . no wonder you're confused about how old you are. Someone like you needs special clocks." I half smile. "I know you, and you're right. It's more than your favorite flowers. Or your favorite tea."

I stand, ready to make hers.

"I do remember you, Nina," she says.

I stop, not far from her.

"I mean it," she goes on. "At the Coffee House, you always had a book with you behind the counter. It was a new one every time: *Frankenstein, The Call of the Wild, In Cold Blood.* You read in between customers, on breaks—every chance you got. I'd never seen someone read so much standing up." My heartbeat gets louder. It's possible that Claire is guessing—most students read those books at some point. But I hear the conviction in her voice. Her eyes beg me to believe her. "So don't tell me that no one noticed you rob the richest school in the world. I noticed you before you found me, before you read my manuscript, before we spent hours on that bench. You really were there at the beginning. Before I was anybody."

"You were always somebody."

"To you, Nina."

I'm standing over her now.

Her chin angles up toward me. Her body's so close I could moan just standing here. I feel every part of me relax except for the hard strip in the back of my pants. My hands are tingling. I'm lifting them toward her, slowly, trying not to scare her away. My fingers are warm, as if she's already in them, as if she's already changing their chemistry. I'm about to touch her shoulders when she stands and walks past me. At the top of the stairs, she half turns and tells me that she's happy to make the tea. "You washed my dishes for four years. And made my coffee for one." Her smile is tired, in profile. "You deserve a break."

~

On the drive home that night, I relive it over and over again.

Claire and I were so close, I could've leaned into her mouth.

I could've tilted her back on that bed and run my hand down her neck, her chest. I could've pulled her dress down and asked, *Does he worship you like I do?* But of course he doesn't. His feelings haven't been tested like mine.

A few days left, but she'll come home with me sooner. I can feel it.

First, we'll call Miranda together. I know them both well enough that I can imagine the details, the tears sticking to their fingers. Claire Ross, coming home. Then, we'll fly to New York—tight aisle, hard Biscoff cookies, and the whole country passing under us, stuck there elbow to elbow for seven hours. With that much time in the air, maybe she'll work on her new story. Then, I'll see something I never have before. I'll watch her writing in real time, each letter appearing in my mind almost as soon as it appears in hers. The connection between an author and a reader doesn't get any closer than that, doesn't get any more intimate.

Before we even land in New York, her return will make headlines in every language. I imagine Claire reuniting with her mom and sister at the airport. I'll give them space, of course. Plenty of people will be trying to pick my brain, anyway. They'll be falling over themselves, dying to know how I did it. My great case, even bigger than I imagined. Because in the end, it didn't just transform my life at work. It transformed my life at home.

Then, Claire and I will live together in New York City. I doubt she'll want to spend more time out East. That town never felt like her. Instead, we'll find a cozy apartment. With her royalties, we could even buy our neighbors' places. Just for the peace and quiet. She'll finish what she's writing, and then, I'll be the first to read it, once every comma's in place. I imagine drinking coffee, reading it in bed with a pen, and underlining hundreds of perfect sentences. Could she ever write anything better than *The Starlit Ballet*? It might take her another decade, but in between, I'd have almost four thousand perfect mornings with her.

And if she doesn't want to come?

As a private eye, I've thought a lot about right and wrong. After all, I tend to find myself in homes that aren't mine, watching people who think they're alone. But I always felt like too much of an outsider to be guilty of something. I was just a spectator, observing other people's lives. My hands were clean because they stayed in my pockets.

Now, I'm involved.

And maybe the only wrong choice would be to do nothing, to ignore what feels right. Like keeping my mouth shut in those lectures when I knew the answer. Like never telling my parents that I needed more from them. Like never correcting my clients that *I'm Nina*, instead of nodding along to the homonyms they gave me—*Tina*, *Rita*, *Anita*.

With traffic, I don't get to the motel for an hour. By the time I unlock my phone, Claire and Leo are leaving the kitchen. Upstairs, I can't hear them anymore.

"Fuck!" I whisper.

She wouldn't sleep with him tonight.

I won't be able to tell, but—she wouldn't. Not after what happened today. She remembered the books I read from ten years ago. She took off her wig. We sat together on the sofa downstairs, drinking tea. She confided in me that she'd never had a real girl*friend* before. That's when I pictured her in the locked box, wood under her fingernails. Terrifying for anyone, but a special hell for the imaginative. She said that boys had always been easier, friendlier . . . until me. Then, she took a long sip of tea, the cinnamon stick gliding around the rim until it touched her cheek. Her throat like a bone in her neck.

Still, I don't like not being able to see her.

I don't like leaving her with him.

I scroll through my missed calls from Roger, Miranda, and Kira. It's been a while since I paid attention to them. Even now, I only read some of the messages. Kira sent the most, including several versions of Where the fuck are you? She says that she's going to sue me for breach of contract. She says that she's going to ruin my name, that I'll never work in the area again. They're all stinging, venomous texts. Can I stall her?

Hi Kira, I'm sorry I've been so hard to reach. I'll call you as soon as I can, which might not be for a few more days. This case is still my first priority, my only priority. I've been too busy to stand still, but I'll have a full update for you and Miranda any day now. Then, I'll explain everything. Thank you for understanding.

Send.

TWENTY-THREE

"I just want a good life with Cady."
—*Claire Ross,* The Starlit Ballet

After Leo drives off the next morning, I step out of my car. This block keeps getting quieter. There are feathers on a few different lawns, poking out of the grass like colorful headstones. The feeder has a couple of birds left on the rim, and unfortunately, they're beautiful—lemon yellow, long black tails. They're still singing, still hungry.

I jog up Leo's stairs.

Inside, I hear glass clinking.

Claire's pulling a plastic bag out of the trash in the kitchen. It's filled with empty green wine bottles. There's a yellow tint in all of them, looking like dirty gold or a rotting algae bloom. Claire's wearing one of Leo's tees and boxer shorts ending at her knees. No wig. Her tan's fading in patches. It's the way a spray tan disappears, leaving where it's been scrubbed, falling off with dead skin. She looks even more vulnerable than yesterday, now in someone else's clothes, in someone else's house, cleaning up his mess.

I sniff the air—fermented grapes.

She passes with the trash, walking it outside. She doesn't make eye contact with me on her way to the front door. If she did, I wonder if she'd break down. It's harder to ignore your pain when someone else sees it, when they're staring at you.

With Claire gone, and nothing but the smell, I'm back in my first apartment. I remember coming home one night to find our front door locked. The 3-J was a shadow in the paint, metal digits long gone. I'd left my keys inside. I remember knocking—knuckling the wood with everything I had—until a neighbor touched my shoulder. *I'm Dee.* She wore purple scrubs. She led me across the hall and fed me chicken noodle soup, spaghetti drifting through the broth. I called it mermaid hair. It was warm and heartbreaking.

She let me sleep on her sofa.

That weekend, I followed Dee—from a distance. She and her daughter went ice-skating in Boston Common, carving cautious circles on the glass. Her daughter looked about my age. I sat on a cold bench, my hands tucked inside my coat sleeves. It was hard to keep track of Dee and the girl, like following cards in a shuffling deck. But I managed to watch them for hours, even when they were nothing but black dots in a snow-covered park. I followed them all the way back to our building. As if I was hoping for seconds.

When Claire returns, she washes her hands hard in the sink.

I ask her if she wants to talk about it.

She shuts the water off.

"I'm going to take a shower," she says on her way upstairs. She still won't look at me, won't let me in. Without any headband, her pink bangs skirt her eyelashes. I follow her to the bottom of the staircase and watch her climb. Her legs look shrunken, the shorts only revealing her calves. Her Achilles tendons are wiry stripes, and then, gone. I still have one hand on the banister when I hear the dull hum of her shower.

Drift toward the noise.

Her bedroom door is open.

Her bathroom door too. She's crying loud enough that I hear her through the water. I rush inside to find her on the floor, back against the wall, forehead on her knees. I reach my arm into the shower to turn it off. Cold water rinses the color out of my white sleeve, until it's nothing but clear film. I sink onto the tile next to her. Her shoulders keep shaking. I hate seeing her like this. I feel angry—worse, responsible. I'm the only one here.

"You need to leave him," I say.

She covers her eyes, revealing a mark on her forearm: four dark smudges in a row. They look like shadowy phases of the moon—fingerprints.

I say her name warily.

She drops her arm.

"Did he . . . ?" I scan for more bruises or worse. She stays crumpled, bent knees under baggy clothes. I can't see much, but I'm not going to unfold her here, a foot from the toilet bowl. I picture Leo's gun in my car, relieved it wasn't in this house. "It's not safe for you to be here. Let me help you. Let me take you back to New York."

"I'm thinking about it," she whispers.

"Let me take you home."

My phone rings. I ignore it.

"Who is it?" Claire asks.

I check.

I can't lie to her.

"It's your sister," I admit.

"You want to answer it?" she asks.

"No, I don't."

"You can," she urges me.

The buzzing stops.

"Claire," I say. "I know your imagination." I picture Logan and Cady in Yosemite Valley. A haze of sunlight and pollen. Standing between infinities. "But you're seeing someone who isn't there. Leo is . . . another character you invented. He only exists in your mind." Red veins in her eyes dull the green. "I know you're strong, but this isn't. This is weak and reckless, and if you don't get yourself out of here, I'll do it for you."

She twists her hands.

I give her a moment to think.

I'm tempted to confront Leo for what he did. My dad taught me how to defend myself. *We have to be prepared.* He gave me lessons in our living room, his feet shifting, fists over his cheeks. I remember the time he begged me to punch him. He kept slapping his jaw, right on the bone. My hands wouldn't move, not even to cover my eyes. Someone in the hallway was trying to get their lighter to catch, snapping the wheel again and again. *We have to be prepared.* Dad kept a pistol in his closet too. It was lighter than I expected, like picking up a box of cereal. He took me to the firing range, taught me not to flinch when it fired.

"I didn't know it would be like this," she says.

I open my hand to her.

She takes it.

"I've thought about leaving," she says.

"Then why don't we?"

"Because what would I go back to?" Her voice is desolate. "I spent my life writing about someone who . . . isn't real. Leaving him, it's more than leaving him. It's admitting that I wasted my time. Think about it," she adds, before I can cut in. "I spent most of my twenties in one room, on one book. Maybe people connect with that story because I had to, because if it wasn't alive, if it didn't *breathe*, then I would've gone insane." She pauses. "Do you know what it's like to give your soul to something, and then it just . . . melts? I don't feel betrayed. Leo didn't do this on purpose. 'Disillusioned' is a better word. Everything I thought about true love—"

"You weren't wrong about that. Just about . . ."

"Him?"

I nod yes.

"I'm not so sure," she says. "I spent so much time on the world I wanted, I never got to know the one that exists." I put my other hand on hers. "Maybe the world is a dark place. Maybe people are heartless and cruel, and at the end of it, we just die. Maybe that's all there is. It's ice cold, and then we die." She lets go of my hands and hugs herself.

"Please don't say that." My wet arm feels a new chill. "You're the reason a lot of people believe in true love. If you start saying it doesn't exist . . ."

"I was wrong about Leo. So why not—"

"I'm begging you."

She lifts her chin.

"You were only wrong about Leo," I insist.

She loops her arms around my shoulders.

"I was such an idiot," she says. "I thought I knew him, but . . . you can't read someone from far away, can you?" I want to slow this moment down and memorize it. Her hair is on my chest, soft as foam—that was her favorite part of the cappuccino I used to make. I'd stir it once with my finger. *You can't read someone from far away.* I couldn't agree more. And now, here she is, closer than ever. I want this for the rest of my life.

"We're going to leave tomorrow," I say.

It's so assertive, I surprise myself.

"It's time for you to pack."

I help her onto her feet.

We walk into the bedroom side by side.

She turns in to the closet, disappearing for a few uneasy seconds. I stand in the middle of her room, my fingers interlaced, thumbs tapping against each other. When she emerges, she's cradling a black duffel bag in her arms. Holding it to her chest like a dark security blanket. She drops it next to the bed, where it lands with a muffled thud.

When I offer to help, Claire asks for water.

I trot downstairs, passing both copies of *The Starlit Ballet* in Leo's bookcase. The spines look like a hole in the shelf. One square crater. It's a grim view, now that I know the couple behind it never got far. All they had were a few conversations, ten years of distance, and then cold disappointment. *My* real-life story with Claire is more romantic than that.

I fill a cup at the sink.

Maybe Claire will write about us one day. The cup starts to overflow. What if I inspire more than a detail—what if I inspire a whole story? Claire wrote *The Starlit Ballet* based only on what she felt for him. If a one-sided relationship can make her feel that way, then what will ours do? What will real love move her to write? When we're living together, she'll be with someone who knows every moon on her finger and still asks her questions. When we're finally together, she'll feel that. Then, she'll write something even better.

I shut off the faucet.

Upstairs, Claire drinks the water in big gulps. Her throat bounces as we sit next to each other in their bed, looking at flights. The plan is to show up tomorrow afternoon and book tickets for the first plane we can get back to New York. As soon as she gives me her word, I find myself staring at her. We're doing it. We're starting our new life.

"What's so funny?" she asks.

"Nothing."

My smile tapers.

"I'm just happy for you," I add.

Happy for us.

~

I stay on the bed while Claire packs what little she has. She might look like she's sleepwalking, but she's doing it. She's kneeling over the duffel, folding her tanks. Meanwhile, I'm trying not to move. I don't want to disturb anything, not even the flow of filtered air. Claire stands without warning and leaves the bedroom. I stare at the empty doorway, telling myself she'll come back. She returns a few beats later with a silver laptop.

Drops it on her clothes.

"Is that—Leo's?" I ask, pointing.

"You stole half a million dollars' worth of school, and I'm the thief?" she asks with a cool edge. "Sorry, I have months of work on there, and he's been a drunk menace the whole time." Her logic doesn't feel sound. But maybe it is—people who break rules lose their rights.

Claire covers the computer in neat green rectangles of clothing. They bury it completely, not a wink of silver peeking through them. "When you were on campus all those years ago, did you really just go to class? Or did you ever . . . take anything else?"

I remember Siobhan. Undoing the mother-of-pearl buttons in her cashmere twinset. Moving her hair off her shoulders, like parting curtains. She was warm—for all the calculus homework still on her desk, razor-sharp lines in every sigma, she was warm. Whenever I leaned back and opened my eyes, she was smiling.

I can't lie to Claire.

But telling her feels disrespectful, somehow.

"It takes skill to deceive people the way you did," Claire says, moving on. "Blending into a Harvard class, surrounded by kids who spent the summer at Oxford, reading everything on the syllabus in advance. It's a high-wire act, pulling off that kind of social fraud. Trespassing on the most entitled. You said it took guts for me to go on those shows. I say that whatever I have, you have the same thing." She looks at me more carefully. "Do you remember when you said we have a window into each other?"

I tell her of course.

She's studying me from the floor, hands on her knees. There's virtually no tan left below her wrists. Naked fingers, bone-colored palms.

"You inhabit people." Her tone is softer now. "When you were walking around campus, I'm guessing you wore crimson?" I nod yes. Of course Alice wore her school's color. Bloodred sweaters, dark plaid scarves. "I don't think you went there just to learn about Faulkner, Nina. You wanted to play dress-up—but *play*'s not the right word. Because it wasn't a game. It was something you needed to do. Sitting in lectures, taking notes, you were . . . disappearing into a dream." I feel like she's inside me, swimming around. "As a private eye, it's not that different, is it? You watch other people for a living. You're not in *your* life; you're in *theirs*. In their failing marriages and secret drug habits and second families."

259

"Who am I inhabiting now?"

"Me," she says.

"Claire Miranda Ross."

"Do you know yourself as well as you know me?" She squints doubtfully. The next part comes out even more slowly. "I think you're being everyone you can except yourself. What are you so afraid of? I could probably answer that for you, but I think you need to answer it yourself." A far-away part of me wants to cry.

~

At the end of the day, it's hard to say goodbye to Claire. She's never looked more like herself, in a black turtleneck and dark slacks. Her tan has faded to the color of sand. There's not a speck of makeup on her face, leaving her eyebrows pale and her lashes faint suggestions. She even has her clear-rimmed glasses back. They catch the light, glittering with specks of pink and yellow. I know that we're going to New York tomorrow, but being so *close* to something makes waiting for it even harder. The sun has just started to set behind us on the outdoor steps. I'm so charged down to my fingernails, though, I can't tell if it's hot or cold. I'm hugging Claire tight enough that she coughs, and I really should let go.

It hurts to pry myself away.

"I don't want to leave you here with him," I say.

"I've been here for months."

"Still—"

"I can handle one more night."

I retreat slowly.

The drive back is difficult.

I keep imagining our new life.

New apartment. New York City.

Maybe she'll fall into a habit of asking for my advice while she's working. What if I become the one she turns to for help with that next phrase? Beautiful enough to quote and simple enough that it doesn't get in the way of the story? Even if I can't offer her insights, I could still be a sounding board, so she can tease the answers out for herself. Asking me could become so second nature, our minds would practically curl around each other. I wouldn't need any recognition for it. Of course, she'd name me in the acknowledgments, but I wouldn't need the public to know who I am. I'd just need her. The Real Claire Ross.

Twice, I find myself drifting into other lanes. At one red light, I slam so hard on the brakes that I close my eyes, bracing for impact. Nothing. Eyes open. Luckily, the next car is still seconds behind me. I must've been driving too fast for them to keep up. In my rearview mirror, they come slowly to a stop.

My phone buzzes. Kira.

The light's still red.

I could answer my phone right here on the console. There's no reason to avoid her anymore. Tomorrow, I'll be escorting her sister across the country, into her family's open arms. I'm in the right—better than that, I *made* something right. The Rosses are going to start treating me differently when they find out what I've done.

I greet Kira on speaker.

Green light.

"Put my sister on the phone right now."

"Tomorrow night, you can—"

"Listen, you fucking creep, I know what happened to your parents. The police found you in a room with both of them dead? You were covered in their blood, and the DA never pressed charges? How'd you manage that?" The headlines come back to me in Times New Roman over my windshield. **The Overnight Orphan. Double Murder Destroys Boston Family.** I didn't come across them until I started working in Long Island, until I googled my own name to see what employers might find. If anyone read the articles, buried on page three of the search results, they never mentioned them to me. Until now.

"Hello?" she asks.

I swallow.

"Hello?" she presses.

"Are you a private eye now too?"

The question comes out smooth.

From Nina the elegant detective.

"Put Claire on." Kira's tone is stone cold.

"I'm afraid that's not possible—"

"Fucking do it."

"—but you can take my word that she's safe."

"Your word doesn't mean shit."

"Actually, it does," I say, still calm. "I've never been convicted of a crime. In fact, I do the opposite. I solve them for a living. And I found your sister. Did you hear me? I *found* your sister. I didn't take her. I didn't hold her here against her will. I *found* her—"

"I saw the photos."

My grip on the wheel is wet.

"What you did wasn't human," she says.

I remember how my dad looked on the floor.

The scissors in his neck had green handles. Mom had been the one to do that. Then, she sat back on her bed, eyes vacant. There were three bottles of wine on her nightstand, each with just a sip left. They made everything in the room smell rancid. She didn't move out of the way when I grabbed one and raised my arm. She didn't even blink. It was almost enough to make me stop and ask her to look at me. She'd just killed him. I was about to do the same to her. What would it take for her to see me? To get out of that cloud and look?

I'd seen Mom slap Dad a hundred times. Whenever she found something new and expensive under their bed—an EMT first responder kit, a five-pound pack of survival garden seeds—she'd swing at him. She'd do it right where I was standing. I could almost feel her footprints under mine, sense her raised arm in my own. Sometimes, she slapped her bosses too. At least that's what she told me when she came home, triumphant that she'd finally stood up for herself. *Fuck you, Jenelle. I smoke wherever the fuck I want.*

I squeezed the neck of the bottle.

I always was a good student. A quick learner.

At the end of my swing, the bottle flung out of my hand and hit the wall.

After, I stood between my parents, crying with rage and suddenly hopeless, because all I'd wanted was their attention. Now, how were they ever going to see me? How were they ever going to stop using, lying, and falling over themselves, and see me now that they were gone? I called 911 and told them to hurry. When the police asked me what happened, I said that I'd found them like that, in their own dark pools. My parents were drunk enough, with pasts crooked enough, that everyone believed me.

"Kira, my record is clean."

"Put—"

"Tomorrow, I'm bringing her home."

TWENTY-FOUR

"His face is fresh and smooth—even though he's lain on a deathbed hundreds of times, even though he's lost everything someone can lose. I want to memorize this view and keep it for the rest of my life. Our last crazy, little life."
—*Claire Ross,* The Starlit Ballet

I stand up in the dead of the night, racked with nerves. I'm not sure if I've shut my eyes since I lay down a few hours ago. The truth is that I *am* worried about her in that house—with him. But she said she'd be safe. She gave me her word.

What's more valuable to a writer than that?

I sit down, cradling my head. My skin slides back and forth over my skull. Every so often, headlights burn across my window. I imagine driving to Claire now. The fast lane would be almost empty. Cars spread out like a search party, flashlights scanning for traces of a body. I can almost see the highway ahead of me. Almost hear my car door open and shut on Mallory Way, no louder than someone talking with their mouth closed. I'd step inside their house, walk carefully upstairs. I'd push their bedroom door open with just my fingertips. But if Claire woke up to find me standing over her . . . I don't want to scare her away.

She gave me her word. There's no reason to panic.

We're less than twenty-four hours from boarding. Less than twenty-four hours from wings. I'm going to sit next to her at thirty-five thousand feet and feel the armrest rattle. We're going to fall asleep on each other, and I'm going to wake up in New York City smelling like her.

But what if . . . ?

The question keeps me awake.

What if Claire gets cold feet? The momentum we have together is so new, so fragile. What if Leo was tame tonight and apologetic in bed? What if he made promises to change, promises I can't compete with? What if my plan falls apart, and no one ever knows that Claire and I meant something permanent to each other? I almost want to tell someone what's happened. Just to nail it down, somehow. Keep it from slipping away.

I sit up, feeling caffeinated.

What if people knew that we spent a week together in San Francisco? That Claire let me into her private escape, where no one else was allowed? She trusted me, like no one had ever trusted me. We were so close, we were a part of each other. If only people *knew* that, our story would take on a life of its own. It couldn't just end tomorrow.

I reach for my laptop. Log into r/ClaireRoss.

My username hovers in the corner, Closer3ader.

I never enjoyed checking this site, even when it was a treasure trove of new photos. I hovered over it like a bodyguard, intervening whenever I felt the need. Protecting Claire from their invasions, their zoom. Even before she went missing, Starlites ravaged her privacy as a three-hundred-thousand-headed creature, as if they could get closer to her just by memorizing her coffee order, her brand of sneakers. As if their one-sided obsession with her could ever be anything more. It was delusional. At times, terrifying. I was never one of them.

Then again, here I am. In Finding Claire.

My fingers rub together over the keyboard.

I remember the photo I took of her writing. I find it on my laptop and crop it until most of the background is lost, until only I know where it was taken. In this shot, the light is generous. Her eyelashes are crisp, blonde crescents. There's a pink stripe over her ear—almost lost in her dark wig, but it's there. A wisp like the inside of a lip.

I upload the photo, on the brink of posting it.

I'm looking in her closest eye. Claire Miranda Ross. My spectacular freak. I always knew I belonged with a loner, someone too socially awkward for normal life. Until I met Claire, I never realized that being exceptional is socially awkward too. It's a glamorous strain, but still, she disturbs every group she joins. People can't relax around her, can't be themselves. So no matter how popular she is, she'll always be an outsider.

She'll never fit in with anyone except lucky, lucky me.

According to the sidebar, there are thirteen hundred other people here. The number flickers to fourteen hundred before settling back down. All these Starlites think that they know her. They might've had her fiction. But Claire was only real with me. Sharing the photo is quick, silent. I shut my computer and lie down before I can see the consequences.

～

The next morning, I check out from the motel and speed to Leo's. I drive with my window down on the highway, one hand on the side of the car. I'm humming—I can't hear the sound, but I feel it. One rush up my throat.

I'm more than excited to see her.

The light is creamy in their neighborhood. All the houses have a champagne-colored glow, lustrous bay windows. Walt Whitman comes back to me: "Give me the splendid silent sun, with all his beams full-dazzling." Then, Victor Hugo: "To love another person is to see the face of God." And then, I hear a dozen more of my favorite lines as if I'm Logan with his kaleidoscope, seeing the most layered and dizzying version of the world. It's a collage of my favorite poems and books, a scrambled mix of literary highs.

I park next to Leo's house.

Catch my reflection in the side view mirror.

From here, I can only see half my face. One unslept eye. Not quite bloodshot, but close. Pinkshot. My lips flake like I'm molting. Maybe I am. Maybe today, I'm the person I always wanted to be, with the one I always wanted to be mine.

Leo's car passes in a silver blur.

Once he's gone, I watch his house, the Golden Gate a red frame around it. I try to savor the view. After all, it's the last time I'm going to see this—aside from the shots that might crop up in the news. *I never know in the moment what's going to matter. It's only looking back that I can tell which days counted a little bit more.* I disagree with you, Miranda. Because here I am, fully aware that today will matter. It's going to etch itself inside me—every weed, every wildflower. It's going to change the rest of my life.

The sun climbs higher.

I'm opening the car door when I glance at the glove compartment. I wasn't planning to take it with me, but . . . what if? It's the same question from hours ago, nagging me in daylight. What if she's changed her mind? I find myself reaching for the gun, tucking it in the back of my pants. I feel its weight as I step outside in perfect silence. Heading for Leo's, I can't even hear the warbler, that one last bird to twinkle through the trees.

I skip up the outdoor steps. Open the front door without knocking.

On the floor, the tulip vase is shattered. Shards glint across ten feet of space, the tulips limp in the center. Some of the petals look crushed, as if someone stepped on them over and over again. Streaks of red paste hang on to their stems. Without wasting any time, I try to jump around the glass, landing on some that split under my sneakers.

I yell for Claire.

A trail of blood leads upstairs.

I jump up two at a time to find her bedroom door half-open. I push it so hard it slams into the wall. Claire is lying face down in bed. She isn't making any noise, but her body's convulsing. I sit next to her, my hands hovering over her shoulders.

I can't see her face.

Her body's hidden under the comforter.

There's a lump where her feet are—red.

"Claire." I'm crying now. "What is it?"

She turns this way, lying on her side.

Her bottom lip is split and bleeding. A dark lump on her eyebrow is already starting to swell. I can almost see the imprint of his hand. She isn't crying anymore, just shaking. I lift the covers from around her foot and see the cut: an inch across the ball. She must've stepped on glass, running away from him. I pull a pillowcase loose and wrap it around her ankle. I tie it off like a tourniquet, then elevate her foot on two pillows.

"I'm going to call 911," I say.

"Don't." I'm about to argue when she adds, "Then everyone will know where I am. I can't handle that now. I just want to go home." Her voice cracks. "You said we were going home." Bandages. I remember them in the medicine cabinet.

I grab them, along with Neosporin and rubbing alcohol. When I'm back, Claire manages to sit up against the headboard. She nods, granting me permission. I unwrap the tourniquet. I want to ask her what happened, but I don't want to make her relive it now, not while she has to feel this too. I clean the cut, wrap gauze around it. Meanwhile, she covers her eyes with her hands. After she's been taken care of, I find a seat next to her in bed.

"He asked where I got the flowers," she says quietly.

"What did you say?"

"The truth." She wipes her eyes. "I told him that you recognized me on the street, that you were a friend. Then, I told him you'd been spending the day here. He asked why I'd been keeping secrets, what else I was hiding. I said he needed to calm down, and then . . ." She points at her face. "He wasn't even drunk this time. This is just who he is. Sorry," she says, interrupting me before I can ask another question. "I can't talk about this anymore."

I offer to get her ice.

She nods okay, but it's hard to leave.

Downstairs, stepping around the broken glass isn't easy. Some shards are almost invisible, clear arrowheads blending into the floor. Others are glass crumbs, only apparent in the split second that they catch the light. A few hang on to the vase's curves, rounding them into frozen hammocks. And no matter how careful I am, I hear tiny crunches under my sneakers. Giving me an unwilling role in the mess, making it worse.

I fill a ziplock with ice and carry it upstairs.

When I'm in bed with her again, she leans on my shoulder and dabs the ice to her face. After a few touches, she lowers the cold bag to the sheets.

"I know it's not my fault—" she starts.

"This is *not* your fault."

"—but I should've known better." Her voice cracks. "He told me things—I should've paid more attention to them. I should've—"

I ask her what things.

"We started driving on September eighteenth. I met him at four a.m., right outside our gates. I was so excited, I didn't even shut my window." When she says the word "excited," she looks even emptier. "We drove for a week, talked the whole time. There wasn't an hour of dead air on the trip—because we hadn't talked since college, not really. In Ohio, he told me he was in recovery. In Wyoming, he told me he got fired from his last job. For 'unresolved issues with rage.'" She grimaces. "It sounds crazy now, but I didn't overthink it at the time. When you're in love with someone, you don't see them the way that you should."

Downstairs, the front door opens.

"I forgot my headphones!" Leo announces.

I freeze.

Claire glances at the Bose pair on the nightstand beside her. They're sleek, all black. In the same second, she checks in fearfully with me, maybe to make sure that I'm not going anywhere. When I hear him walk closer, I stand up silently and glide into the closet. I remove the pistol from my waistband and turn the safety off. Downstairs, Leo mutters something to himself. It's short, incoherent. A sentence left unfinished.

He shouts for Claire.

The stairs creak. Every one makes her flinch.

Leo enters and stops short with his back to me. I've never been this close to him before. His shoulder blades are like balled fists stretching out his polo. His arms are massive, hands ominous. Even just hanging at his sides, they're loaded with potential. I take a closer look at his knuckles. Is Claire's blood still on them?

He steps toward her.

"Freeze!" I shout, raising the gun.

When he spins around, I shake the pistol in his direction. He raises his hands and steps back until he's against the blackout shade. He's blinking furiously, managing his shock. It feels surprisingly good to stand here and watch him twist. His fingers are curling over his palms, as if they're trying to protect themselves, be a little less exposed.

I nod my head toward Claire.

"You realize *she's* closer to me now than you are?" Her bleeding foot is just a couple of steps away. Leo and I have five more yards between us. "You left her right there, and you have no idea who the fuck I am."

"Who are you?" he asks.

Claire starts to cry.

He inches toward her.

"Stay the fuck away from Claire," I shout.

Something lodges in his brain.

I realize it's the word "Claire."

He lowers his hands.

"You know her?" he asks Claire.

He points at me.

"Claire, who the fuck is this?" He walks toward her.

"Stop!" I shout. But he keeps moving.

I shoot without flinching. As soon as I pull the trigger, the bullet whips his shoulder back. He hits the shade, his pupils wide. It wasn't a fatal shot, just enough to stop him in his tracks. I keep my feet planted and stare at his face around the barrel.

"Do it!" Claire shrieks.

She's so loud I almost pull the trigger on reflex.

She wants me to kill him?

"Please." She looks me in the eye. Her split lip is bleeding again.

Leo starts to slide sideways, leaving a dark trail on the shade. He's stunned but—not foggy. I know what an addict's eyes should look like. Leo's brow is still a strong ledge over a focused stare, even with a bullet in his shoulder. He has the same morose intensity that he had in every rowing headshot, the same sharp attention.

"Do it!" Claire repeats.

At this distance, there's no missing.

When I pull the trigger, glass shatters. It's so loud and high pitched it sounds like the house is screaming. I spin away from the noise. Pieces of the window keep colliding, keep stabbing the street, until eerie peace overtakes the room. I turn back around and face an open wall. The last scraps of glass are a jagged frame around the edges. At the bottom, the blackout shade is a dark mess over Leo's body, like dirt over a corpse. He must've pulled it down when he fell. The soles of his sneakers face me, but otherwise, he's shrouded.

And Claire is—smiling.

Nothing and no one moves.

Claire continues to smile—but it's too much like a scratch on a photograph, something that can't be real. Her expression doesn't change even when the light shifts over her face, when something blocks the sun for a split second. She stays blissed out, opiate.

"What?" I ask, breathless.

She reaches for the landline on her nightstand.

Dials three numbers.

"Help!" Claire shouts her address into the phone. "She's killing him! Please, help, I'm begging you!" She hangs up. I look at her, confused—but I'm too shocked to put a sentence together, to say anything at all. Her smile returns, and it's like watching one of her soulmates shift into a new identity. Watching every hair, birthmark, and piece of her heart turn over until it belongs to someone else. She becomes impossibly serene.

"What are you doing?" I ask.

"Watching you perform."

My cheeks feel cold.

"'Perform'?"

"You are my grand finale."

I feel dense trying to process it.

Her words are in order, but they don't make sense. She's always spoken straight to my soul, but now, nothing is getting through to me. Nothing is clicking the way that it should. *You are my grand finale.* I wait for it to mean something.

"When the police come, you're going to tell them a story." Her tone is dreamy, almost childlike. I feel a strange urge to *blink* my ears. "You'll say you were planning to kill Leo all week. You've been in love with me for years, and you wanted him out of the way. So, you started stalking the house, getting close enough to breathe on the windows. Today, you finally made your move. Your fight broke out downstairs with the vase. It continued up here, where you shot him dead. You're going to say this was all your beautiful idea."

I squint at her, mystified.

It almost sounds like she's trying to write over what this is, over everything that's led us here. She always did invent people, choose their emotions. She always did stage elaborate scenes and make them persuasive, permanent. Is she trying to do that now? Is she trying to rewrite history? I stare at her, at the shining eyes that don't match the bruise, at the smile that doesn't match the bleeding lip, wondering if she's trying to write into the fabric of the world, if she's trying to change its code right in front of me.

I try to focus on the truth.

Keep it from slipping away.

And the truth is that we're in Leo's house in the Marina District. The floor is hard under my feet. My hand is still tingling where the gun kicked back onto my palm. I didn't spend the week plotting to kill Leo. I didn't press my body against his windows, fogging them up from the outside. Right? I watched the two of them from my motel, and that was miles away. On the feed, it always looked like Claire loved him. Didn't she? I almost can't remember. My mind feels like it's melting down the back of my neck.

"But you loved him," I confirm.

"Did I?"

"You wrote your book about him."

"Your life's about to end, and you want to talk about my book?" She looks at me with gentle, amused surprise. "Books are like horoscopes. Don't you know that by now? Everyone sees what they want to see—and he wasn't the first one to think it was all about him. I mean, come on, Nina, really?" Her sense of pleasure deepens. "I wrote a book about someone who didn't talk to me for ten years? How desperate did you think I was?"

"Not desperate," I say.

"Then what?"

"Special."

"But you know better than that," she says. "Don't you, Detective? Your job almost requires you to doubt everyone, even the people who hire you." I don't admit that she's right. "And then, you defy all that to believe *I'm* the exception to the rule?"

"But . . . ," I start.

If she didn't love Leo . . .

"Then why are you here?"

She smiles at my question.

"It started last year, when I had the strangest idea." Her voice is mild with a tinge of brightness. "I wanted to write something—bigger." Her *b* and *g*'s come out firm, giving the word two hard bumps. "I didn't know how. But the idea kept creeping back, tugging my sleeve. Bigger." Again, she gives the word two bumps. "I started to wonder, What if my characters didn't just feel real; what if they *were* real? What if they had beating hearts?"

Her eyes are fascinated.

"It was just an idea, though, until Leo reached out. He said everything you did—that he knew *The Starlit Ballet* was about the two of us—and that he'd matured. That he was ready to put our relationship first. I realized he was the character I'd been looking for. The first page of my next story. I asked for his help to sneak away, and it really was as simple as that." She smiles even wider, as if she's built something beautiful.

"Naturally," she goes on, "I became a character too. The person he wanted me to be. All of a sudden, I was Claire Ross, avid hiker. Claire Ross, lover of the great outdoors. Who enjoys nothing more than sweating her way up a mountain. She felt like a brunette." She shrugs, lifting one shoulder a lazy inch. "I'd written a love story, but *this* was life size. Rich and dense. I wasn't sure where to take the plot . . . until you showed up."

"Me," I whisper.

"Yes, you. Madly in love with me. Desperate to be cast. I knew you'd play a part. I wasn't sure *what* until I saw you with the birds." She pauses, and in the quick silence, I hear their absence. "That's when I knew you'd be the villain. You have what every great villain needs, don't you? A demented moral compass. You can convince yourself that you're doing good, even when you're killing." She tilts her head to one side, as if she's reading my distorted north. "Pitting you against Leo was the perfect drama."

My gaze drifts to his headphones.

"A plot device, you're right," she says, as if she can read my mind. "I held on to them so he'd come back. So you two could finally meet, and you could give the performance of your life." She smiles pleasantly. "I've been writing our story down, you know. A memoir that's also fiction. Something entirely true and entirely scripted."

"He wasn't hurting you?"

"No, he was . . . sweet." I glance at the soles of his sneakers. They're an innocent white. "And of course I remembered what you told me in Cambridge. Your parents were too drunk to notice you? You sure got noticed in the end." There's a wicked spike of interest in her tone. "So, I knew what kind of problem he needed to have."

"He wasn't an alcoholic."

"Well, he *was*, years ago. When I got here, he still went to meetings once a week. After you arrived, I started asking him to go every day. Sometimes, twice a day. He didn't like that." Her whole body is relaxed. "It wasn't too hard to stage. Besides, he had so many bottles of olive oil—all green glass, long necked. So much red wine vinegar, white wine vinegar . . . a little work in the middle of the night was all it took."

I don't understand.

"Even if you lied to Leo," I say, thinking out loud. "Even if we're . . . in some kind of story, we're still connected. Aren't we?" But I'm slowing down, my words getting heavier and heavier with doubt. "We still have a window into each other. Don't we?" *You inhabit people.* When she said that, she was kneeling right here on the carpet. *Whatever I have, you have the same thing.* But yesterday, she sounded different. She wasn't this dreamy, this distant. She was someone else. "Even our flaws are the same," I realize.

"Are they?"

I think through every version of her. The feisty sister, battling with Kira. The beloved fiancée, with gentle Roger. The reclusive author, only emerging in uniform, on repetitive walks. Indulging paranoid habits, guarding her work and shredding every page. I wonder if she knew what she was doing. If she knew she was vanishing into characters, long before her masterwork—when she made other people characters too.

"Yes," I say quietly. "And like it or not, we're closer than ever now. Because if this is who you really are—" She looks at me, impossibly serene, her youthful voice waiting its turn. Sunlight splashing lime green on her stare, like drops of sour juice. "Then I'm the only one who knows the truth. I still understand you better than anyone else."

"Don't fall for your own tricks."

"What does that mean?"

"It means . . . don't be the thief who gets robbed." She licks blood slowly off her front teeth. "You've been impersonating someone else your whole adult life. With your omissions. With what you let other people believe. You can *say* that you know me better than anyone. But you of all people should realize that you only just met me. This is the first time we've ever spoken. These are our first five minutes."

The smooth words cut deep.

Like a knife dipped in honey.

Sirens approach.

It's too easy to imagine how this will play out in headlines and comment sections. I'll be one more celebrity stalker. In the same category as Dana Martin, the man so incensed Justin Bieber didn't return his fan mail that he conspired from prison to castrate him. The list will be Nina Travers, Dana Martin, and a host of others: the man who showed up at Keira Knightley's home and meowed at her front door; the man who stalked Gwyneth Paltrow for twenty years; and the man arrested feet from Lana Del Rey at one of her concerts, where he planned to kidnap her. I'll look like one more disturbed civilian, ruined by my fantasies.

"And now you expect me to lie for you?"

"I know you will," she says smoothly. "Because you still love me. More important, you admire me. That's the trouble with writing something powerful, isn't it? It gets inside you. It changes the texture of your mind. Even if you don't understand what I'm doing, even if you don't agree with it, something in you trusts it because I wrote your favorite book." She sounds impenetrably confident, not a crack of doubt between her words. "You feel like I understand you, like we have something in common, but it's more than that. You don't just think that I speak for *you*, but for all people, that I'm here with a divine purpose."

A divine purpose.

Is that what I think?

"Do you know what reading is?" she continues. "If you boil it down, what it *really* is? It's giving up control of your mind. When you read my book, you lent your inner voice to me—and that's very similar to what you're about to do. When the police arrive, and when they question you, you'll be lending your *actual* voice to me."

Her lip is still bleeding.

If Leo didn't beat her up, Claire must've hurt herself. She must've destroyed the vase, crushed the flowers, and then looked for the perfect weapon. Something to leave a mark. Did she use one of her own books? I wonder if she felt any pain, or if she was so swept up in her new story, she felt nothing but awe. *Because you still love me.* But the Claire I love never would've done this—and that's because the Claire I love doesn't exist.

The front door opens downstairs.

Footsteps stream inside.

"You should know," I say.

"What's that?"

"I didn't shoot Leo the second time."

Her smile vanishes.

"He just heard every word."

~

I step toward Leo's front door, my hands shaking.

An officer talks to Claire upstairs.

I haven't heard her voice since they got here. She never once tried to plead her case, role-play any victim. Only her eyes moved, surveying the uniforms around us. It was eerie to see someone so deft with words suddenly think she was better off without them.

At first, Leo was too stunned to confirm my story—which came out of me reflexively, before I'd even chosen to tell it. Claire watched me as I spoke, her hands folded. Every now and then, the corners of her mouth turned down, as if she was resisting a smile. Maybe she was amused to hear a story so mangled, the dull and ugly words thrown together, the arc bent and wretched. Maybe she felt a shred of superiority, even in her dwindling freedom, to hear me botch it. No glitter, no witchcraft. She was still the best storyteller in the room.

Leo did finally second me.

He was on his way out with the paramedics when he told the police I was acting in self-defense. I'd been misled. I was just trying to protect myself and Claire. I heard the pain in his voice, but he seemed intent on minimizing damage. Reducing the number of victims. After that, the police talked among themselves. I sat in the living room, staring at photos of the man who'd just saved me. Who'd just used his limited strength to do some good. I'd been spying on him all week, living in his home, and I never realized he was the hero.

Then, the police took my information.

They just told me that I'm free to go.

I reach for the doorknob with two hands, before pulling one back and rubbing my temple. I don't feel like myself. I'm off-balance, lighter on one side. A dull roar is coming from the road, but I'm so disoriented it sounds like the ocean. It sounds like I'm back at Miranda's, alone in her house, hearing salt water scrape the sand.

I open the front door to a crowd.

The street is full of—Claire.

I'm facing a hundred copies of her. Everyone has the pink pixie cut. Clear glasses. Black turtleneck. They're all shifting from foot to foot, shoulders colliding in a dense and rippling mob. Some reach over police barriers, pearls on their ring fingers. Everyone is similar but slightly different, like reflected images or leaves on the same shaking tree. They all look starved for something specific, something just out of reach—but they seem convinced that they can touch it, scrape some of it under their fingernails.

I shut the door.

Shit. *Shit.*

The photo—of course the Starlites put it together. They must've pinpointed this spot from the sliver I gave of the view. I check through the peephole. This house is surrounded, fans coiled around it like a noose. The only way out is through them.

I open the front door, step outside.

I've never felt my spine straighter than right now, inching toward this group. Their shrieks get louder the closer I get. One police officer at the front barks into a walkie-talkie on his shoulder, waving me forward. I brace myself. They're all reaching for me, as if Claire might've left her scent or something more substantial behind—as if Claire is always shedding parts of herself, leaving a trail of unique personal debris.

"Clear a path!" the officer shouts.

They don't listen.

I step into the crowd.

Surrounded by Claire, the costume.

Did you is she? See her okay? Questions overlap, scrambling each other. The voices are desperate and impossible to trace. Someone yanks my elbow, and I stumble left into a row of bodies. Someone else yanks me in the opposite direction.

"Where is she?" a woman demands, holding my wrists. She faces me, her pink wig askew. An auburn tuft of hair peeks out over her ear. I try to get away, but she's stronger than I am. She tightens her grip, choking my arms.

"Stop it!" I beg. "What are you doing?"

Her intensity doesn't flicker.

You. I realize my mistake. *You.* Because right now, there is no *you.* She's not thinking about herself. She's only thinking about Claire. I lean to one side, so far that we both lose our balance. She lets me go, and

I fall into the mob. It's so loud my scream is silent. A trampled pink wig lies flat on the road, the only pop of color down here. I reach for someone—anyone—trying to scramble out of the mass of black elbows, dark knees.

Someone takes my hand.

On my feet again, I'm facing a woman my height. There's a crooked bend in her nose—a lot like mine, as if there's a distorted mirror between us. Her braid has fallen out of her wig. It runs down her back, fraying like old rope. Her lips are moving, struggling to put a thought together. It looks so important to her that I wait.

"Is Claire okay?" she manages.

She raises a shard of broken glass. Its edges shimmer.

Other Starlites are too lost in their own minds to grasp that she's holding a clear blade. It flickers in and out of invisibility. I step back, even though she doesn't look like she's going to hurt me. The only one she might hurt is herself. Her fingers bleed on either side of the shard. I rub my eyes. *Is Claire okay?* Claire asks, surrounded by Claires. I've found a point in the universe where logic collapses. Where the weight of massive celebrity has broken a rabbit hole into the ground, and we're all tumbling down the chute.

"Is she?" she presses.

I blink hard.

For once, I can see straight. The question was never supposed to be, *Is Claire okay?* It was always supposed to be, *Am I okay?* What am I avoiding with this obsession? What have I neglected in my own life to salivate over her trivia and log into r/ClaireRoss? Looking at this woman—her wrist turning red—all I feel is compassion for the person she's ignored. Because I've been in her shoes. I know what it's like to need that anesthetizing distraction. And I don't want to take it away if she's not ready to live without it.

"She is . . ." I consider how to respond. "Perfect."

"Really?" She smiles through tears.

"More than perfect. Claire Ross is a dream."

TWENTY-FIVE

Two weeks later

Right before going home, I stop in Betsy's Cookhouse and order two fried eggs over easy. From my seat at the window, I see a quiet, Sunday-morning slice of my building. Lauretta's sitting on her balcony with her feet up. The white bottoms of her snow boots face me, as clean as if she's never worn them outside.

I check my phone.

A new email just arrived from Miranda. Subj: Wire Transfer Complete. She did pay me for finding her daughter—even though, strangely, her daughter won't be coming home. As far as I know, Claire's still recovering in East Hampton with family, but she's not the same Claire who left. The legendary Claire Ross is gone for good.

I remember her face as police streamed into the room. Her lip was still bleeding. She had red crevices between her teeth and a raspberry streak on her tongue. She didn't make a sound, didn't move, not even to spit out the blood. Even frozen in place, though, she changed right in front of me. She hardened. The amazement left her eyes, and her wounds became the brightest parts of her. I don't know who she was becoming. But with the press still telling her story, I'm sure everyone will find out eventually. Claire's newest character. The latest chapter in her fiction. *She started to make things up.* I wonder if she ever stopped.

I'm lucky. I know that I'm lucky.

Because if things had gone just a little differently, I could've become the villain she imagined. Said my lines, played my part. But when Leo turned to face me—at *that* angle, in *that* light—his eyes were clear. Crystal clear, as if he hadn't had a drink in weeks. I shot the glass on a hunch, buying time until I figured it out. Claire shouting *Do it!* was enough to keep him still under the blackout shade, figuring things out for himself.

Her 911 call got him the attention he needed.

Leo walked out of the hospital last week. I saw the photos online. In every one, an extra-large green hoodie hid most of his shoulder cast. The white plaster kept his forearm lifted and parallel to his chest. The only comment he gave the press was that he doesn't plan to press charges. What will he do now, alone in San Francisco? Maybe he'll try to forget the past few months. Go back to the life he had before she revised it.

The waitress delivers my breakfast. I thank her and cut a wedge out of the eggs, clipping both yolks. The yellow runs like water. Passing a hand through my hair, I notice that she's still next to me. She has red glasses, round as the bottoms of Coke bottles. Her copper hair is half-up, half-down. The ponytail on top is a short, perky sprout.

"Sorry, do I know you?" she asks.

"Crazier things have happened."

"Wait a minute. You found Claire Ross." She crosses her arms, her blue eyes wide with discovery. "I'll be goddamned. What's your name?"

"I'm Nina."

"Travers, right. How's it feel?"

I decide how honest I want to be.

The truth is that two weeks later, I still don't feel like myself. I feel like I've lost a limb, like I'm missing an organ on one side, leaving me off-balance. It took me a while to figure out that what I'd lost was my fixation. After I'd pushed through the Claires—my arms bruised and clothes torn, one sleeve hanging by a thread—there was nothing left.

I woke up the next morning with space. That's the only way to describe it: internal space, room for thoughts that weren't about her.

Looking in the mirror, I noticed how long my hair had gotten, how I'd let it rot in its braid. My nails were overgrown, jagged. I took the shower that I desperately needed until my skin was red. I got a haircut in San Francisco, and as soon as I left the salon, I realized how little time I'd spent outside.

For the next week, I gave interviews. I'd already told the police the truth. There was no hiding from it anymore. Every reporter who wanted time with me got it on a silver platter. The story fueled headlines around the world. It was everything I used to want: my great case, as famous as Claire Ross. Everyone who'd heard of her had suddenly heard of me. A few papers even called me "the literary Sherlock," as if I could bring his powers of deduction to books, as if I had a habit of solving crimes in fiction. Maybe a villain like Claire needed a worthy hero, someone just as right as she was wrong. People who read the articles must've thought I was superhuman, having the week of my life.

In reality, I was wearing out my shoes, wandering through San Francisco. I walked so deep into the city I landed at the Sutro Baths. Formerly the world's biggest swimming complex. Now, nothing but holes filled with rainwater, ruins on a rocky cliff.

I sat there for a while, the wind beating on my face. Pelicans covered a distant rock. White feathers in the air looked like snow. Not thinking about work, and not thinking about Claire, I kept thinking about my parents. How little time I'd spent remembering what happened. It was as if I disappeared the same day they did, and someone else took my place. Someone in charge of surviving. Over ten years later, and I hadn't stopped to wonder—a hundred things, but first among them, if it was safe enough to come back.

Sitting there, I phoned into my first Al-Anon meeting. My hands were sweaty, jittering. When I joined, there were only four others on the line. No one spoke for five, six, *seven* minutes, until our chair finally said, "Welcome, Al-Anon family."

One by one, everyone introduced themselves. I wanted to say my name. It was in my mouth, but I couldn't get *Nina* out. So, I stayed on mute, listening to them chime in, hearing every mispressed key and windshield wiper in the background. I heard the wounds in their voices too. Even in a word or two, the pain was there, distorting and familiar. People read from the twelve steps, treating each other with royal respect. *Thank you for letting me read that.* And, *Welcome to the newcomers. We love you in a very special way.*

Then, people started to share.

It was all so *real*, it made everything I'd done for the past decade feel like games on the surface. I listened to stories I could've told, but not that slowly. Not that kindly. Because I hadn't sat with my own stories for long enough. I'd never acknowledged the power they had over me, down to the condition of my bathroom mirror. I wanted to say that, but I couldn't move. The air was thick and briny. Pelicans looked like gray letter *Z*'s.

I went to my second meeting in person. *Welcome, Al-Anon family.* Sitting there, with my hair cut, hands clean, and wide-open space in my head, I felt like I was finally in the right place. I was in the company of people who understood. People who reached me like no one else ever had before. For too long, I'd wedged an obsession between myself and *this*, all this complicated heartache and unfulfillable longing. Everything I should've faced years ago.

I stopped interviewing with reporters.

At my third meeting, I came so close to speaking that my lips moved. I wanted to tell them about my parents. Vanilla ice creams on cold days with Dad. The times I gave my mom baths, holding her chin up. My whole life, I'd never done anything violent. And then, I remember the neck and shoulders of that bottle. The black stripe of wine over the screw cap. The siren-red glass above it. I was going to do it. I really was going to swing, the way she had a hundred times. But I couldn't. I threw the bottle into the wall instead, and something happened to her when it shattered. She fell back on the bed.

And never got up.

I didn't look in a mirror for weeks afterward. I even tried to avoid my own hands. Then, the email arrived from her medical examiner. CAUSE OF DEATH, IMMEDIATE CAUSE: Variceal Hemorrhage. UNDERLYING CAUSE: Cirrhosis. I didn't believe it at first. I thought I'd shocked her. The broken glass. Wine dripping down the wall. Even when I understood, I still felt responsible—not for what had happened, but for how. For the last thing she saw. I worshipped novels for the next ten years, as if they could save me.

I wanted to tell that group *something*. I sat up straighter, leaned forward. *I'm done hiding from what's already happened.* Or, *I'm ready to come back to my own life. I'm ready to face everything unfair and unstoppable about it without an obsession.* The words were on my *teeth*, but I couldn't get them out. I cried into my fingers until I felt hands on both my shoulders. It almost felt like they were catching me.

I landed in New York this morning. It wasn't until I passed Hudson News that I realized I'd lost my copy of her book. I must've forgotten it at the motel. Or maybe in the rental car. Either way, I walked right past the bookstore. I didn't even glance at her covers to see what the stars looked like today—gleams on black fur, edges on a dark gem.

But even when you make the right choices during the day, your dreams can still betray you. For the past two weeks, I've dreamed every night of what almost happened—shooting Leo, then reciting her lies. Every night, I've dreamed of watching the movie version of *The Starlit Ballet* from prison, on a twelve-inch flat-screen in my cell. In my dream, I'm holding a *TV Guide*, where I circled the program announcement: The Starlit Ballet, PG-13, Soulmates reincarnate and find each other in every lifetime, an epic love story based on the worldwide bestseller by Claire Ross. As soon as the opening credits roll, I let the music overtake me—so elevating and transcendent that it feels religious. In my dream, I save her legend. And every time, I wake up sweating, scared, and grateful that I made the right decision.

How much should I share?

"It felt like . . ." I smell smoke on the waitress. "Sorry, do you smoke?" She nods yes. "It felt like having your last cigarette. Your very last one."

"Damn," she says.

She taps the table.

"Eggs on me," she says. "I insist," she adds, before I can protest.

She leaves with the gossip.

It's not the first time I've been recognized, but it's a first in my hometown. I scan the room and notice people swivel away, giving their attention back to short stacks and steaming coffee. One couple continues to stare, as if I have important answers.

I leave a tip on the counter, then walk home.

The cold is familiar, comforting. It's not California cold. It's real, honest cold. Snow brightens rooftops across town. The air smells like ice and grabs my hands with a pleasant throb. Later today, I can start to sift through the hundreds of emails from potential new clients. In the end, I didn't just find Claire Ross. I found out who she really is. That seems to have drawn the eye of everyone with an impossible case, everyone who's almost lost hope—but has enough money to buy a little more. I'll have to sort out authentic requests from the rest, attempts by the few remaining Starlites to pick my brain. Maybe some of them will just want to shake my hand, lean in, and try to smell her.

Lauretta comes into view.

Sucking on her cigarette like it's a juice box.

I reach into my pocket and pull out the envelope addressed to her. Inside, there's a four-by-six photo, taken just last week. I see a watered-down version through the paper. In this shot, I'm leaving my last interview. Photographers surround me on Mission Street, crowding out access to a food truck. Flashing cameras white out their faces. My chin slants away from the glare, down toward my relaxed-fit tee and jeans. I don't look like I'm trying to impress anyone. For the first time, the only person I'm trying to be is me.

When Lauretta sees me, she dabs her cigarette out in a snowy ashtray. The butt hisses and steams. She gets on her feet.

"The literary Sherlock!" she calls.

I can't help but smile.

"You don't have to call me that."

"Got a better idea?"

"I like the sound of Nina."

~

I head to a local hardware store that afternoon. Every tree is padded and white. Snow is a lacy border around the sidewalk. Maybe winter is the brightest season. On my way across town, I stop in a Starbucks and take my place at the back of the line. One barista grinds beans behind the counter. It sounds like paper shredding, a whole tome through metal teeth. A young girl smiles at me on her way out, holding her mom's hand and a cake pop.

My line moves forward.

Tall windows frame town.

I find the menu on the wall. Parts of it read like an Italian love letter—*ato, ino, esso.* The woman in front of me takes another step, into a torrent of natural light.

She's wearing a beige felt skirt and black tights. One half of her cashmere scarf dangles down her back. It's pale as steam, swaying between us in shapely figure eights. She checks her watch, holding car keys in her left hand. As she turns, I notice her braided headband. Her long, dark hair seems familiar now. It's been almost a decade, but it looks exactly the way I remembered it. Like oil dripping over her shoulders.

Someone pays. The line advances.

I step forward, smelling all the coffee beans I never tasted. One barista swirls inches of whipped cream onto a milky brew. Someone else leaves with a caramel-soaked drink. The woman in front of me fidgets with her keys. Maybe she's stopping here on her way out East. That would be a long drive, if she started in Connecticut. There's a chance that she's hungry for a late lunch. I reach forward and tap her once on the shoulder.

As she spins around, her midnight hair catches the sun.

ACKNOWLEDGMENTS

First, to my agent, Eve Attermann, for being my Day One. Thank you for championing my work since the first draft of my first book. I cannot overstate the impact of your transformative insights and belief. Many thanks to the whole team at WME—Rivka Bergman, Nicole Weinroth, and Caitlin Mahoney. I am honored to be working with the best.

Thank you to my superhuman editor, Carmen Johnson, for leading a metamorphosis in this story. I am thrilled to partner with you on my next novel! I am indebted to Shari MacDonald Strong for your sharp eye and illuminating suggestions. To everyone at Amazon Publishing, especially Tamara Arellano, Lauren Grange, and Tree Abraham.

Zibby Owens, your visionary work with authors has been an uplifting force and nothing less than a revolution. Thank you for empowering a vibrant community of writers and for including me. Carrie Feron, I cannot fully express my gratitude for your exceptional guidance on multiple projects. Our creative winter together was a blessing.

Dan Brown, your advice over the years has given me courage when I needed it. Thank you for helping me navigate countless bends in the writing path. Blake Crouch, your storytelling tips changed how I approach every idea. To other authors, editors, and friends who have generously shared their time along the way, thank you: Jennifer Bardsley, Lisa Barr, Amy Blumenfeld, Sophie Cousens, Jill Davis, Karen Dukess, Tracey Garvis Graves, Kristy Woodson Harvey, Helen O'Hare, Hannah Orenstein, Kyle Owens, and Suzanne Park.

In addition, thank you to those who supported my earlier books, including Jessica Ambrose, Lara Blackman, Fiona Davis, Avery Carpenter Forrey, Emily Giffin, Emily Henry, Kaitlin Olson, Carl Radke, Jill Santopolo, and Wendy Walker. Thank you to my friends in bookstores, especially Jesse Bartel at BookHampton.

Finally, thank you to my family—Mom "Minkey" and Dad, Parker and Michael, and Emil and Cara—who have always encouraged me. To my in-laws, Julie and Jim, Francie and Will, Stephen and Mary Kate, and Betsy. And most of all, most most *most* of all, thank you to my husband, David.

ABOUT THE AUTHOR

Photo © 2021 Lea Cartier

My Favorite Terrible Thing is Madeleine Henry's third novel. Her work has been featured in the *New York Times*, the *Washington Post*, the *New York Post*, and *Entertainment Weekly*. Previously she worked at Goldman Sachs after graduating from Yale. She lives with her husband in New York, where she is at work on her next book. For more information, visit www.itsmadeleinehenry.com.